A day in the life of a single dad.

Zeke ran a hand through his hair, suddenly conscious he needed a shave and he was wearing his oldest pair of jeans. Trust his daughters to bring home a beautiful woman when he looked his worst.

He hurriedly buttoned his shirt, aware that an undercurrent of tension stretched between him and the red-haired woman on his porch. She seemed to be avoiding looking at his chest.

Finally he extended his hand. "Hi. Zeke Blalock."

She drew in a deep breath. "Paige Watkins. I live next door." She reached for one of the fliers sitting in his daughters' little red wagon. "I thought you might want to see these before the girls finished giving them out." A smile curved Paige's lips and attraction hit Zeke square in the gut. He had the insane urge to reach out and stroke her hair.

Then he looked down and read the crayoned writing on the flier, and blushed for the first time in all his thirty years.

He'd known single fatherhood would be difficult. But what on earth could he ever have done to prepare himself for this?

Dear Reader,

Spring is coming with all its wonderful scents and colors, and here at Harlequin American Romance we've got a wonderful bouquet of romances to please your every whim!

Few women can refuse a good bargain, but what about a sexy rancher who needs a little help around the house? Wait till you hear the deal Megan Ford offers Rick Astin in Judy Christenberry's *The Great Texas Wedding Bargain*, the continuation of her beloved miniseries TOTS FOR TEXANS!

Spring is a time for new life, and no one blossoms more beautifully than a woman who's WITH CHILD.... In *That's Our Baby!*, the first book in this heartwarming new series, Pamela Browning travels to glorious Alaska to tell the story of an expectant mother and the secret father of her child.

Then we have two eligible bachelors whose fancies turn not lightly, but rather unexpectedly, to thoughts of love. Don't miss *The Cowboy and the Countess*, Darlene Scalera's tender story about a millionaire who has no time for love until a bump on the head brings his childhood sweetheart back into his life. And in Rita Herron's *His-and-Hers Twins*, single dad Zeke Blalock is showered with wife candidates when his little girls advertise for a mother...but only one special woman will do!

So this March, don't forget to stop and smell the roses— and enjoy all four of our wonderful Harlequin American Romance titles!

Happy reading!

Melissa Jeglinski
Associate Senior Editor

His-and-Hers Twins

RITA HERRON

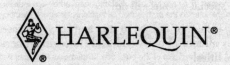

HARLEQUIN®

TORONTO • NEW YORK • LONDON
AMSTERDAM • PARIS • SYDNEY • HAMBURG
STOCKHOLM • ATHENS • TOKYO • MILAN • MADRID
PRAGUE • WARSAW • BUDAPEST • AUCKLAND

To my Mom,
For raising a set of devilish twin girls herself and surviving
with very little gray hair. For continuing to encourage me to go
after my dreams. And most of all, for keeping my refrigerator
clean so I can sit at the computer and pound at the keyboard—
Thanks, Mom, I love you....

Always,
Rita—one of those devilish twins

ISBN 0-373-16820-9

HIS-AND-HERS TWINS

Copyright © 2000 by Rita B. Herron.

Visit us at www.romance.net

Printed in U.S.A.

ABOUT THE AUTHOR

Rita Herron is a teacher, workshop leader and storyteller who loves reading, writing and sharing stories with people of all ages. She has published two nonfiction books for adults on working and playing with children, and has won the Golden Heart award for a young adult story. Rita believes that books taught her to dream, and she loves nothing better than sharing that magic with others. She lives with her "dream" husband and three children, two cats and a dog in Norcross, Georgia.

Books by Rita Herron

HARLEQUIN AMERICAN ROMANCE
820—HIS-AND-HERS TWINS

HARLEQUIN INTRIGUE
486—SEND ME A HERO
523—HER EYEWITNESS
556—FORGOTTEN LULLABY

Thumbkin Special
Chocwit Chip Cookies

2 sticks margarine
1¼ c. brown sugar
1 tsp vanilla
1 egg
2 cups self-rising flour
2 cups chocolate chips

2 cans frosting
Candy—M&M's,
red hots, sprinkles
Raisins

August
Blalock

Beat margarine with brown
sugar and vanilla. Add egg
and beat until creamy.
Gradually beat in flour.
Stir in chocolate chips. Drop
on ungreased cookie sheet.
Bake at 375° for 10-12 minutes.

Decorate with
thumbprints. Or use
icing and candies
to make your
own face.

Summer
Blalock

Henrietta

Chapter One

"The house next door is definitely jinxed." Paige Watkins sighed dramatically into the phone, aware she sounded irrational. But she didn't care—she had to talk to someone.

"What are you talking about?" Paige's best friend, Amelia asked. "You think it's haunted?"

"No, that would be better," Paige said in despair. "Another single man moved in."

"In Eric's house?"

Paige winced. "That's the one."

"Oh, that *is* terrible," Amelia drawled sarcastically. "I suppose he's cute, too."

Paige rolled her eyes when she heard Amelia's bracelets jangle. Amelia collected a bracelet as a going-away gift from each of her former boyfriends. So far she had three silver, two gold and one jade. "I don't know if he's cute or not and I don't intend to find out."

"Are you delirious, Paige?" Amelia sputtered. "'Cause if you need a doctor, I'll be glad to drive you."

"I don't need a doctor *or* a shrink." Paige chuckled. "But my new neighbor has kids, and I'm not jumping into a relationship with a single dad—not ever again."

Her friend clucked sympathetically. "Look, Paige, just because Eric went back to his ex-wife—"

"His gorgeous ex-wife with the double D cups."

"Yeah, well, just because he went back to his gorgeous ex-wife with the double D cups doesn't mean you have to give up on all men."

"Why would I want to repeat the same mistake? Besides, I still haven't gotten over what happened with little Joey."

"That wasn't your fault, Paige. Kids can sneak away from you in a minute."

"Still, if that car had hit Joey..." Paige shuddered, forcing away the memory. "I don't want the responsibility of children, especially someone else's. It's too scary."

Amelia exhaled noisily. "Forget the kids, just tell me, *is the dad cute?*"

"How should I know?" Paige wound the phone cord around her fingers. "I've been avoiding him."

"You're a pathetic excuse for a female," Amelia said in obvious disgust. "If you haven't met him, how do you know he's single?"

"Mrs. Spivy across the street." Paige laughed as she remembered the day the good-natured, well-meaning woman had dropped the news. Mrs. Spivy was such a gossip she'd probably protested when the phone company did away with party lines. "She's the neighborhood welcoming committee. She took him an apple pie when he first moved in."

"Well, there's a thought," Amelia said. "Why don't you make your favorite chocolate mousse and take it over? You could put whip cream and a cherry on top."

Paige scoffed. "I am not going to bake my way into the man's bed."

"I guess that would be a little sexist," Amelia admitted. "Okay, then design yourself a sexy new outfit, something short, you know, show off your legs."

"And that's not sexist?"

Amelia laughed. "Well, I'd tell you to fix me up with the guy, but things are going pretty good with Derrick—"

"You really like him?" Paige asked, grateful for the change in subject.

Amelia cooed dreamily. "He's almost perfect. I'm surprised you set me up with him instead of keeping him for yourself."

"We've been friends since grammar school," Paige said. "But there wasn't any chemistry between us."

"Good," Amelia said, emphatically. "'Cause he might be the one."

"You're a hopeless romantic, Amelia. I've given up on men for a while."

"Gee, Paige. There're a few good ones out there. You have to keep looking."

"And get my heart broken again? I don't think so."

"Trust me, it's worth it."

Paige laughed, then shook her head. "Listen, I need to deliver these fliers. I promised Mrs. Spivy I'd head up the committee on the neighborhood watch program."

"Still having trouble with vandals?"

"Yeah. Maybe this watch thing will help."

"Hey, a perfect excuse to meet your new neighbor."

Paige rolled her eyes. "You *are* hopeless. He's probably a geek with monsters for kids." She hung up the phone, shaking her head at Amelia's laughter, then grabbed the fliers and headed toward the door. She meant what she'd told Amelia. She was through with men for a while, especially ones with children and pets. No more kitty litter on the carpet. No more car pools. No more back seat squabbles. No more being used for a fill-in mom. She intended to heed her mother's advice and focus on her dreams.

She'd finish her degree, then become a dress designer. Then she'd travel and make her mark in the business world.

Outside, as Paige stuffed fliers in people's boxes, her thoughts strayed to the neighbors out tending their spring flowers and yards. Thirty miles north of Atlanta, the residents of Crabapple had access to all the city offered, but land was cheaper and trees plentiful in the suburbs. Quaint antique shops lined the downtown area, which consisted of nothing more than a church, a gas station, an elementary school and a two-lane highway. Several small horse farms bordered the edge of town. But the close-knit community, famous for the crabapple trees flanking the town square, had recently been plagued by a series of mysterious vandalisms, making residents nervous and edgy.

She'd almost finished distributing the notices when she noticed pigtailed twins pulling a bright red wagon, walking an overweight, floppy-eared dog. Or the mutt might be walking them. The child holding the leash yelled, "Whoa, Henrietta!" but the dog moaned pathetically and tried to lie down. The urchin tugged until the dog begrudgingly ambled along behind her, its head drooping, its movements labored. The girls were probably four or five years old. One wore yellow overalls, the other blue.

Where were their parents?

Stop it, she chastised herself silently. They aren't your responsibility. Thank goodness. After Joey...

Besides, except for the break-ins, this was a quiet, safe

neighborhood. Teens were probably responsible for the vandalism.

Still, she couldn't help being curious about the girls. She turned the corner and headed toward them. The twins had stopped by a telephone pole. The one in yellow struggled with the dog to keep it from charging into the street to chase a bird while the other one pulled out a hammer and a flier from the wagon. She clumsily attempted to hang the paper on the pole. They were probably having a garage sale, or they'd set up a lemonade stand.

She chuckled again as the child slammed the hammer down and missed, then tried again. The dog howled, and the other girl brushed his long brown ears lovingly. Suddenly a gust of wind blew the paper from the second little girl's hands.

"Oh, no, get it!" she cried.

Her sister pointed to the flailing paper. "Stop!"

"I'll get it!" Paige's mothering instincts automatically kicked in when she saw the paper swirling toward the road.

The girls halted, their eyes wide as the wind hurled the flier into the street. The mutt barked, perked his ears, and darted to chase it. So, the dog could run, after all.

"Girls, don't go into the street," Paige warned.

The one in yellow pulled the leash, struggling against the dog's weight. Her sister grabbed her waist to keep her from being dragged into the road. The dog moaned and flopped to the ground. The twins tumbled over each other, landing on top of the dog.

Paige snatched the paper from the ground and fought laughter as the girls and the dog sought to untangle themselves. Her gaze strayed to the flier and a smile curved her lips as she saw the crayon childish scrawl. Then she deciphered the words and her mouth dropped open in surprise.

WIVE AND MOMMI WANTED
Rite Away
for Hansum Daddi & Dorabl Twins
Must like anmuls and make chocwit chip cookies
Zeke Blalock 555-1200

Paige studied the girls—strawberry-blond hair, huge green eyes, with a smattering of freckles dotting their noses—they *were* adorable.

But why were they advertising for a mother?

She handed the flier to them. "I guess you need this."

"Thanks, but you can keep it," the girl in yellow said with a hopeful smile.

Her sister wrinkled her nose. "That is, if you don't already gots some little girls of your own."

"Can you make chocwit chip cookies?"

"Well, yes—"

"You don't gots a daddy?"

The twin in blue poked her sister. "You mean a hus...bund. He's *our* daddy."

Paige smothered laughter. The little girls were obviously serious. Did their "daddi" know what they were up to?

"What are your names?" Paige asked. She noticed the one in yellow was missing a front tooth. *Good, a way to tell the girls apart.*

"I'm August," the child with the missing tooth answered.

"And I'm Summer." The twin holding the wagon pointed to herself. "Our mama named us that 'cause we was born in the summer."

"But she wents away," August said in a sad voice.

"And we don't ever see her anymore," Summer said. Both girls' bottom lips suddenly trembled and Paige's stomach clenched into a knot. They looked as if they were going to burst into tears any second.

"I'm Paige Watkins," Paige said, deftly changing the subject as she petted the mutt's head. "Great dog, you've got there." Surely, the topic of the dog was safe.

"Her name's Henrietta," Summer said brightening.

"Yeah, first we called her Henry, but we found out he was a girl."

"Girls are different from boys," August said.

"See, boys gots a—"

"Yes, honey, I know the difference," Paige said, with a grin. *So, the dog topic wasn't such a good idea either.* "I haven't seen you two before. Where do you live?"

The girls exchanged worried looks. One of them pointed in the direction of Paige's house. "Thataway, I think."

"In a brown house."

"It gots a porch."

"We just moved in."

"We'd put the fliers up 'fore now, but daddy just bought us some new crayons."

"He washed the others with his underwear. My red crayons turned his shorts pink."

"I see." Paige chuckled and glanced down the street. The only brown house on Maple Street was the one next to hers. These were her new neighbors! They were monsters, all right—adorable, precious little monsters.

"Do you gots a dad…I mean, a husbund?" August asked.

Paige's heart squeezed. "No, honey, I don't." She studied the flier again. "Has your daddy seen this?"

Both girls shook their heads emphatically, their pigtails swinging wildly. Summer leaned toward her and whispered, "It's a surprise."

"'Sides, he was asleep," Summer added.

"I see," Paige said again, touched by the girls, but suddenly irritated with the man. What kind of father slept the day away while his children roamed the streets? And he'd given his children the idea he needed a wife so badly they'd advertised for one!

More than likely, he wanted a cook, maid, and baby-sitter. Maybe he was a geek who had trouble meeting women, she thought hopefully. But if he left the girls alone a lot…well, he needed to take responsibility for his daughters. And what about the girls' mother? She'd actually deserted them! How could a mother do that?

Paige gritted her teeth as anger churned through her. "Let me walk you home."

The girls traded looks again. "We're not sposed to go with strangers."

Paige patted Summer's back. "That's true. But I'm not really a stranger. I live in the yellow house beside yours. So we're next-door neighbors."

Both girls' eyes danced with mischief, matchmaking wheels obviously turning in their little heads. A bad premonition sank in the pit of Paige's stomach—the house was definitely jinxed. She couldn't give the girls any false ideas about being their mother. She would walk them home. Then she would have a talk with their father, and be out of their lives for good.

ZEKE BLALOCK awoke with a start. He hadn't meant to fall asleep at all, but between the move, unpacking and nursing an ailing golden retriever all night, he'd been completely exhausted. The silence in the house alerted him to trouble. He jumped off the sofa, shoved his tousled hair from his forehead and panicked. Where were the girls?

In the backyard with Henrietta—it's fenced in, a quiet, safe neighborhood, that's why you moved here—they're fine.

But his heart pounded anyway, and he had to see his daughters' darling, innocent faces before he could relax. Still blurry-eyed from sleep, he raced through the den, dodged the sleeping cat on the floor and almost stumbled over the maze of unopened boxes. Damn. He needed to finish unpacking. He stubbed his toe, but ignored the throbbing pain and rushed to the back door. His pulse raced when he spotted the empty yard and the gate swinging back and forth.

They were gone! Had they been kidnapped while he napped on his living room couch? Should he call 911?

He hurried up the stairs, yelling their names as he searched the house, but no answer. Remembering they liked to play hide-and-seek, he checked every closet, even under the bed. They were nowhere to be found.

Feeling sick to his stomach with panic, he almost yelped in shock when the doorbell rang. Who could be at the door? He didn't know a single soul living on the street. Unless it was some salesmen. He sure as hell didn't have time for that. Or maybe it was that nice elderly lady, Mrs. Spivy with some more pies. Or maybe she'd seen his children!

Unless the police had found his daughters and—

Don't overreact. Maybe they're playing in the front yard.

The bell rang again and he bolted, not caring that he was barefoot and his oxford shirt was unbuttoned. He swung open the front door and squinted through the screen. A gorgeous redhead stood on the front stoop, wearing a scowl the size of Texas. Was she selling something? If so, she certainly needed to perfect her demeanor.

"Mr.—"

"Daddy!"

"Girls!" Relief ballooned inside him at the sight of his daughters. He yanked open the screen door, dropped to his knees on the porch, and pulled them into his arms. "Where have you two been? I told you to stay in the backyard." He leaned back to examine each of them, spot-checking to see if they'd been injured in any way, totally forgetting about the frowning woman standing in his doorway. They looked okay. They sounded okay. They hadn't been kidnapped. "I was worried about you," he said in a firm voice.

"We're sorry, Daddy," Summer said.

"Yeah, but we was busy," August argued.

Zeke frowned and adopted his serious-dad expression. "I don't want to hear excuses. You gave me a scare. The rule is you don't leave the yard without me. Do you understand?"

Both girls bowed their heads and studied their colored sneakers. "Yes sirrrr," Summer said.

"August?"

"'Kay, Daddy."

"But we found somebody." Summer pointed to the woman. "She lives in the yellow house."

"Right next door," August added. "She walked us home."

Zeke glanced up to see the woman still standing on the stoop. Her frown had disappeared, and her light green eyes seemed troubled.

"Thanks for bringing them home," he said.

August pulled at his sleeve. "Her name's Paige. Like a book."

"This is our daddy," Summer said proudly. "He's a mess today, but that's 'cause we was unpacking, and he didn't sleep last night 'cause he's a dog doctor."

"A beterinarian," August clarified, wrinkling her nose. "Daddy, your face is all fuzzy."

Zeke ran a hand through his dark brown hair, trying to smooth the disheveled ends, suddenly conscious of his unruly appearance. He needed a shave, his shirt was hanging open and his jeans were full of holes. On top of that, he was running on two hours of sleep, max. He probably looked like a stray animal that had been digging in the yard. Leave it to his daughters to bring home a beautiful female when he looked his absolute worst.

He hurriedly buttoned his shirt, aware an undercurrent of tension stretched taut between him and the red-haired woman who seemed to be avoiding looking at his bare chest.

Finally he felt clothed and extended his hand. Maybe now she would look at him. "Hi. Uh, I'm Zeke Blalock."

"Hello. Paige Watkins." She drew in a deep breath and her short cropped T-shirt stretched tight across her small but ample breasts. For the first time since he'd opened the door, he noticed her running attire. Bright red letters boasting the slogan Free To Be Me emblazoned the front of her shirt. Black running shorts hugged her slender thighs and she wiped at a bead of perspiration on her forehead. Was she hot, or nervous?

"I hope my girls didn't disturb you," Zeke said.

"We didn't, Daddy," August said.

"No, they were fine," Paige said. "Actually—"

Henrietta flopped onto the porch and whined. "My dog didn't dig up your flower bed or something, did she?"

"Oh, no, nothing like that." Paige reached for some papers in the wagon. She was selling something.

"We're gonna go play," Summer said.

"Yep," August agreed.

"Girls, wait," Paige said.

Uh-oh. They *had* done something. He'd hoped he'd be lucky enough to find neighbors who liked kids. Maybe Paige Watkins didn't. "Look, Ms. Watkins, if the girls upset you, I'm sorry, they're just—"

She handed him a flier. "The girls were putting these up in the neighborhood. I wondered if you'd read them."

The girls had made fliers? Guilt flashed onto his daughters' faces as they backed off the porch. "We're taking Henrietta to the backyard," August said in a low voice.

"Yep." Summer dropped her chin forward, avoiding his eyes.

"Wait, girls." Zeke motioned them to stop as he recognized the familiar crayoned writing. Then he read the words and the sun grew hot on his neck and the porch spun in circles.

Chapter Two

"Oh, my God!" The paper rattled in his hands as Zeke waved it at the girls.

August poked his arm. "Daddy, you're not sposed to say that."

"'Cept in church," Summer added.

Zeke glanced in horror from one innocent set of green eyes to another, then back at Paige. A smile curved her lips and he momentarily forgot his daughters' latest stunt. Attraction hit him square in the gut. Paige was breathtaking. Sunlight glinted off her auburn hair, and he had the insane urge to reach out and touch it.

Summer tugged at his sleeve, bringing him back to reality. "Daddy, Paige don't gots a husbund."

"And she can make chocwit chip cookies."

"Daddy, be nice." August cupped her hand to her mouth and stood on her tiptoes. "And comb your hair. You look like a poodle-head."

For the first time in his thirty years, a blush crept up his neck and scalded his face. He wanted to throttle his darling daughters, then crawl in Henrietta's doghouse in the back and hide. Instead he gestured at the flier. "Uh...I didn't know anything about this."

Paige's light green eyes twinkled. "That's what the

girls said. I thought you might want to see it before they finished distributing them."

"Giving them out?" Horror struck Zeke anew. Exactly how many had they displayed? He turned to the twins, trying desperately to control his soaring temper. "Summer, August, where did you put these fliers?"

Summer chewed her lip in thought and shuffled from one foot to the other.

August piped up. "In the mailboxes."

"All along that street," Summer added.

"How *many* did you give out?" he asked, his vision blurring at the thin stack remaining in the wagon.

"I dunno know," August said, twirling her pigtail around her finger.

"'Bout a hundred," Summer said.

"Oh, my God!" Zeke's stomach rolled.

"Daddy!" both girls shrieked.

Zeke pressed his hand over his racing heart as he mentally counted mailboxes. What would the neighbors think?

"You're never gonna find us a mommy if you keep talkin' like that," August whispered with a frown.

Zeke clenched his jaw. Paige caught her lip between her teeth as if she was fighting laughter. He'd barely moved into the neighborhood, and now he'd have to move again.

"Girls, we have to get these fliers back," Zeke said, his voice laced with mortification.

"But why, Daddy?" August asked.

"We just do," Zeke said in a firm tone. "I'll explain later."

"Uh-oh." August's eyes grew wide. "Are we gonna have one of those long talks?"

"Yes, we are," Zeke said matter-of-factly as he waved

the disastrous paper in the air. "This is not the way to go about finding a wife. Or a new mommy."

"Then how do we do it?" Summer asked, looking crushed that he hadn't liked their idea.

Zeke's throat closed at the confusion in her small face. He knew single fatherhood would be difficult, but this...well, he hadn't been prepared for this kind of scene. And right in front of pretty Paige Watkins. "I don't know, but we'll talk about it later." He knelt in front of them and softened his voice. "Now, put Henrietta in the backyard, and we'll go for a walk so you can show me which houses you gave fliers."

"'Kay," both girls said. They pulled and tugged at the leash until the lazy dog groaned, then lifted her bulk and waddled behind them.

Zeke searched for some way to salvage his pride. "I...uh, thanks for bringing the girls home," he finally said. "This parenting business is harder than I thought."

"I know," Paige said sympathetically.

He narrowed his eyes. "You have children?" He hadn't seen a wedding ring. Not that he was looking, but the girls said she didn't have a husband. The big, yellow two-story seemed plenty spacious for an entire family. Did she live there alone? Or did she have a string of boyfriends or a live-in? Maybe she was divorced with kids of her own.

Paige shook her head. "No, I don't have kids. But there're several children in the neighborhood."

"Really? Maybe you can give me some pointers."

She wobbled on one foot, giving him the distinct feeling she wanted to leave. "I don't think so."

His ex-wife had felt the same way. A frown marred Paige's heart-shaped face, and something about her tone bothered him, but he didn't have time to analyze it.

The twins barreled around the corner. "Henrietta's in the yard," August said.

"Okay, let's go." Zeke pointed to the driveway. Summer and August skipped ahead. He closed the door, and he and Paige walked across the lawn to the sidewalk. When they reached her driveway, she paused, chewing her bottom lip.

"Well, it was nice to meet you, girls."

"Aren't you coming with us?" Summer asked.

"No, thanks," Paige said. A wary expression streaked her slender face. "I have homework to do."

"You go to school?" August asked.

"We're going to kindergarten next year," Summer said.

Paige laughed. "I'm finishing a college degree," she answered. "And one day I'm planning to study in Europe."

August's face lit up. "Our mommy went there. She lives in that big town with that river running through it."

"But she never came back," Summer said softly.

Zeke's heart squeezed as he remembered the day Renee had left. Both girls had cried for hours.

"I'm sorry," Paige said gently. She gave him a forlorn look and he shrugged, trying to mask his feelings. It sounded as if Paige had high aspirations, just like his ex-wife. Well, he wouldn't travel that route again. No matter how sexy and delectable the female, looks weren't the most important thing. If and when he ever became involved with another woman, she'd want a family—she wouldn't be more concerned about her career than him or his daughters. Besides, he didn't need the complication of another female—he had his hands full with the two he had.

Paige gave him a slight wave. "Well, I'll see you later, Zeke."

Zeke nodded and their gazes locked, the magnetism between them instantly sparking his body to arousal. A sweet sensuality darkened the light irises of her eyes, and she caught her bottom lip with her teeth again, a gesture he wanted to remedy by touching his lips to hers. She exhaled, then folded her arms beneath her breasts, her cropped shirt accentuating her subtle curves. Then she turned and he made a futile attempt not to stare at those dynamite legs and her curved backside as she strode toward her house.

August tugged at his arm and he dragged his gaze from Paige to see a fuming, three-hundred-pound man storming toward him. To his horror, the man had one of his daughters' fliers clutched in his beefy hands.

PAIGE STOOD ON her porch and watched as Zeke attempted to explain his daughter's *surprise* to Mr. Larkin, a heavyset man who, from his loud voice and the way he kept waving his mammoth arms around, was obviously very possessive about his wife. Finally, after a few minutes of conversation, the twins joined in and the irate man turned to mush. Before they parted, she heard him asking about Zeke's veterinary practice and agreeing to bring his bulldog to Zeke's clinic for shots. He also promised Summer and August he'd let his dog visit Henrietta.

The munchkin girls had stolen Mr. Larkin's heart, just as they had hers. All the more reason for her to stay away from them.

She sank onto the porch swing and rocked herself back and forth in an effort to get a grip on her emotions. The precious girls had matchmaking up their sleeves, and she didn't intend to raise another family. Standing on Zeke's front porch had brought back painful memories of Eric and Joey. She could still see three-year-old Joey riding his tricycle in the driveway next door, toddling along with that stuffed bear he always liked to carry, curled up on her couch, snuggled with her grandmother's afghan.

But Eric and Joey had deserted her, and she had her own goals now. Giving up her menial office job had been the first step. Taking a job at a boutique and enrolling in college was the second. Not dating any more single dads ranked next.

She laughed as the twins attempted cartwheels on the sidewalk while Zeke frantically removed the fliers from the neighbors' mailboxes. Some geek. Big and brawny Zeke Blalock was nothing like the man she'd pictured. He obviously cared a great deal about his daughters. She had to give him points for that. As far as rating him in the sex appeal department—he'd rank up there with Tom Cruise and Tom Selleck. A definite one hundred and ten plus.

Handsome and tall, broad shouldered and muscular—she'd barely been able to resist staring at his naked chest before he'd buttoned his shirt. His chocolate-colored eyes had melted her insides and rendered her tongue-tied. His strong chiseled profile, big rough hands and olive skin suggested he worked outside, instead of inside a clinic. And his backside was firm and muscular, especially in those tight jeans, she noted, as she shamelessly watched him bend to pet Mrs. Blue's small gray cat.

Stop it. He's not for you. He has a ready-made family, and you're not mommy material. Your own mother resented the sacrifices she made to stay home and take care of you.

Renewed determination filled her and she hurried inside to finish her project. She paused when she realized she'd forgotten to tell Zeke about the vandalism and the neighborhood watch meeting. She'd been too sidetracked by his good looks. Darn, she'd put a flier in his box later.

For now, she decided to tackle her design project. But when she touched the scraps of black satin fabric she'd collected for her textile project, she moaned.

She had planned to design an evening gown with the fabric. But an unbidden image came to mind—the shimmering fabric would make a perfect bed covering, with Zeke Blalock lying on top, naked as a jaybird.

ZEKE CLEARED A spot on the oak kitchen table and plopped the cardboard pizza box on top, using his foot to gently usher Henrietta away from the table. He'd tried to explain his reaction to the mommy-wanted fliers to his daughters, but he wasn't sure they'd understood.

"Well, daddy, if we can't adver..."

"Advertise," Zeke supplied. "No, we don't advertise for a mother or wife." He dished Summer a slice of plain cheese pizza and August pepperoni, willing himself to be patient.

"Then how will we ever get a new mommy?" August asked, nibbling at the gooey cheese.

August picked a pepperoni off her pizza, licked it, then popped it into her mouth. "And how will you get a wive?"

"A wife," Zeke corrected. "Honey, I don't want a new wife. I'm happy being with the two of you." He raked his hand through his hair and shook his head at Henrietta as she pawed at his feet. "No, Henrietta, pizza will give you heartburn." Ignoring Henrietta's woeful look, he turned his attention back to his daughters. "Listen, girls, I know you miss your mom, but we've talked about this before. You have me, and we're a family—all by ourselves.''

August poked out her bottom lip. ''But you're a boy,'' August said as if it were a news flash.

''Of course, I'm a boy,'' Zeke said patiently.

''But boys can't be mommies,'' Summer protested.

Zeke's throat clogged. ''Honey, I'll try my best to be both a mother and father to you.''

''But boy mommies can't come to our Mommy and Me Tea at preschool. Only girl mommies!''

Zeke felt as if he'd been punched in the stomach. How could he have forgotten that Mother's Day was coming up? Because he was an idiot.

At least he'd finally discovered the crux of the problem. ''When is the mother tea?'' he finally asked.

''Next week,'' Summer said, sounding stricken. ''Friday.''

''Yeah. Everybody else's mommies will be there.''

Drive the knife in a little deeper, girls. Henrietta added to his guilt by whining and giving him a pitiful flop-eared look. He gritted his teeth and tossed her his pizza crust. If he could find Renee right now, he'd throttle her.

''I have an idea.'' He forced a cheery smile. ''Your grandmother can come. I'm sure she'd love to visit your school.''

Both girls' faces fell.

''You can call her yourselves.'' Zeke tried to brighten his voice with enthusiasm. ''Maybe you could even spend the night with her.'' *And you could have a night out,* a silent voice whispered. *Call Paige. Have a date. A conversation with an adult, not a child or an animal.*

Summer's eyes lit up. ''All night long?''

''Yep. Wouldn't that be fun?''

August nodded. ''Grandma lets us eat cookies for breakfast.''

Grandma would. Zeke ran a hand through his hair. Oh, well, it would only be one morning. And he had to do something for his heartsick daughters. He couldn't allow them to be the only ones at school without a mother figure.

He handed them the phone. ''Here, dial Grandma's number. She's been begging me to let you spend the night.''

Together the girls punched in the number. When he heard his mother's voice screeching over the phone, he assumed by the pleased expressions on his daughters' faces she'd accepted the invitation.

One more problem licked. At least temporarily.

When they hung up the phone, the girls' moods had drastically changed. August gobbled another piece of pizza and Summer gulped her milk, then ran to the bathroom. He breathed a sigh of relief but the feeling disintegrated when Summer screamed. ''Daddy!''

He sprinted through the house to find her. August trotted behind him, stepping on his heels in her haste.

Summer was standing in the bathroom, her eyes dazed. Her little hand shook when she pointed at the cat huddled in the bathtub. ''What's...wrong with Buffy?''

Zeke swallowed nervous laughter. ''There's nothing wrong with her,'' he said gently. He knelt down beside the fat, panting calico cat and wrapped his arms around his daughters' shoulders. He'd barely survived one traumatic moment before another struck.

Now, he had to explain the facts of life to his four-year-old daughters. Buffy was having kittens.

THE CREATIVE SIDE of design and the actual sewing intrigued Paige. She started sketching various ideas for the design project, considering fabric choice, cost and accessories as she worked. For this project, she only needed to design one outfit, but for her final, she'd design an entire wardrobe, taking into account the busy lives and schedules of the women who might wear her creations.

Several minutes later, she stared at the sketch, crumpled the paper and tossed it into the trash. The dress looked all wrong. Too high of a neckline. Not tapered enough. She started another drawing, but the telephone rang, disturbing her concentration.

Maybe it's the sexy guy next door, calling to ask you for a date.

She reached for the phone, ordering herself to decline the invitation, then sighed in disappointment at the sound of Amelia's voice. "Hi, Amelia."

"Hey, Paige. You have to come to my party next week!"

"A party?" Paige blinked in surprise, searching her mind to see if she'd forgotten an important date. No holidays coming up. No birthdays. "What brought this on?" she asked, when nothing special registered.

"I'm getting married!" Amelia squealed so loudly Paige had to hold the phone away from her ear.

"Married? When? To whom?"

"To Derrick, of course. He asked me this afternoon!" Another bout of squeals filled the line. "We're having an engagement party next Friday night. Can you come?"

"I wouldn't miss it for the world. But Amelia, this is happening so fast. Are you sure?"

Amelia laughed. "I am. He's definitely my soul mate."

"That's great." Paige twisted the phone cord around her fingers. So, now *she* was the last of the dying breed of single women among her friends. It shouldn't bother her. And she was happy for Amelia.

"I would ask you to be my maid of honor, but we're eloping," Amelia continued. "He's taking me to Paris on our honeymoon, I can't wait, Paige. Life is wonderful."

Paige's hands instantly moved across her sketchpad as she began sketching a wedding dress. "I wish you were having a big wedding though. I'd like to design your dress."

"I know." Amelia sounded faintly disappointed. "But Derrick wants to get married right away and I'm afraid to wait. You know how guys are, he might change his mind."

Don't I? Eric had canceled their wedding the morning of the ceremony.

"Paige, I'm sorry, I know how that must have sounded."

"Don't sweat it," Paige said. "I'm not going to rain on your parade, Amelia. And we are not going to talk about my failed love life."

"Thanks, Paige, you're the best," Amelia said softly. "I'll see you next Friday."

The phone clicked into silence before Paige could think of a way to beg out of the party. She turned back to her project, but the house seemed unusually quiet. Growing up as an only child, she should have been used to be being alone. But she'd craved a big boisterous family with lots of sisters and brothers. In retrospect, maybe her need for a family was the reason she'd become so attached to Eric and his son.

But the silence hung in the air, echoing off the walls. Eerie, cold, almost smothering her with the emptiness.

Stop it. You have to get used to it.

Determined to forget Amelia's wedding, she flipped on the radio and decided to make a batch of brownies. Comfort food always spurred her creativity. She threw the brownie ingredients into a bowl, stirred the thick rich batter and popped the mixture into a pan.

A loud howling sound caught her attention and her gaze strayed to the Blalock house next door. She'd still forgotten to tell Zeke about the neighborhood watch. She'd take them brownies and tell Zeke about the meeting. After all, a welcoming basket of food was only neighborly, and she didn't want anyone to accuse her of lacking in Southern hospitality.

"DADDY, THAT'S GROSS." Summer covered her eyes with her hands and peeked through the finger holes as the fourth kitten popped out. Buffy, following her normal motherly instincts, licked the kitten clean.

"They look like skinny rats," August said, watching the other three kittens burrow underneath Buffy.

"Yeah, they do." Zeke hoped this kitten was the last. The girls refused to go to bed until all the kittens had been born. But Buffy started panting again, signifying the onset of another birth.

Henrietta sniffed her way in and dropped into the corner, her tongue lolling out as she joined the scene. The doorbell rang and August and Summer both sprang up from their perch on the floor by the tub.

Zeke rose, but August pointed her finger at him. "No, Daddy, you watch Buffy. We'll get it." August and her sister scrambled through the door at the same time. Zeke heard their feet padding on the hardwood floor in the foyer as the doorbell rang for the second time.

"Paige!" both girls chimed.

"Hi, girls."

A second of elation gathered inside Zeke at Paige's soft musical drawl, but his smile instantly faded when he realized the house was a mess. Boxes cluttered the den, laundry littered the sofa, blankets and kittens filled his bathtub, and pizza sauce spotted his shirt where Henrietta had licked him. He pinched the bridge of his nose. He didn't have to worry about Paige being attracted to him. She'd never be able to wade through the tornado-strewn house to find him.

"Daddy, Paige brought a treat," August yelled.

Summer raced into the bathroom. "Daddy, look!"

Buffy's panting quickened and she dropped another kitten just as Paige and Summer stepped into the doorway.

"We're having kittens," August announced proudly.

Paige's expression turned wary. "I hope I didn't come at a bad time. I brought over some—"

"Brownies! Yum!" Both girls reached for the basket and Henrietta lunged against Paige, almost knocking her over.

Zeke grabbed Henrietta while Paige held the brownies in the air. "Get down," Zeke yelled.

Henrietta chowed down on the chocolate chunks that spilled from the basket. Paige's rich laughter rang through the crowded bathroom, joined first by August's, then Summer's.

Zeke lost himself in the moment. It was the first time Summer had laughed in ages. She'd taken the divorce harder than August, having bad dreams and moping around. "Thanks, Paige, those look great," he said, reaching for a brownie.

"Sure." Paige leaned over and peeked inside the tub. "The kittens are precious. How many so far?"

Summer held up five fingers.

"The spotted one's called Callie," August said.

"And the white one is Cotton."

Paige nodded. "Do you think she's finished?"

Zeke shrugged. "Probably." His pulse hammered as Paige knelt, her bare thigh brushing against his. She reached a finger inside to pet the baby calico's fur.

"They're beautiful," Paige said softly.

The girls gobbled a brownie, dropping chocolate flakes all over the floor. Henrietta quickly lapped up the crumbs.

"Take Henrietta and put her in the yard," he told the girls. "Then put on your pj's and brush your teeth. *With* toothpaste. I'll be right in to kiss you good-night."

The girls scampered out, leaving Paige and Zeke alone. Paige watched the kittens nurse and Zeke forced his hands to remain on the tub when they desperately itched to touch her. "Thanks for the brownies," Zeke said. "My favorite."

Paige's gaze locked with his, but she quickly looked away. "I...I meant to tell you earlier that we've had some vandalism in the neighborhood."

"What?" Zeke's pulse raced. "I thought this neighborhood was safe. That's why I moved here."

"It is." Paige placed a reassuring hand on his arm. "We think the vandals are teenagers. So far, they've been sneaking into houses, playing video games, generally messing up people's homes."

"Sounds like some real troublemakers," Zeke said.

"Anyway," Paige continued, removing her hand, "We're organizing a neighborhood watch program. The first meeting's next week at my house." She absentmindedly ran her tongue over her lower lip as if she were nervous, drawing Zeke's gaze to the spot. "I hope you'll come."

Zeke tried not to read anything personal into the invitation, though he wondered why Paige suddenly averted her gaze again. "I'll try to make it. That is, if I don't get hung up at the clinic."

Paige nodded. "I left a flier on your kitchen counter."

He winced, wondering how she'd found the counter.

Paige laughed as if she'd read his mind. "It's by the pizza box."

He chuckled, aware her eyes darkened when she gazed at him. His body tightened at the undercurrent of attraction strumming between them. Her soft strawberry scent invaded his senses, making him momentarily forget all the reasons he shouldn't touch her. A dollop of chocolate batter dotted her cheek and he reached out and gently brushed it onto his fingertip. She glanced up in surprise, her eyes widening when he licked the tip of his finger.

Paige's expression filled with uncertainty, but her lips parted slightly as if in invitation. She was so close her warm breath mingled with his own. Tension, tight and sensual, radiated between them, drawing her closer, dragging him into a web of desire he hadn't felt in a long time. A year of celibacy surged into need. He didn't miss the sex as much as he missed the affection, the tender look a woman could give a man, the sweet satisfaction in hearing her whisper his name. Temptation made him tilt his head, and the sensuality and innocence in her expression shocked him.

"We're ready!" August shouted.

His children's voices jarred him back to reality. "I'll be right back," he said in a husky voice. *Don't move.*

He took the steps two at a time, ushered his daughters back upstairs and into bed, then said good-night in record time. He forced himself to walk back down the steps. He didn't want to act too eager. After all, he'd barely met the woman. He didn't even know if she had a boyfriend.

But when he stepped into the bathroom, Paige had disappeared.

Chapter Three

Paige avoided Zeke all week. Still, the memory of his masculine scent and his breath whispering against her face made her heart pound with excitement. And turmoil.

Why did all the handsome ones have to be married, divorced with kids, or already committed? Not that she was actively manhunting, but a date here and there would be nice. She deserved some fun. But Zeke Blalock definitely didn't fit the idea of footloose and fancy-free. Even if he wanted a no-strings relationship, it wouldn't be fair to his children. They wanted a mother.

And she was not mommy material.

She tried to recall the negative aspects of her neighbor—his house was a mess, he had animals everywhere, and he had no sense of style. For heaven's sake, his pants and shirt hadn't even matched.

Still, she'd worked late two nights in a row at the dress shop so she wouldn't give in to temptation and visit him. The other two evenings she'd stayed up well past midnight working on her design project. The black satin dress had proved to be more of a challenge than she'd expected—especially since every time she pinned the material around herself to assess the fitting, she imagined Zeke unpinning it.

Thursday afternoon, she stood in the window of Beverly's Boutique, redressing the mannequin. She'd chosen a forest green linen suit and elegant accessories to complement the outfit.

"That looks great." Beverly traced a finger over the paisley silk scarf she'd used to accessorize the suit.

"Thanks." Paige changed the belt for the third time.

"You have a hot date tonight?" The thirty-five-year-old entrepreneur who owned the store had become a good friend and confidant in the past few months.

"Not even a cold one," Paige said with a wry laugh. *Not a possibility either.* "The neighbors are coming over for a meeting. I am going to an engagement party for a friend tomorrow, though."

"Great." Beverly tapped her polished nails on the counter. "Maybe you'll meet someone there. You're single and free now, you should be dating a different guy every night."

"I don't have time." Paige stepped back to scrutinize her work. "I'm working my way through school, remember?"

A customer slipped into the shop and Beverly's posture straightened as she recognized the possibility of a sale. The tall brunette flitted through the store, choosing several outfits to try on, then meandered over to the jewelry counter. Beverly would be off to brownnose any second. Talk about the pot calling the kettle black. Beverly worked seventy-something hours every week. Her social life was more nonexistent than Paige's.

Beverly gave her a forlorn look as if she hated to run out in the middle of such an important conversation. Paige laughed, nonplussed. "Go on, make your sale."

Paige cleaned up the window area, closed out one of the cash registers and waved goodbye as Beverly ran the customer's credit card through the machine. She could almost hear Beverly's squeals of excitement as the dollar signs brringed. She admired Beverly. After her husband had deserted her for a younger woman, Bev had borrowed money, opened the shop and made a success out of it.

Paige intended to make a success out of herself the way Bev had with the shop. Her high school home ec teacher had raved over her sewing projects, and a couple of her college professors had encouraged her dream of becoming a designer. Even if she never made it big with her own designs, she could work as a buyer for a big department store.

As she pulled into her driveway, she noticed Zeke and the girls' empty driveway. As a veterinarian, Zeke probably had to work long hours. Shoving thoughts of them from her mind, she strolled up her driveway and went inside to enjoy the peace and quiet. Zeke probably wouldn't even make the meeting.

WHAT HE WOULDN'T give for five minutes of peace and quiet before the meeting, Zeke thought as Summer and August battled over who would push the grocery cart. But hoping for peace was futile with two exhausted, hungry, irritable girls in tow. He tried to ignore his daughters' next argument—which kind of cereal to purchase—as he wove his way through the aisles searching for something nutritious to serve them that could be nuked in the microwave and ready to eat in five minutes.

"I'm starving," August said, dragging the toes of her sneakers.

"And I'm tired," Summer whined.

"I'm almost done." Zeke ignored the boxes of sugar-coated cereal the girls sneaked into the cart. Dinner, bath, the baby-sitter—he wondered how fast he could manage it all once he arrived home.

The young girl behind the counter snapped her gum as she rang his purchases, her gold nose ring dangling precariously. He inwardly cringed, feeling a million years old. How would he handle it if Summer or August grew up and wanted their bodies pierced or tattooed in ungodly places?

"Did you have fun at day care today?" he asked.

"No, Charlie stoled my finger-paint picture," Summer said.

"But I smacked him one," August said.

"You did what?" Zeke's gaze shot to August.

"Right between the eyes," August said.

"He bledded and everythin'," Summer mumbled in a low voice.

The girl behind the counter laughed, flashing a mouth full of braces. "Fifty-two dollars and thirty-five cents."

Zeke sighed. What kind of school allowed children to steal and hit each other?

"Yeah, Ms. Edie said she's gonna call you," August said. "But I tolded her you'd want me to 'tect Summer."

Uh-oh. Zeke paid for the groceries and hauled his girls toward the minivan. On the ride home, he heard them nibbling on the dry cereal, and his thoughts drifted to his uncertainties about parenting. The girls were only in preschool and he was already receiving discipline calls from the teachers. His stomach knotted. He needed a woman's help. What if he totally screwed up this parenting thing? Would his kids wind up on some daytime talk show one day?

As soon as they pulled in the driveway, the twins ran to check on the kittens. He fixed soup and sandwiches, eating quickly so he could make the meeting next door.

He tried to stifle a tingle of excitement at the thought of seeing Paige again.

Zeke showered and quickly changed, choosing his clothes carefully. Being color-blind made matching his wardrobe difficult, so he'd pinned simple tags inside. He carefully matched the tags, then dragged on fresh army green slacks and a cream shirt. By the time the sitter, a teen from down the block, had arrived, he had minutes before the meeting was to start. He strode next door, wondering if he would have a few minutes alone with Paige before the neighbors descended.

PAIGE OPENED THE door and tried not to react to the sight of Zeke's handsome face grinning at her. Then she noticed his dark gray slacks and brown shirt, and a frown wrinkled her brow. And his socks—one navy, the other brown. The poor man, someone needed to dress him!

"Is something wrong? You're frowning."

"No," Paige said, quickly recovering. "Come on in. You're the first one here." *Even with mismatched clothes, you look sexy as hell. Darn it.*

Zeke entered, sweeping the comfy room with his dark gaze. "Nice house. A little neater than mine."

"I live alone. That makes all the difference."

"Yeah." He jammed his hands in his pockets. "I guess it does."

She ignored his adorable dimple and offered him a soda as they worked their way into her den. Thankfully the doorbell rang again and Paige hurried to answer it, grateful not to be alone with Zeke.

Within minutes, neighbors filled the room, chatting easily. Zeke smiled politely to the guests as Mrs. Spivy introduced him. A slender, plain woman with short brown hair sat on his left and Dannika, a tall, leggy divorced brunette, maneuvered her chair close to his right. Paige caught Zeke's panicked look and almost felt sorry for him. Then Derrick came in and swooped her into a hug.

She threw her arms around him. ''I'm so happy for you and Amelia,'' she whispered. ''I just knew the two of you were perfect for each other.''

Derrick kissed her cheek. ''I love you, you know that! You are the greatest, Paige.''

Paige laughed, but the two of them pulled apart when she heard Mrs. Spivy clucking. ''Can you two put your love life on hold while we get this meeting under way?''

''CAN YOU TWO put your love life on hold while we get this meeting under way?'' Mrs. Spivy's words reverberated in Zeke's mind like a yelping cocker spaniel. The macho guy who held Paige simply grinned and pulled her onto the couch beside him, slinging an arm around her in a too-cozy move that rattled Zeke's teeth. The guy loved her—he'd said so right in front of the whole neighborhood.

So much for wondering if Paige had a boyfriend. And he'd thought they'd had chemistry between them. She'd probably been suffering from shock over his messy house and sloppy appearance. And that flier—he was mortified.

''Let's get started,'' Paige said in her silky voice. ''We're all aware there've been some break-ins recently.''

Heads nodded in agreement. Zeke's attention strayed as he studied Paige's den. A comfortable leather couch, beige and red plaid recliner, pine tables. Everything neat and orderly. Paige's voice broke into his reverie.

''And the police are doing all they can.'' Paige folded her hands together. ''But we've always been a close neighborhood, so Mrs. Spivy suggested we start this neighborhood watch program.''

''I still can't get the ketchup out of my white sofa,'' Myrtle Simmons said with a sigh.

''They took my car, drove it around and left it dead on empty,'' Bert Collins added.

''One of 'em left a pair of unmentionables on my floor,'' June Bailey said, patting her neatly coiffured hair.

''The police are investigating each incident. But as citizens, we can help prevent crime. We want to keep our kids safe.''

A hushed chorus of agreement filled the room. The woman beside Zeke offered him a shy smile. ''I want my Daryl to be safe. Especially since his father's not around.''

He nodded, wondering if he'd been pegged as potential father material.

Paige cleared her throat. ''We have a large neighborhood so we've decided to pair off and run regular checks on each other's homes. Derrick assures me that posting a sign announcing our watch program will deter some crimes.''

A hearty discussion followed, including who worked and who stayed home, how Genie Atkins would watch anyone's house when she was bedridden, who to call if someone saw something suspicious, and how old Mr. Pirkle could dial the phone on a bad day with his arthritis. Mrs. Spivy silenced the room with her hand. ''I've already made a list to pair people up.'' She stood and handed out the papers. Zeke glanced at his and saw he'd been paired with Paige. He felt as if he'd won a small lottery.

''In setting this up, I took into account homes with working parents, elderly people at home who might need help, the proximity of neighbors.'' The leggy brunette beside him had been paired with Derrick. Good.

''I'm the new vet in town,'' Zeke announced. ''Watchdogs help in deterring break-ins. If anyone wants a dog or pet, let me know and I'll match you with an appropriate animal.''

''That's a great idea,'' the woman beside him whispered. ''I want one of those little terriers.''

''I'll see what I can do,'' he said, avoiding her come-hither look.

''I own a security consulting business,'' Derrick added. ''I'll be happy to install new dead bolts on doors and windows. If anyone wants a security system, we'll work out a special deal.''

''That would be wonderful.'' Mrs. Spivy pressed her hands to her cheeks and tittered. ''We feel so much safer with you around, dear.''

Zeke ground his teeth. He was going to provide dogs to people and help teach the animals how to pee outside while Derrick installed security systems.

An hour later, the crowd dispersed and Zeke couldn't think of a reason to stay any longer, especially when Derrick cornered Paige in a private conversation.

It was better Paige had a boyfriend, he told himself as he left via the back door. She wanted a career, he wanted a wife and mother for his girls. And Renee had already taught him about the heartbreak involved when you tried to combine the two.

''I'D LOVE TO help you find a house for Amelia,'' Paige said, grinning at Derrick.

''I thought you might help me choose a bracelet as an engagement gift, too.''

Paige winced, hoping Amelia wasn't already banking

on another failed altar attempt, but she smiled and patted Derrick's arm. "I'd love to, Derrick."

Derrick's smile grew wider. "Great. Now what about you, Paige? Are you interested in anyone?"

Paige shook her head emphatically, pretending nonchalance as she scanned the room for Zeke. "I'm concentrating on finishing my degree."

"How about that guy who moved in next door?" Derrick raised a dark eyebrow. "He was giving you the eye during the meeting."

Paige brushed at a piece of lint on her shirt. "You're imagining things. He wasn't looking at me any certain way."

Derrick's warm laughter boomed. "Look, Paige. I know that predatory gleam when I see it."

Paige rolled her eyes. "He's a neighbor, that's all. Besides," she said, trying to hide her disappointment over Zeke leaving without saying goodbye. "He has kids."

Derrick nodded knowingly. "You think it'll be a repeat of Eric?"

Paige shrugged. "I can't take any chances."

ZEKE PAID THE baby-sitter, watched her walk across the street to her house, then grabbed a beer and sank onto the sofa. He flipped on the TV, grimacing when he noticed old reruns of the syndicated show, *Father Knows Best,* playing. His insecurities about single parenting kicked in again.

He knew what to do with a sick animal, could perform surgery on a traumatized cat or dog, but would he know what was best for his children?

They needed a mother. And as much as he hated the dating game, he should make himself look for someone suitable. Paige's image quickly surfaced, but he blotted it away like an unwanted ink stain, then flipped the channel again and groaned as *The Brady Bunch* piped onto the TV. Now, that was exactly the kind of woman he needed. A stay-at-home mom, cook, housekeeper.

But his body curled in distaste. Not very modern thinking. Aggravated with himself, he stood, ready to take Henrietta for a walk and settle down for the night. Henrietta was nowhere in sight.

He noticed his front door swinging open and glanced outside to see a shadow that looked like Henrietta trotting toward Paige's. He groaned, hoping Henrietta hadn't gone in search of more brownies. He certainly didn't want to interrupt Paige, especially if loverboy was still there drooling all over her like a lovesick St. Bernard.

"HENRIETTA, WHAT ARE you doing here?" Paige watched in surprise as the bulky dog wiggled through her pet door and sniffed the kitchen floor. Henrietta turned up her nose and her eyelids drooped in a pitiful begging expression. "Sorry, I don't have any brownies tonight," Paige said sympathetically. She studied the pet door, wondering if she should board it up against the vandals. But the door was so small, only a child could crawl through.

The dog whimpered and Paige stepped from her stool and walked awkwardly toward her, clutching the black satin around her body. After the neighbors had left, she'd decided to experiment with a new design. She barely had the fabric pinned above her shoulder.

Henrietta sprawled on her floor, looking woeful. Feeling sorry for her, Paige unwrapped a leftover biscuit from her counter and handed it to her. The mutt accepted it happily, thumping the floor with her short, stubby tail.

"Come on, Henrietta. I bet the girls are looking for

you.'' Paige opened the back door and almost bumped into Zeke.

''She's here,'' Page said. ''I guess she came looking for more brownies,'' Paige said.

Zeke reprimanded the dog. Too late, Paige remembered she was wearing nothing but her panties and the scrap of black silk wrapped turban style around her body. Zeke's gaze flashed with heat as he skimmed her attire. Paige felt exposed, as if the silk were as transparent as cellophane. Her nipples beaded beneath the skimpy fabric and desire curled low in her belly. He had to know she was naked under the fabric. A slow smile spread on Zeke's face, revealing that killer dimple in his left cheek. She was a goner.

Paige backed away, panic bubbling inside. Warning bells chimed in her head like a police siren, screeching for her to run—to avoid impending danger.

''Nice outfit,'' Zeke said with a broad grin.

Paige ignored the flutter in her stomach. ''It's a project for my clothing class.''

''Hmm.'' Zeke folded one arm across his middle and grinned wickedly as his gaze rested on her bare shoulder. ''I think you should get an A plus. Maybe even extra credit.''

Paige shivered at the flash of hunger in his eyes, then swept her hands down the sides of the satin. A mistake. The slippery material drooped off her other shoulder, making her feel bare. ''It's not finished yet,'' she said taking another step back inside her house.

Henrietta must have realized she was being ignored because she suddenly lunged against Paige's knees, begging for another biscuit.

''No, Henrietta,'' Zeke ordered.

Paige shrieked, pushing at the animal. But Henrietta's

paws caught the fabric and became embedded. Zeke
yanked at the dog, but Henrietta snatched the silk between her teeth and jerked it so hard the material ripped,
then dropped completely to the ground. Paige shrieked
again and Henrietta took off running with the fabric
clenched in her mouth as if she'd found a fresh ham bone.
Paige brought her hands up to cover herself.

"Henrietta, come back here!" Zeke glanced at Paige
and hesitated. She bit down on her bottom lip as he zeroed in on her skimpy black bikini panties and bare
breasts. Then he swallowed visibly, sweat beading on his
lip. If Paige hadn't been so utterly mortified, she would
have admired the gallant way he brought his face up to
hers. "I'll get her."

"I'll be inside," Paige said in a voice that squeaked
out. Then she ran in her house to safety, her face burning.

ZEKE'S HEART pounded as he chased Henrietta across the
yard. Not only had his children humiliated him, now his
damn dog had embarrassed him.

Of course, Paige looked pretty embarrassed herself.

He'd known from her running attire she had a nice
figure, but her firm, high breasts had taken his breath
away, and her muscular thighs and slim legs stretched
out from those bikini panties like a man's dream. Exhausted or not, after seeing Paige half-naked, he'd never
be able to sleep tonight.

"Henrietta, give me the fabric!" he ordered.

Henrietta growled, darted into the backyard and
dragged it into her doghouse.

He knelt on his hands and knees and crawled toward
the entrance of the doghouse. "Here, Henrietta. Here,
doggie. Give me the fabric."

Henrietta growled again. The dog acted as though the

material was a security blanket, like the ones his daughters slept with. A brainstorm hit him and he ran inside, grabbed an old blanket and hurried back. Dropping to his knees again, he stuffed the blanket inside. "Here, nice warm, cozy blanket for Henrietta. Give me the other one."

After several long minutes of coaxing, he finally exchanged the material for the blanket and examined it. It was wet with dog slobber, dirty and grass stained—what was he going to tell Paige?

Before he faced her, he rushed in to check on the girls. Thankfully they were both snuggled in their beds sound asleep. He practiced an apology as he walked back to Paige's house, trying desperately not to think about how sexy and enticing she looked wearing nothing except black lace, with her auburn hair feathered around her bare shoulders, her dusky nipples pouting for attention.

When he reached her porch, he exhaled a shaky breath. As if she'd been standing with her hand on the doorknob, she opened the door, but only wide enough for him to see her blushing face and the big, green furry housecoat she'd pulled to her chin. He almost laughed, but the memory of her bare breasts remained imprinted in his brain and arousal strummed through his body, throwing him completely off center.

"I'm afraid Henrietta ruined the material," he said sheepishly. "I'll replace it if you'll tell me where to find the fabric, or I can write you a check to cover the costs."

Paige narrowed her eyes in disappointment. "No, I don't want money. Besides, the project's due tomorrow."

"Tomorrow?" He jammed his hands in his pockets, realizing the stores were probably closed. "Well, um, you want me to wash it for you?"

Paige shook her head. "No, this fabric isn't washable."

"Paige, I'm sorry. At least let me take it to the cleaners?"

She patted his hand in a sympathetic gesture. Her fingers were soft and warm and he fought the urge to wrap her dainty hand in his. "Don't worry, Zeke. I have some extra fabric. I'll make a short dress instead of a long one."

Zeke read the uncertainty in her expression as she studied the stained material, but admired her easygoing nature. She should be furious with him.

He felt even more guilty. "Well, I guess I should go then."

"I guess."

"Good luck with the project."

"Thanks."

He stared into her eyes, a picture of her naked flashing through his head like an erotic magazine photo. "Are you sure there's nothing else I can do?" *Maybe help pin the material around you, then take it off and touch you all over?*

"I'm sure," Paige said softly. "Go on back to the girls."

"Oh, yeah, right." *The girls.* Geez, he'd almost forgotten. What kind of father was he?

"Well, I'll see you."

"Yeah, see you."

"Good night, Paige."

"Good night."

Zeke slowly walked back to his house, his thoughts jumbled. He liked Paige, and he was undeniably attracted to her. But he had to focus on raising his daughters.

Back inside, he yanked off his clothes, took a quick

shower and collapsed into bed. It had been an exhausting day. As he closed his eyes, images of Paige's flushed skin, her rosy lips, her high cheekbones and dainty nose, her glorious auburn hair, her curvy, sexy legs taunted him. He missed having a woman's body snuggled up next to his, his legs tangled with her silky, smooth skin, her soft breath whispering against his face.

Problem was, he didn't just want any woman. He wanted Paige Watkins.

Reality shattered his dreams when he rolled over to the empty space beside him and felt the crisp cool sheets. He couldn't have Paige. And if he pursued her, he'd be on a collision course with trouble.

So once again, he went to sleep. Alone.

PAIGE SHOVED THE embarrassing memory of Zeke seeing her practically naked from her mind and tried to salvage her project. Unfortunately, Zeke's heated gaze and sexy smile popped into her head at the most inopportune times. She'd stuck herself about twenty times with a pin and had almost sewn her finger on the sewing machine. Finally, around 3 a.m., she finished the dress and sat back to admire her work. She'd fashioned a tea-length semi-formal dress that dipped off one shoulder. The tapered skirt accentuated a woman's normal curves while drawing attention to her best features. Around 4 a.m., she stumbled into bed and closed her eyes.

Zeke's unbidden image drifted through her dreams but this time, Zeke was undressing her. And this time, she blushed from excitement and passion. Then she undressed him, savoring every delightful moment as his bronze skin and rippled muscles were unveiled.

At 5 a.m., Paige woke up from her dream with the sheets tangled around her, her head throbbing from lack of sleep. Shocked at her lustful thoughts she leapt out of bed, threw on her jogging clothes and ran out the door.

Forty-five minutes later, she returned to the house, her energy renewed. The neighborhood had been filled with early morning walkers and runners and the fresh air had cleansed her senses. She showered, planning to have breakfast and study her marketing before she headed to her 9 a.m. class. But when she stepped into her kitchen, there sat the troublemaker—Henrietta.

"COME ON, GIRLS, we need to leave." Zeke buttoned his white shirt, tucking it inside his pleated navy trousers.

"But I can't find my shoes," August said.

"Try your feet." Zeke pointed to her bright yellow sneakers.

"Not these." August rolled her eyes. "They don't match my blue dress."

"I see." Actually, he didn't. Being color-blind definitely had its limitations.

"Here they are!" Summer held up another pair of shoes.

"Bailey's bringing his grandma, too," August said. "'Cause his mom is a 'portant psych...head doctor."

Zeke clamped his mouth together to prevent a chuckle, grateful at least one other child had a substitute mom for the tea. The telephone jangled and Summer and August raced to it, fighting over who would answer. After a few seconds of wrestling, they finally compromised and held it between them. But their faces instantly crumpled before him.

"Grammy can't come to the tea!" August wailed.

"She's throwed up her waffles." Summer's lower lip trembled, then she promptly burst into tears.

His heart jumped into his throat as he grabbed the phone. "Hello, Mom. Are you okay?"

"Listen, Zeke, I'm so sorry, but I have the flu." His mother's voice sounded weak. "It's one of those twenty-four-hour bugs, but I don't want to expose the girls."

"Oh, Mom, I'm so sorry you're ill." Zeke rubbed his temple, trying to talk over the sound of Summer's wailing. "Sure, Mom, I understand. I hope you feel better."

"Tell the girls I'll make it up to them. They can spend next weekend with me."

Sympathy for his mother softened his voice. "It's okay. These things happen. The girls understand." He grimaced, hoping he sounded halfway convincing. He had a feeling his mother could hear Summer bellowing and August kicking her feet against the steps. He expected August to start throwing things any minute.

"You know I'll be glad to keep the twins if you want to go out sometime, son. There's a couple of attractive single women in my church, women who like to stay home—"

"I'm not interested, Mom."

"You're not still pining for that awful woman, Renee, are you?"

"No." Zeke gritted his teeth. "I don't care if I ever see her again."

"Good. I told you she wasn't right for you. But I'll help you find someone—"

"Mother, I don't need you to help me—" he paused to rein in his temper "—except with the girls occasionally. Now get some rest. I'll call you in a day or two." He hung up the phone, uncertain how to handle his daughters' disappointment.

"I'm not going to school!" August yanked off her

shoes and tossed them into the corner. The shoes banged against the wall and bounced off with a loud thud.

"Me neither." Summer poked out her bottom lip.

"Girls, listen," Zeke said, feeling forlorn himself. "Grandma can't help getting sick. I know you're disappointed—"

"You don't know anything!" August yelled. "You don't have to go to school without a mommy, not even a subst...a pretend one!"

Zeke sank into the chair beside the phone and dropped his head, despair momentarily filling him. Maybe he didn't know anything. He kept telling himself he was doing the best he could. *But what if it's not enough?*

The doorbell rang, giving him a moment's reprieve, and when he opened the door, Paige stood on the other side, Henrietta in hand.

Was she still upset about the night before?

Paige pointed to the ground where Henrietta lay sprawled on her belly. "Henrietta seems to like my place."

Summer's bellowing drowned out his reply. August ran over and flung herself at Paige, knocking her off balance.

"What's wrong?" Paige's brows crinkled in concern.

"We don't wanna go to school," August wailed.

"We can't go today." Summer sat up and rubbed her puffy, swollen eyes.

Paige patted August's back. "Why can't you go, sweetie?"

Zeke frowned, a headache forming behind his eyes. "They're having this Mommy and Me Tea at school and my grandma was supposed to go—"

"'Cept she's sick," August said, sniffling.

"She's upchucking," Summer cried.

He frowned at the girls. "You have to go to school, girls. Dad's already late for work. You don't want the sick animals to get sicker because I'm not there, do you?"

August hedged, chewing her lip. Summer sniffed and swiped at her nose with the sleeve of her dress.

"We could go to work with you," August suggested.

Frustration welled up inside Zeke. "Girls, I can't keep you there all day. I have surgery scheduled—"

August tightened her grip around Paige's legs. Summer leaned over and whispered something in her sister's ear. August nodded to her twin, then spoke up, her eyes wide. "Okay, we'll go, Daddy, under one 'dition."

"A condition?" Zeke ran a hand over his jaw. "I don't believe this. I'm bargaining with my four-year-olds."

"You want us to go to school?" August folded her arms as if preparing for battle.

Zeke nodded.

"Then Paige has to come to the tea with us."

Chapter Four

Paige quickly searched Zeke's face for his reaction. Kids! They had no idea how awkward they'd made things for both of them. Zeke looked as if he'd been strung up and left dangling over a tank of hot oil. "Um, girls—"

"I'm sure Paige is busy," Zeke cut in firmly, giving the children a stern glare.

Paige hesitated. She *was* busy. She had to turn in her project at ten. But Zeke's haggard expression and the twin's swollen eyes tore at her heart. She couldn't help but sympathize, and she'd always had trouble saying no, especially to innocent children. Another reason she wouldn't make a good mother.

"I'm sorry you walked in on all this, Paige. We'll work it out somehow." Zeke shrugged, then took Henrietta by the collar and pulled her inside. She flopped at the girl's feet and covered her furry face with her paws, letting out a whine of her own that added to the saga of sobbing.

"I do have class," Paige said, hoping the girls would be all right. "My project's due today—"

"You don't like us," August blurted, poking out her bottom lip.

"It's 'cause we're lots of trouble." Summer swiped at her puffy eyes. "Just like Mommy said."

Paige's chest tightened at the misery in the girls' expressions. She chewed her lip, not knowing what to say. Fury streaked Zeke's face, but he seemed to mask it quickly as he knelt before the girls. He patted both their backs, then spoke in a calm husky voice, "Listen here, girls. I don't know why your mother said that, but I'm sure she didn't mean it the way it sounded. Your mom loves you."

Summer's lip trembled. "She said we make too much messes to go with her."

"That we'd get in the way. That's why she won't come back," Summer's voice cracked as another onslaught of tears slipped down her cheeks. "Eber."

Moisture pooled in Paige's eyes but she blinked to stem the tears, shifting uncomfortably. She felt like an intruder to a private conversation. Zeke clenched his fists by his sides and her heart went out to him. She should retreat to her own yard, give the threesome time to discuss the situation, but her feet refused to budge. She remembered how her mother's absenteeism from the events in her life had made her feel. And Summer and August's mother had *chosen* to leave when they were small. They couldn't possibly understand.

"I'm sure Mom was just in a bad mood when she said those things, honey." Zeke tipped Summer's chin up with his thumb. "She loves both of you very much. We'll call her tonight and you can talk to her, okay?"

"We tolded her we'd be good," Summer whispered. She stuck her thumb in her mouth and chewed on her fingernail.

Paige's own nails dug into the palms of her hands. She cleared her throat before she spoke, sympathizing with

Zeke. How could any parent explain or defend another parent who'd deserted their child? Zeke's broad shoulders stiffened, his chocolate eyes dark with anger. And some other emotion she didn't recognize. Hurt? Was he still mourning over the loss of the woman, or did he hate her for leaving them?

"What time is the tea?" Paige finally asked.

Zeke's gaze locked with hers and he shook his head, his voice hard when he spoke. "Look, I appreciate the offer, but you don't have to do this, Paige. The girls are my responsibility, I can take care of them."

"I know you can." Paige blushed, suddenly aware how handsome Zeke looked in his white shirt and navy slacks. "But I want to go to the tea. For them." She forced herself to stop staring at him, then knelt beside the girls and patted their hands. "I haven't been to a tea in ages. What time should I be there?"

"Twelbe o'clock," Summer and August said in unison.

"You're really gonna come?" August asked in disbelief.

"Paige—"

"I'm really going to come." Paige tucked a strand of the little girl's red hair behind her ear, ignoring Zeke's brittle look, "that is, if it's okay with your daddy."

Zeke's smiled tightly, his voice low, "I guess so."

"We promise not to pester you too much," Summer said in a shaky voice that tore at Paige's heart.

"You could never pester me too much, girls. We're friends," Paige said gently. Both girls threw their arms around her neck and Paige fell backward with the impact, almost toppling to the floor.

Zeke's tender look sent butterflies shimmying through her stomach. "Hey, you, two, you're going to wear Paige out before the tea.'' When Zeke had settled the twins on the floor, he reached out a hand and helped Paige up. His hand was hot and rough, his olive skin a sharp contrast to her pale complexion, his hand almost swallowing hers in size. The irises of his dark eyes sparkled with awareness, traces of the emotional ordeal with his daughters still lingering in the soft set of his mouth and the tight lines around his eyes. Paige's heart thumped a strange pitter-patter, his masculine touch sending a trace of awareness rippling through her, igniting an undercurrent of emotional and sexual energy that she refused to acknowledge.

"Thanks, Paige, I appreciate this." Zeke squeezed her hand, holding it a fraction of a second longer than she thought necessary.

"Sure, it'll be fun," she said, praying she didn't make any mistakes. The girls would be in school, teachers would be there, nothing could happen. They would be safe.

She could be the girls' friend and Zeke's, but not his lover. If she let herself get attached to them, and they left, she'd never survive. Not a second time. Eric had claimed to despise his ex, but had taken her back the second she'd come groveling. And when Paige had made a mistake with his son, Eric had immediately pointed out that Paige wasn't Joey's real mother.

She was simply going to be neighborly to Zeke and his children, nothing more.

The girls grabbed their shoes, then tugged at Zeke's pant leg as if they suddenly couldn't wait to go to school. "Daddy, we're gonna be late." August charged toward the door.

"Yeah, let's hurry." Summer pulled at his hand. "We

have to decorate the…'' She clamped her hand over her mouth, her eyes glowing with excitement.

August poked her. ''Shh, you're not sposed to tell.''

Summer giggled. ''The surprise for the tea,'' she finished.

Paige stood and met Zeke's gaze. His dark eyes held hers and for a moment she forgot the girls were in the room. Turmoil hardened his angular features and his shoulders slumped. He seemed tired and sad and angry at the same time. Did his heart still belong to his ex? Or did he have a sixth sense about not trusting her with his daughters?

He raked a hand through his hair, the longish ends brushing the collar of his shirt, then clenched his teeth when he spoke. ''Thanks, Paige. I owe you one.''

Paige shrugged and swallowed the sudden nervous tension wedging itself between them, barely noticing when Summer ran outside. He sounded as if he'd bitten the words out, as if he hated being indebted to her. Had she made a mistake? Had he hoped she would decline? She finally shook her head, breaking the moment. ''No problem. That's what neighbors are for.'' She glanced at her watch, trying not to dwell on the masculine scent wafting around her. His aftershave reminded her of the outdoors—rugged, woodsy, and intoxicating—and the smattering of dark hair she noticed peeking through the top of his white shirt warmed her insides, suddenly making her feel hot. ''I really need to go though, or I'll miss my first period class.'' Her legs quaked as she stumbled toward the door.

''Come on, Daddy!'' Summer and August screamed from the driveway.

Zeke chuckled at the girls, some of his tension draining

away. "This is really nice of you," he said quietly. "I know you had your day all planned."

Paige shrugged again. "I told you, it's no big deal. I still have time to make class, turn in my project, go to the tea, then come home and get ready for my date tonight." As soon as she said the words, Zeke's jaw seemed to tighten again. Or maybe it was her imagination. Then his expression turned blank and he turned and walked toward his car. She followed, trying not to stare at his delectable behind or the way his broad shoulders filled out his starched shirt.

"Oh, by the way. Where is the tea?" Paige called.

Zeke pivoted slightly as he opened the car door for the girls. "At Riverwood Day Care. Do you know where it is?"

Paige nodded, her stomach cramping. Of course, she remembered the day care. She'd gone there herself as a child. And she'd absolutely *hated* it.

PERSPIRATION TRICKLED down Zeke's collar and dampened his shirt. He had to force himself to remain calm and concentrate on the sutures needed to repair the Maltese's battered leg, but his jaw ached from clenching it. Damn Renee. She'd actually told the twins they were too much trouble. How could she have said something so cruel to her own daughters? Tension churned through his stomach, and he gripped the needle, his fingers trembling with anger. Taking a deep breath, he exhaled, the pent-up air from his lungs wheezing out shakily, then set to work repairing the animal. Thank God the shot had worked and Snowball now lay limply on the table. He wasn't in the mood to struggle with the dog or be bitten, and although she was normally a sweet, friendly little thing, any animal reacted differently when in pain. He stroked Snowball's soft white fur, then swabbed antiseptic on the nasty wound to clean it before he added the stitches. His best estimate—she'd need about fifteen. She had taken quite a beating from a much larger German shepherd, no doubt coming out the loser. Just the way his daughters had from someone who was *supposed* to love them.

He swallowed, blotting the girls' early morning crying jag from his mind. At least Paige had agreed to serve as their temporary mother figure for the day. But they didn't need a *temporary* mother figure. They needed a real mother, someone who'd be there at night to hold them, someone who would cuddle them when they were sick or scared, someone who wouldn't desert them for her own selfish interests. And Paige wasn't that someone. Knowing she had a career in mind, he couldn't let them become too attached to her or raise their hopes, or they would be hurt even more.

"Dr. Blalock, call on line two." His receptionist, Clara, poked her head in the treatment area.

"Can you take a message?" he asked threading the needle with the synthetic suture thread.

Clara frowned. "It's from the day care."

Zeke's heart paused, then began beating frantically against his chest. What if one of the girls were hurt? He instantly dropped the needle on the table and hurried across the room. "I'll take it in here."

Clara shut the door and he picked up the phone in the lab area. "Dr. Blalock here."

The second it took for the woman on the other end to answer seemed like an excruciating eternity. "This is Edie Benson. I'm one of the four-year-olds' teachers."

"Yes, Ms. Benson, is something wrong with Summer or August?" he asked impatiently.

"No, oh, no, they're fine." She hesitated, the silence unnerving him. "But we're having some problems at school with the girls."

"Problems? What kind of problems?"

"Well, Summer seems to get upset over little things. She cries a lot."

Tell me something I don't know.

"And August has become quite volatile lately," she continued. "The other day she hit another child."

Zeke relaxed, leaning against the whitewashed walls. "Yes, I know. She told me you'd be calling. Do you really think hitting someone is that abnormal for a four-year-old?"

"Not really," the woman said in a sympathetic voice. "Some children are naturally more aggressive than others. But lately August has been hitting a lot. And this morning she punched a little boy in the stomach. I thought it might help if you'd talk to her."

"Now?"

"Yes, she's sitting right here."

Zeke sighed. "Put her on."

"Daddy, he's a big fat meanie," August argued.

"Sweetheart, if you're upset or he's bothering you, tell your teacher. You can't go around hitting other children."

"But it's no fair, he called me a dummy."

"I'm sorry, honey. But you still can't hit him." He ran a hand through his hair, exasperated. "August, sweetie, put your teacher back on the phone. We'll talk some more tonight."

"'Kay, Daddy," August said in a pouty voice.

Zeke sighed when he heard the teacher's voice. "Ms. Benson, August says this boy is being mean to her."

"I know, and we've reprimanded the boy and are also calling his parents."

"Good. I'll talk to August again tonight."

"Thank you." Relief lightened the middle-aged woman's voice. "She's a precious little girl. I know being a single parent isn't easy."

Zeke's fingers encircled the handset so tightly his knuckles ached. "You think I'm not a good parent?"

"Oh, heavens, I didn't mean that," the woman said kindly. "But parenting is hard on everyone. And sometimes when there's a change at home, children's behavior is affected." She hesitated, then spoke softly. "I don't mean to pry, but have you considered counseling for the girls?"

Zeke's stomach clenched. "No."

"Well, it might be worthwhile. I'm afraid this mother-daughter tea we're having may have triggered some emotions. Holidays are always difficult for kids from single parent homes, especially at first."

Zeke swallowed, his voice thick. "Did the girls tell you my neighbor's coming today?"

"Yes, that's great. But still, Dr. Blalock, consider counseling. Some of the local churches offer support groups, as well as seminars and counseling for divorced families."

"Fine. I'll think about it." He rolled his shoulders to relieve the ache coiling in his neck. And he would consider counseling for the girls, he decided, as he hung up the phone. But first, he'd talk to August and see if he could understand why his sweet, darling little daughter had suddenly become a four-year-old terrorist at nursery school.

Because her mother had left her?

Renee had been gone less than a year and had said she

was moving back this summer, but he didn't harbor hopes of her returning for good. Even if she changed her mind and decided she wanted family life, he wouldn't want her. His taste for flighty blondes had run its course with their disastrous short marriage. And they'd only married because of the pregnancy. When the girls had been born, he'd grown up and accepted responsibility for them. Too bad his former wife hadn't done the same.

Since the divorce, he hadn't had the time or energy to pursue a woman, nor the desire to put his own heart on the line to be crushed again. Over the past few months, he'd avoided dating, thinking if the girls saw him with another woman, it might upset them. Now they'd advertised for a mother, and they obviously needed one. He had a few single clients, but no one he could think of sparked his interest. His mind automatically strayed to his sexy next-door neighbor. He'd definitely felt a strong physical reaction to Paige. This morning, her sweet feminine scent had invaded his entire being and had lingered with him all the way to work.

But Paige wanted to travel and work. He strode back to the stainless steel table, threaded the needle through the dog's skin, making the stitches as even in length as possible. No, Paige was simply filling in for today. He wouldn't repeat the mistakes of his past, couldn't force a woman to be a mother if she wasn't ready to be one. Renee had taught him that painful lesson.

"Are you about finished with Snowball?" Clara poked her head in the treatment area.

"In a minute. How's the waiting room?" Clara's face puckered into a frown. At forty-seven, the woman was attractive in a brash sort of way, with dark eyes and hair, but her problems had taken a toll on her appearance. Worry lines fanned beside her bloodshot eyes and gray streaked her hair. Today, he could truly sympathize. He felt as though he'd aged twenty years since the divorce.

"Only one Siamese in the cat room. But the dog side is packed. It sounds like a war zone in there." She clicked her teeth. "Almost as bad as my house."

"Not the kids again?"

She shook her head. "I should have stuck with dogs. Two teenagers are killing me. Jake wants a car and Lori had her first date. She didn't come in until two in the morning."

"Geez, I bet you were frantic." Dark circles deepened the lines below her eyes, and he wondered if she'd slept all night. He wouldn't have if it had been Summer or August out all night. Just the thought of it made him dizzy.

"She's grounded for the rest of her life," Clara said with a tight laugh. "But I don't know what I'll do with Jake. He's so angry all the time."

Like August. "I'm sorry, Clara. I wish I could help. You think it's just a teenage stage?" Zeke finished the last stitch and secured the Elizabethan neck brace on the dog so she couldn't chew on his handiwork when she awoke. Lifting her from the stainless steel table, he gently eased her down in one of the beds for recovery.

"I don't know." Clara blew out a frustrated breath. "He blames his dad for losing his job. And me for everything else." The uncertainty in her voice reminded him of his own misgivings about parenting. "I'm doing the best I can, but it doesn't seem like enough."

I know the feeling. "Maybe you should take some time off work." Zeke gave her a sympathetic smile. Her kids had problems and they had two parents. Would his daughters grow up to have even worse problems because he was a single dad?

BY HER THIRD period class, Paige had almost driven thoughts of Zeke's dark, mesmerizing disturbing eyes from her mind. *Almost.*

Dismissing the lingering sound of his deep, husky voice proved almost as difficult. She kept imagining him repeating her name in the throes of passion, while she gently erased the turmoil from his eyes with hot sultry kisses.

"Great project," Jan Roberts said, interrupting her thoughts.

"I like yours, too," Paige said, admiring the young girl's unusual design. She'd used denim fabric to create a bikini with a cover-up of sheer lace.

"I hope we get our grades back soon," Jan said as they left the classroom and headed outside. "When we see the things Professor Davidson likes about these projects, I'll have a better idea how to approach the final."

"You're right," Paige said, although she already had sketches of ideas floating through her mind.

Jan flipped her long brown hair over her shoulder, her sun-bronzed skin glimmering in the morning sunlight. "Hey, I'm meeting some of the guys for happy hour this afternoon at the pub by Arty's Antiques. Want to hang out with us?"

Paige glimpsed the two guys Jan pointed to across the landing. The tall muscular guy with brown hair looked cute in a boyish way, and the striking blonde wearing a Braves baseball cap winked at her. The year she'd taken off to save money for school and help Eric with Joey might have been ten. Both guys seemed too young for her.

"I can't," Paige said, wishing she'd meet a single, childless man who lit her fuse the way Zeke did. For now though, she had a tea to attend.

"Are you sure you don't want to come?" Jan asked.

"No, but thanks anyway. I'll see you Monday." She quickly crossed the grassy quadrangle, passed the student center where dozens of students lounged around on blankets and picnic benches enjoying the beautiful spring sunshine, then raced to her car. Sliding the key in her ancient VW Bug, she puttered out of the parking lot and drove toward the day care, rolling down her window to enjoy the sweet scents of blooming pansies and freshly cut grass as she neared the suburbs. Mothers pushed their babies in strollers, while joggers, and small kids riding bikes filled the sidewalks.

Paige spotted the day care and her palms began to sweat. As a child, she'd cried when her mother had left her in day care because the rooms were dark and dreary and crowded. She quickly parked and ambled up the sidewalk, smoothing down her black denim skirt and making sure her hair was neatly secure in the combs at the nape of her neck. She'd chosen a sleeveless, lightweight lavender sweater, hoping to create a stylish impression, but also wanting something classy enough for a mommy tea. She wanted the girls to be proud they'd invited her. Or was she trying to impress Zeke, she wondered, disturbed at the thought.

When she opened the door, the sounds of children's voices and laughter spilled out, greeting her with warmth. Bright walls painted in blues and reds and oranges and greens took her by surprise. The day care had changed drastically since she'd been small. Or had she only remembered it as dreary because she'd wanted to stay home with her mother?

Hmm. She ventured inside and noticed several adults already gathering in the foyer. A poster with a child hugging a big brown teddy bear drew her eye and she relaxed.

"Hi, I'm the director, Vanessa Ann Whitfield." A tall, attractive woman with creamy dark skin ushered them into a large open area where Paige noticed child-size furniture, posters and letters of the alphabet decorating several doors, and children's artwork displayed on bright bulletin boards. Tables had been draped in pastel-colored paper tablecloths, and punch bowls filled with red punch and pitchers of tea had been placed in the center of each table. Small chairs had been situated around low tables and the children had decorated place cards in the shapes of flowers and printed their mothers' names on them. Paige's heart squeezed slightly, seeing the crayoned scrawling of her name in between Summer's and August's.

She suddenly felt like an impostor, yet at the same time, she imagined how awkward and uncomfortable the girls would feel if the chair between them were vacant. Then the door sporting a purple dinosaur opened and children rushed out. Excited voices and chatter wafted around her as the children searched for their mothers. When August and Summer spied her, their small urchin faces lifted into a grin that Paige would never forget.

"Paige!" The girls squealed, then raced over and dragged her to the chair. "Look, we made you a tulip," August said.

"You can sit between us." Summer pointed to a bright orange child-size chair.

Paige grinned and made a show of examining the jagged edges of the paper flower. "It's beautiful. Purple tulips are my favorite."

"August cutted it," Summer said hesitantly.

"And Summer wrote your name," August said.

"It's perfect," Paige said, her chest tightening at the insecurity in the girls' eyes.

"No, it's not," Summer said. "The *g*'s crooked."

And they'd left out the *i*, but Paige would never tell them. She chewed her lip, wondering if their mother had criticized them instead of praising their efforts. She scooped up Summer, then August and gave them both a hug. "Well, it's perfect to me because you took the time to make it." She kissed them on the cheek, wondering if her momentary display of affection had embarrassed them. "And I love it," she added.

But instead of embarrassment, Summer beamed, her little cheeks rosy pink, and August grinned so wide her tongue popped through the hole where she'd lost a tooth. Then August dropped into the chair with a thud and pointed to the cookies the kids had decorated. "Sit down, Paige. We made cookies, too." The two-inch thick icing had run down the sides of the sugar cookie and sprinkles loaded the top, but Paige squeezed into the small chair, willfully ignoring the messy decorations and the calorie content as she smiled and nibbled on the gooey desserts. "Yum, these are delicious."

"Ladies and children," a smaller fair-haired woman said. "I'm Ms. Benson, the four-year-olds' teacher. I'd like to welcome you."

Everyone broke into applause. "We hope you enjoy the refreshments and short program we've planned. Feel free to browse around the center before you leave."

Everyone clapped again and Summer and August raced to the food table for drinks. Paige studied the proud moms as they exclaimed over their children's artwork. A couple of grandmothers sat at another table, and Paige relaxed slightly, grateful she wasn't the only fill-in.

The children served the punch with a minimum

amount of spillage. Paige thumbed through the booklets containing Summer's and August's drawings, concerned when she noticed August had used the color black for her family portrait. She'd obviously been upset when she'd drawn the picture. Then she scanned Summer's and frowned. Summer looked forlorn and was standing alone in all her drawings.

The teacher called the kids to the front, then introduced the music teacher who'd organized the program. August and Summer waved, then took their places, singing with animation to a litany of silly children's songs. As the children burst into the last song, they invited the moms to join in. Paige willingly followed as August and Summer dragged her between them. To the tune of "Twinkle, Twinkle, Little Star," the children substituted their own words, "Mothers, mothers, here we are, dancing near, dancing far, Thank you for all you do, You are great, we love you!"

The children hugged their mothers, then presented them with small books they had made entitled, "All About Me." Paige blinked furiously to control her emotions, knowing she would need to return the prized booklets to Zeke, but touched to be included in the girls' special day. She understood now why the twins had been so upset about the idea of coming to school without a mother or even a stand-in. It would have been devastating for them.

When they took their seats, August ran up with a friend. "Paige, this is Betsy." Betsy bit into her cookie, dropping crumbs all over her ruffled dress.

Betsy's mother, a short, pudgy woman extended her hand to Paige. "I'm Amy. We'll have to get the girls together to play sometime." Before Paige could respond, Janet ruffled August's hair. "You girls certainly do favor your mother. You have the same red hair and green eyes—it's amazing.''

Paige caught her lip between her teeth. She hadn't considered the possibility people would mistake her for the girls' mother. ''I'm Paige Watkins, I live next door to the girls.'' She saw Summer and August watching her carefully. ''I'm afraid their mom couldn't make it today, so I came as a friend.''

The woman gave her an uncomfortable smile and Paige tried to smooth over the awkward moment by suggesting the twins invite Betsy over to play one afternoon.

''But Daddy works all the time,'' Summer grumbled.

''Yeah. He gots mergencies and stuff,'' August croaked. She stuck her finger in the icing on her cookie and smeared it around in circles.

''Well, I'm sure we can arrange something,'' Betsy's mother said. ''We'll give him a call sometime. Maybe I could pick you up from school and he could get you on his way home from work.''

''Hey, if you want something bad enough you'll figure out a way to get it,'' Paige said. ''Maybe you could play together on a Saturday or Sunday.''

Summer nodded, brightening to the idea. August licked the icing off her finger. Paige gobbled up the cookies, making a big deal about how well the twins had decorated them, then allowed the girls to give her a tour of the center. Computers, TVs, tape recorders and video games lined the walls of the media room. Listening centers and comfy beanbag chairs created small cozy areas for reading. A separate section housed blocks and games, a housekeeping corner filled another area and an art center equipped with easels, paints and a child-size sink served as a separate activity center. The day care had obviously undergone a face-lift since her childhood.

Paige's admiration for Zeke Blalock rose a notch. He had chosen a safe and friendly atmosphere for his children.

Better off here than with her.

Paige hugged them both as she started to leave. "You girls have a good day."

"You wanna come over later?" August asked.

Paige's hand settled on her purse strap. "I can't tonight, sweetie. I have plans."

"Oh." The disappointment in the girl's voices worried Paige. Had she given them false ideas by coming?

"Besides, I bet your dad has plans for you tonight," Paige said.

Both girls threw their arms around her neck. Paige glanced up and saw Zeke standing in the doorway. His gaze captured hers, his eyes dark pools of honey and trouble all at once, and his sexy mouth curved slightly into a heart-stopping smile that nearly snatched the air from her lungs.

Zeke stared at Paige, a current of sensuality rippling between them, a thread of need materializing that he tried to banish from his thoughts. For the last few minutes, he'd watched the scene in the day care with growing unease and a tightness in his chest that wouldn't go away. When he'd stopped by to talk to the day-care director, she'd encouraged him to watch the girls during the tea, thinking he might see some of August's inappropriate behavior himself. Instead he'd watched the girls fawn all over Paige, and he'd seen her talking and laughing comfortably with them, as if she belonged right there at the mother-daughter tea. She'd even danced and sang to that silly song they'd performed, something his ex-wife would never have done. His daughters had loved it.

Summer and August suddenly spied him and broke into a run, throwing themselves at his legs and wrapping their arms around him. "Daddy, daddy, what are you doing here?"

He stroked their pigtails, his gaze still trapped by the elusive emotions in Paige's dark green eyes. "I just stopped by to see if you two were okay."

Summer giggled. "We've been having fun."

August looked a little contrite from their earlier conversation. "But you're not sposed to come to the mother tea. We're having Doughnuts with Dad on Father's Day."

Zeke laughed, shooting Paige a sideways glance as she said goodbye to the teachers and started toward the door.

"I'll come back for doughnuts," Zeke promised.

Paige's sweet scent wafted toward him and he straightened his shoulders, every nerve cell in his body tingling with awareness as she approached.

"Hi," she said softly.

"Hi." He was acting like a tongue-tied idiot. He gazed into her eyes as if thirty kids weren't running around behind them and his own two weren't clinging to him, chattering mindlessly about their morning.

"Thanks for coming," he finally said.

"No problem. It was fun." Paige smiled as she hugged both girls, then said goodbye.

"See you later, Paige," Summer and August yelled.

Then Paige disappeared out the door, and Zeke thought he called goodbye, but he was so mesmerized by Paige's sexy legs and the confusing feelings swirling inside him that he wasn't sure he'd actually vocalized the words.

ALL AFTERNOON AS Paige waited on customers in the boutique, she tried to shove thoughts of the girls from her mind. They weren't her responsibility and if she let herself become involved, she could get hurt. Besides,

Zeke Blalock probably *did* have plans. He hadn't invited her over—his children had. An attractive, single man with a respectable job most likely had women chasing him. Although the idea of Zeke in a serious relationship made her stomach sour. Probably all that icing she'd eaten, she finally decided.

Still, as she drove home after work, bathed and dressed for her date for Amelia's party, she kept peeking out her bedroom window. At six forty-five, when the Blalocks hadn't arrived home, she chewed her thumbnail in worry. Her navy dress swished by her sides as she walked back and forth from the window to her mirror. She checked her appearance, forcing herself to remember she was a free woman. The people next door were not her business. She'd invested two years of her life in her relationship with Eric and Joey, and it had cost her a heartache that had cut to the bone. But Eric and Joey had been gone for months, and it was time she rejoined the dating scene.

She strode to her closet, slid her feet into her navy pumps, checked herself in the mirror again. The strait-laced outfit made her look like an old biddy. She jerked the dress over her head, searched her closet for something more fashionable. The red dress. No, too loud. The purple, no it made her hips look huge. The dark blue linen skirt, hmm. The length was good; it would showcase her legs. And the straight skirt made her hips appear thinner. She chose an ivory shell top and pulled it on. Classy, but sexy. After all, Amelia had set her up with this guy. She didn't want her friend to be disappointed.

And she refused to give in to the ridiculous desire to check the Blalock driveway again. If Zeke had a date, she was happy for him. After all, his daughters deserved a woman in their lives and so did he. And she wouldn't have to feel guilty about possibly misleading the girls today.

She sank onto her bed and placed her hand over her suddenly churning stomach, an image of Zeke's dark chocolate eyes popping into her mind. Why did the idea of Zeke with another woman make her feel queasy?

Minutes later, her doorbell rang, jerking her from her troubled thoughts. She drank a glass of water, hoping to calm her stomach as she blotted Zeke from her mind. Then she opened the door and saw her date standing at her front door, outlined by the lights of Zeke's minivan as he pulled in the driveway next door.

Chapter Five

"Daddy, we're gonna see Paige!" August leapt out of the car into a full run with Summer following on her heels.

"Wait!" Zeke zeroed in on the expensive sports car parked in Paige's driveway. "You can't go charging over there! Paige has company." Zeke juggled a bag of groceries, the contents almost spilling as he darted after the girls. Then he noticed a tall, thin guy standing on Paige's front porch and paused. The man's long hair was clasped into a ponytail, making him look artsy. And he was driving a Ferrari sports car. Paige's date? Apparently he had money.

Damn. He didn't want to intrude, but August and Summer were already barreling up the steps, their faces animated. They'd talked nonstop about Paige and the tea, and he'd spent the last half hour trying to tamp down their hopes.

He put the groceries on the porch and hurried to retrieve his daughters before they embarrassed him further by inviting themselves along on Paige's date. The ponytailed man stepped aside as Summer and August sideswiped him and nearly bowled him over, bombarding Paige with their chatter.

The man's impeccable designer slacks and polo shirt suddenly made him self-conscious of his clothes. He wished he'd had time to clean up before seeing Paige again, especially since the guy on her doorstep looked like a model for a men's clothing magazine. The cat and dog odor permeating his clothes had become second nature to him, but the animal hair and blood staining his dark slacks might turn off a woman. Paige's soft voice wafted toward him as she spoke to Summer and August, then her whimsical laughter filled the air and heat spread through his veins.

He climbed the steps and edged near the stranger. Zeke stood a good foot taller than the man, and outweighed him by thirty pounds, making his ego swell slightly. Would Paige notice the difference?

"Hi." Paige grinned sheepishly at him. "Zeke, this is Dash Huntington."

He instantly assessed the man's pale, lean face. Family money. If he owned a dog, he probably had a white poodle he kept clipped and adorned with bows.

Zeke extended his hand and pumped the guy's hand vigorously, biting the inside of his cheek to keep from laughing when Dash winced slightly. Dash Huntington didn't look as if he'd worked a day in his life. His hands were bony thin, soft skinned, and his nails manicured.

"Nice to meet you," Zeke said. "I live next door."

"Hello," Dash said in a cultured voice. "Your children were just introducing themselves."

"Daddy, did you see his car?" August asked wide-eyed.

"It's a 'vertible," Summer said.

"Yes, I see." Zeke unconsciously noted the comparison between his practical minivan and the customized red sports car. "Nice wheels."

"I like it." Dash's grin revealed straight white teeth.

August pointed to Dash's hair. "How come you gots a ponytail?"

Summer wrinkled her nose and cut Dash off before he could reply. "It looks like a girl's."

"And you smell funny."

"Do you gots on perfume?"

"August." Zeke fought a smile as Dash's eyebrows arched into peaks above his startled eyes.

"It's cologne, imported from Italy," Dash said, patting his jaw.

"Well, uh, girls, Dash and I have to be going." Paige shifted on her right foot, the hem of her skirt rising to reveal trim long legs. And that no-nothing top hugged her curves in all the right places. Zeke had the sudden urge to ask her to change. Did she have to look so damn sexy to go out with this guy?

His gaze locked with hers and a moment of insanity passed between them—desire, hot and bold, flamed in the sparkling green irises of her eyes and heat pummeled through his body. Paige licked her lips and swallowed, the fine column of her throat working as she took a deep breath, her enticing breasts falling and rising with such gracious aplomb that his eager body hardened with lust.

Somewhere in the recesses of Zeke's befuddled brain he felt one of his daughters tugging on his sleeve. Still, he was reluctant to break the moment, because he realized in that split second of time, Paige was attracted to him. The thought brought a surge of unexpected emotions—desire, lust, protectiveness and something else… tenderness. And a longing so deep he suddenly ached with it.

Then August jerked his hand. "Daddy, are we still gonna roast hot dogs?"

"And camp out?" Summer asked.

He shook off the spell and Paige blushed, then turned toward her date, the moment lost in time, but imprinted in his memory forever, straining at his consciousness while he deliberately tried to shake it away.

"Yes, girls, we're going to camp out," he said. *While the two of them go off and do who knows what?* Dash placed his hand at the small of Paige's back and spots flashed behind Zeke's eyes. Red, fiery spots, bursting into flames, exploding like tiny firecrackers.

"That sounds like fun, girls. Roast some marshmallows for me." Paige backed away from the guy's touch and stumbled inside her front door. A gratifyingly barbaric reaction hit Zeke when he realized she'd shied away from the other man's touch. "I'll find my purse and we'll go." Her voice sounded shaky and he wondered if she might change her mind and stay home. Wishful thinking on his part.

He had to forget about Paige, had to curb his desires and concentrate on making his children happy. His girls were the reason he hadn't asked her for a date.

"Let's go, Daddy," August whined, tugging at his sleeve. "I wanna make a fire."

Summer didn't seem as anxious. She simply stared at Paige as she walked out.

Paige knelt and brushed Summer's hair with her hand. It was such a loving, automatic response that Zeke's chest tightened. "I had fun today, girls. Thanks for letting me come to your school."

A wealth of emotions bombarded Zeke. His daughters were starved for a woman's attention, they were already getting attached to Paige. But Paige had made it clear she didn't want a family.

"Mr. Turner and June Bailey called and want watch-dogs," Paige said. "Maybe a golden retriever or a Lab."

Zeke nodded. "I'll give them a call and see what I can find." Then he turned to the twins. "Let's go, girls. We need to set up the tent before the sun fades."

"Enjoy your little backyard outing," Dash said, leading Paige toward the flashy car.

A snarl curled on Zeke's lips and the word that froze on his tongue was one he definitely couldn't voice with his daughters present. Instead, he led the girls away and encouraged them to help him gather kindling to light a fire in their outdoor brick barbecue pit.

A few minutes later Zeke stared into the flickering flames, contemplating this wild attraction he had for his neighbor. The burning embers popped and cracked, sending off a wave of heat that had him sweating and imagining long lazy nights with a certain woman in his arms. He grimaced as he backed away from the heat. The flames were sizzling hot, almost as hot as the fire Paige had ignited within him. And he needed to stay away from both of them.

PAIGE TRIED TO relax and make small talk as Dash zipped the sports car in and out of traffic, but her mind kept straying to the Blalock backyard camp-out. She'd never had a family to speak of, just her and her mother. Family evenings like the one the Blalocks had planned were something she'd always wanted to have growing up.

Minutes later, Dash maneuvered the sleek car into the parking lot of the country club where the party was already underway. They climbed from the car and Dash guided her through the lovely garden up a winding sidewalk toward the pool area. Loud rock music blasted from inside, spilling onto the patio and filling the balmy spring air, and dozens of people filtered back and forth from the indoor room to the wooden deck. A creek gurgled nearby, and dogwood and honeysuckle blossoms added a heavenly fragrance to the air. Tables laden with a variety of food and beverages seemed to be drawing a crowd. Couples danced on the patio and voices and laughter drifted to the walkway. "How do you know Amelia?" Dash asked.

"We met at the boutique where I work," Paige said. "And Derrick and I grew up together. How about you?"

"Well, I haven't actually met Amelia. Derrick and I belonged to the same fraternity in college at Stanford."

"Are you in the security business also?"

He shook his head. "No, investments. I was raised abroad. Dad always dabbled in the stock market. I guess I followed in his shoes."

Paige wound her fingers together. Her date's upbringing was so vastly different from her own that she wondered if they had anything in common. She studied his features, hoping for a spark of attraction to surface, but his slender build and polished tone gave him an air of stuffiness, especially compared to Zeke's muscular frame, husky voice and easy grin.

But Dash was single and unencumbered by family. Zeke wasn't. He had two adorable daughters and...well, he was adorable himself, but that was beside the point, she thought, frustrated.

Dash took her hand and she tensed, then forced herself to relax, willing herself to focus on his positive features. He was well-dressed, probably had his suits custom-tailored. Heck, he might even have contacts in the design field. He folded her hand into his, and she tried not to wonder if he had other things in mind. Hand-holding—no big deal.

But his palm felt smooth and slightly damp, and the scent of his sweet, cloying cologne enveloped her, stifling the warm night air. As they climbed the steps, she spotted Amelia and relief swamped her.

She waved at her friend. "I'm going to talk to Amelia."

"Fine. I'll find Derrick and get us a drink." His lips brushed her hair as he leaned close so she could hear him over the noise. Paige flinched slightly, unsettled by his touch and vaguely aware that if Zeke had brushed his lips against her hair, she would have stopped breathing in anticipation of more to come. All she could think about now was putting distance between Dash and herself. Thankfully, he went to the bar to get them drinks.

"Paige!" Amelia threw her arms around her, a glass of champagne tipping precariously to the side.

"Congratulations!" Paige hugged her. "I'm so happy for you."

"I'm happy for myself," Amelia said with a giggle.

Paige laughed and pulled her aside. "So when is the big day? And where is that hunk you talked into commitment?"

Amelia laughed again. "He's around here somewhere. Guess what?"

"What?"

"Instead of eloping, we decided to get married in the church and I want you to make the wedding dress!"

"That's great!" Paige's heart thumped in excitement. "When's the wedding? I hope you've given us lots of time to plan so I can make you a special gown."

"Early August," Amelia said. "I'm having my dream wedding—bridesmaids, flowers, the works."

"August? That's only eight weeks away," Paige said

in alarm. "We'll have to shop for a pattern, look at different styles—"

"I know, it's going to be so much fun!" Amelia squealed, her bracelets jangling.

"Let's look at dresses soon so I can see what you want," Paige suggested. "Traditional? Something old-fashioned? Low-cut? A long train?"

"Don't worry tonight." Amelia gestured toward Dash as he approached with the wine. "Just have fun, Paige. You work too hard, you know."

"Yeah, I know." Paige grinned at the sincerity in Amelia's voice and thought of the friendly argument they'd had repeatedly over the past few years. Amelia had always been the partyer, Paige the loner.

Derrick sauntered up and grabbed Amelia, swinging her around for a lip-locking kiss. The crowd cheered. Paige blushed as Dash's gray eyes twinkled with mischief. A Jimmy Buffet tune wafted from inside and couples filled the patio using it as a makeshift dance floor.

"Come on." Dash grabbed her hand, tossed down the rest of his drink and practically dragged her to the dance floor, swooping her around in circles. For the next hour, they danced and gyrated to a dozen songs. In between, Dash allowed her to rest long enough for him to down another scotch. Paige stopped counting after his sixth drink. She also switched to soda, deciding without a doubt she would be driving herself home.

Two hours later, she decided she'd had enough of the party life. Booze flowed freely among the crowd and as the night wore on, her impatience with her date flared. They whirled through a round of popular tunes, but when Buffet belted out with "Why don't we get drunk and screw..." Paige excused herself and found the ladies' room.

When she emerged, ready to go home, Amelia and Derrick were snuggled in a corner in a passionate embrace. To her horror, she noticed some of the guests had decided to go skinny-dipping in the pool. Even worse, her date was playing sharks and minnows with the party animals, wearing nothing but his Rolex and silk boxers.

Paige retreated to a corner alone, contemplating whether or not to call a taxi, or borrow Amelia's car and head home. But the tiki torches flickered in the inky darkness of the night and her thoughts strayed until she found herself dreaming of roasting marshmallows over a campfire, singing silly songs with four-year-olds, and cuddling up to her handsome, sexy neighbor. When her dreams shifted to include a relationship and marriage with more babies, she decided she'd gone insane.

She found Dash and finally coaxed him into letting her drive home. As soon as he climbed into the car, his head fell back against the seat and a loud, undignified snore rumbled through the air. So much for his charm.

Disgusted, she realized she had no idea where he lived. As drunk as he was, how could she in good conscience let him drive himself home from her house? There was only one answer. And she didn't like it—not one bit. She couldn't.

He would have to spend the night.

ZEKE AND THE girls had charred the hot dogs, scorched the marshmallows and accidentally dribbled melted chocolate all over their shirts. The girls had eaten so many s'mores Zeke worried they would have stomachaches, if they slept at all. He tucked them into the sleeping bags, rushed to check on the kittens and the salamander the girls had adopted, glanced next door for the zillionth time to see if Paige had returned, then dragged Henrietta out of the garbage and settled her into the tent for the night. At least the dog was sleeping. But she'd gotten into the chili he'd put on his hot dog, and it hadn't agreed with her stomach. She would probably keep *him* awake all night.

If the thought of Paige not being home didn't do it first. He checked his watch.

"Is she home yet?" Summer whispered.

"No." He winced, realizing he'd given himself away.

"Think she's all right, Daddy?" August asked.

"I'm sure she is. I'm just keeping an eye on her house because of that neighborhood watch thing I told you about." He hoped his voice sounded sincere.

"Uh-huh." August giggled as if she'd seen through his white lie.

"I didn't like that man with the 'vertible," Summer piped in.

"He gots an awesome car," August said. "But he looks like a girl."

"And he gots beady eyes."

"And he stinked, too."

Zeke thumped his fingers on his watch. "Go to sleep, girls."

"Night, Daddy," both girls chimed.

"Night, sweethearts." Zeke kissed them again, then turned off the flashlight just as headlights beamed in the driveway next door.

"That Paige?" Summer whispered.

"I don't know," Zeke said in a soft voice. "And we shouldn't keep tabs on her."

"Don't you like her, Daddy?" August asked.

Zeke glanced through the tent window to watch Paige climb out of the car. "Of course I like her. But she's only a friend."

"Don't you think she's pretty?" Summer asked.

"Well, yeah, sure."

"You wanna kiss her?" August said.

Summer made a hissing sound. "Oooh, kissin's yucky."

"We're not going to talk about kissing. Now, good night, girls." Zeke chuckled. He had no intention of opening up a can of worms by answering that question. Plus he wanted the girls quiet so he could hear what was happening next door. Straining to see without being too obvious, he arched forward and peeked through the bottom opening, unzipping the tent slightly for a better view.

To his surprise, Paige exited from the driver's side, went around and opened the car door for Dash. Then she leaned over, put her arm around him, and the guy draped his arm over her neck. The man was holding her so close Zeke thought they were going to fall on the ground together. Geez. Was the guy going to paw her right in the yard?

And where were his clothes? He was in his boxers!

"Why's that man got on his underwear?" August asked.

Zeke swallowed. *Exactly what I'd like to know.* "I don't know, honey. Maybe he spilled something on his clothes or something."

Paige hit the garage opener and the door slid open, then the two of them walked slowly inside, still holding onto one another as if their bodies were cemented together. He scrubbed his hand through his hair, lost his balance and fell forward on his nose.

Just as he righted himself, she must have hit the button again and the garage door descended, blocking their bodies from his view.

"She's home now," August said.

"Yeah, you can go to sleep, Daddy."

Yeah, right. Sleep was the last thing he could do. He glanced over his shoulder to see both girls spying through the tent window. He shot them a stern look and they quickly dropped down and snuggled into their sleeping bags. Within seconds, both girls drifted into sleep. Zeke's gaze once again strayed to Paige's house, his thoughts jumbled and confused.

A light flicked on in the kitchen window and he spotted Paige's silhouette, then Dash's shadow as they walked out of the room. The charred dinner he'd consumed earlier sank into the pit of his stomach.

Paige wasn't the woman for him, but he hadn't pegged her for the party type either. She'd been so sweet and kind to the girls, but he had to face the facts. Attracted to her or not, she had simply been doing him a favor. He yanked his sleeping bag over his legs, wondering why he felt disappointed in her. They weren't involved, had never dated, she hadn't even pretended to want to get involved in his little family. He fisted his hand and punched his pillow, the lumpy bunched up mass suddenly irritating him beyond reason. It was a good damn thing he'd decided not to get involved with her.

Any woman who'd let a strange man spend the night with her wasn't mommy material. At least, not for his daughters.

PAIGE SUDDENLY jerked awake, startled at the scratching sound from downstairs. Slivers of early morning light sliced the room through the venetian blinds and she glanced at the bedside clock. 6 a.m. Someone was in her house?

A low whine echoed from downstairs. She threw off the comforter, slipped on her bedroom shoes and tiptoed toward the stairwell, then listened again. Someone, or *something,* was definitely in the kitchen. Was it Dash?

No, she'd called a taxi and sent him out the front door as soon as she'd weaseled his address out of him. A thumping sound drifted up the stairs and she froze again, clutching her robe. What if those vandals had broken in? Or a robber?

Her heart racing, she grabbed her portable phone, spotted a glass vase on her dresser and grabbed it to use as a weapon. She eased her bedroom door open, careful so her footsteps wouldn't make a sound as she quickly scanned the hallway. Then she tiptoed down the steps, barely breathing as they squeaked beneath her feet. When she pushed the door to the kitchen open, soft rumbling filled the air. It sounded as if someone was…was *snoring.*

She held her breath, the vase poised at her side, then peeked inside. Henrietta? Zeke's dog was lying in her kitchen, sleeping like a baby. And snoring like an old man.

She sighed in relief, then put the vase on the kitchen table and clutched her stomach as a bout of nervous laughter escaped her. The lazy dog had stretched out beside her kitchen table, making herself perfectly at home. But she'd scared the bejeebies out of her.

"Paige, help!"

Paige swung around at the cry, then covered her hand with her mouth to mask her surprise when Summer's head bobbed through the pet door.

"Honey, what are you doing?" Paige raced over and knelt in front of her, afraid she would get stuck.

"Hunting Henrietta," Summer said as if her early morning visit made perfect sense.

Paige scooted closer, grabbed the child's arms and tugged her through the doorway. Summer wiggled and squirmed, finally squeezing through the small opening, and they both fell forward onto the floor from the force.

"That was fun," Summer said with a giggle.

Paige shoved her tousled curls from her eyes. "Well, next time knock, sweetie. You could have gotten stuck."

Summer hopped up, brushed off the ends of her pink shorts and petted Henrietta's head.

Paige began making coffee. "Where's your sister and your dad?"

"They was asleep. I woke up and Henrietta was missing so I went looking for her, then I saw your gate open and I came over."

"So you're the early bird?"

"Yep." Summer rubbed her stomach. "'Sides, I'm hungry. Daddy burned the hot dogs last night. August and I fedded ours to Henrietta."

Paige chuckled. "How about some strawberry pancakes? I'm cooking myself some and I can never eat them all."

Summer's eyes lit up. "Yum."

"Come on," Paige whispered. "You can help me. We'll eat before your dad even wakes up and knows you're missing."

"Wake up, Daddy. Summer and Henrietta's missing!"

Zeke squinted against the morning sun blazing through the tent, then grunted again as August bounced her body up and down on his stomach. "What, who's missing?" Zeke bolted upright as August's words sank in. Then he gently lifted August from his chest, and searched the tent. Panic sent the blood roaring in his ears.

"I bet she's in the yard." August skipped outside, laughing at the sunshine as it played across her face.

Zeke rushed behind her, scanning the yard. No Henrietta. No Summer. He spun in circles, calling her name. "Summer! Summer! Answer me. Where are you?"

After searching the house high and low again, he remembered the last time the girls had sneaked off on their own—the little red wagon and the fliers. He ran to the garage. Nope. The red wagon remained parked beside the lawn mower.

"Daddy," August yelled. "Maybe she went to Paige's."

Zeke raked a hand through his hair, then hurried out the back door, praying August was right. But the red Ferrari still sat in Paige's driveway and anger churned in his stomach. Paige's date from the previous night was still there. And it was six-thirty in the morning!

He crossed the driveway in long strides. "I'll be right back, August. You stay here."

"But why can't I come, Daddy?"

Zeke paused at her innocent expression and bit back the real reason for his request. His girls were too young and impressionable for the kind of scene they might find. Hell, he didn't even want to see it. Just the idea of Paige sharing breakfast with that Dash guy made bile rise in his throat.

"Go get us some orange juice and doughnuts," he finally said. "I'll get Summer and Henrietta and we'll have a picnic breakfast in the backyard."

"Yippee. Sugar doughnuts!" August raced into the house.

He stomped over to Paige's, his pulse beating wildly. As soon as he stepped on the landing, he heard voices. And laughter. Paige's and Summer's. So she did have his daughter in there while she entertained a man!

Not that he had any right to tell her what to do, but when his daughter was involved, he certainly did. He raised his hand to knock, not bothering to mask his anger. His polite knock turned into an incessant pound.

The door swung open seconds later and he stared into Paige's sensuous green eyes, momentarily lost. Her hair lay in a mass of red curls tumbling around her oval face and she was wearing a soft blue robe which parted midthigh, exposing her gorgeous slim legs. No bra. He could see her breasts jiggle when she lowered her arm. Damn.

Her sexy early morning rumpled appearance only fired his anger more. While he'd been next door with his girls in a tent sleeping on the hard ground, thinking about her and wishing he was with her, she'd been next door sharing her bed with another man. And from the looks of her puffy eyes, she hadn't been *sleeping* either.

Chapter Six

"Summer, you need to come home," Zeke said, his voice sounding harsher than he'd intended.

"But Daddy—"

"No, buts, Summer."

Paige folded her arms beneath her breasts, accentuating her curves even more. "Zeke, what's going on? Did you wake up on the wrong side of your sleeping bag?"

He pinned Paige with a mutinous stare, furious with himself for still being attracted to her when she had another man in her house, probably in her bed at that moment. "We'll talk later. Right now I want my daughter to come home."

Paige took a step backward, her lips parting slightly in surprise at his hostile tone. Summer merely stared at him from Paige's round oak table, a fork hanging in midair over a plate of something that appeared to be homemade pancakes, one of Paige's dolls tucked tightly beneath her arm. The bright cheery kitchen and bench full of country folk dolls irritated him even more. And Paige's wounded expression made him feel like a heel.

But he didn't want his little girl in the house with Paige and a stranger while they were cavorting between the sheets. Another unexplained bout of fury streaked through him. The man was probably upstairs, waiting for his breakfast in bed. Paige's sleep-flushed skin and near-nakedness advertised her sexuality like a billboard. He needed to leave before he made a fool out of himself.

"I said come on, Summer." He hooked his thumb toward the door.

"Zeke, what's wrong?" Paige's voice sounded so innocent he wanted to strangle her.

"I don't wanna go, Daddy. I want seconds."

The door squeaked open and August suddenly ran in, her eyes widening when she saw the plate of hotcakes. "Yum! Can I have some?"

"Sure." Paige reached for another plate.

"No," Zeke said at the same time.

August's stomach growled. "But I'm hungry, and you never make us pancakes."

"Yeah, Daddy, you use those frozen ones in the box."

Zeke raked his hand through his hair in frustration. "Look, girls, you can't just drop over here any time you want and eat with Paige." He pointed to Summer. "You aren't supposed to leave the yard without asking my permission."

Summer's lower lip trembled.

A low sound tore from Paige's throat. "Zeke, maybe she should have told you, but—"

"I don't think *you* should be giving me parenting advice." Zeke made an exaggerated point of glancing around her kitchen, speaking through gritted teeth. "At least not under the circumstances."

Paige's shoulders tensed, her mouth tight with anger. "Exactly what do you mean by that?"

"Well, for starters you're not even dressed." His gaze raked over her satiny robe, pausing briefly on the yellow fuzzy duck bedroom shoes swallowing her dainty feet.

She planted one foot over the other as if the movement could hide the duck's beaded eyes, then looked back at Zeke, arms akimbo. "I'm perfectly covered. And I hardly think there's anything wrong with Summer seeing me in my bathrobe."

But it's driving me crazy. He suppressed the erotic images her outfit conjured. "It's not appropriate, Paige."

August yanked on the leg of his sweatpants. "Daddy, don't yell at Paige!"

Zeke gestured toward the hallway. "August, stay out of this." He faced Paige, toe-to-toe. "Besides, Paige has company," he said in a harsh whisper. "You can visit her another time."

"You're being mean," August accused.

"Company?"

Paige's perplexed expression riled him even more. Why was she pretending innocence? "The Ferrari," he snapped, jerking his head toward the driveway.

He saw the minute the light flicked on her in her beautiful head. Her rosy lips curved into a slight smile, adding fuel to his temper. "Oh, you think…you mean—" She pointed her index finger toward the driveway.

"Yes, I mean…" He allowed his voice to trail off, hoping not to blurt out the issue just in case Summer hadn't already seen the man.

"Daddy, the vertible guy isn't here anymore," Summer said through a mouthful of strawberries.

"We seen him come in last night with you," August said. "We was watchin' from the tent."

"Yeah, Daddy fell on his nose—"

"Girls!" Heat climbed Zeke's neck.

"Why was he wearing his underwear?" Summer asked.

Paige chuckled softly. ''Because he fell in the pool and got his clothes wet, sweetheart.''

''Girls, we'd better go,'' Zeke said tightly.

Paige's gaze locked with Zeke's. ''He's not here, Zeke.''

''He's not?''

She shook her head, the tangled curls flopping into her eyes.

''But his car...''

''He took a taxi home last night.''

''Why'd he do that?'' August asked.

The aroma of coffee and food and Paige's sweetly scented body wafted around Zeke, dancing through his nerve endings, tying them in knots. She flicked her tongue over her upper lip and he had to fight the temptation to wipe the dollop of syrup from her mouth. She seemed to be having trouble tearing her gaze from him, too, but finally she answered August in a matter-of-fact tone.

''Dash wasn't feeling well last night so he took a cab home, honey. He'll pick up his car later.''

''Oh. Pancakes are yummy.'' Summer rubbed her stomach as if Paige's answer completely satisfied her. But Zeke wanted to know what had happened, or rather, what *hadn't* happened.

''Can I have some?'' August dropped the box of powdered doughnuts on the counter, eyeing the syrup and hotcakes.

Zeke's tongue felt thick in his throat. He'd made an idiot of himself for no reason. ''Uh...I guess it's all right, if Paige has enough, that is. I'll just eat crow.''

''What's crow, daddy?''

''It's a bird,'' August whispered in horror.

Summer made a face. "Gross, you're not gonna eat a bird, are you?"

August gulped. "Won't the feathers get stuck in your throat?"

"Yuk!"

Paige and Zeke laughed. "No, sweetie, it's just an expression," Zeke explained.

Paige narrowed her eyes at him. "You can have crow on top of your pancakes, instead of strawberries, Zeke."

He winced. "Look, Paige, I'm really sorry."

She tapped her foot on the floor, hurt lingering in her eyes.

"I don't know what else to say, but I was wrong," he whispered sincerely.

One corner of her mouth finally lifted into a smile. "All right. Apology accepted."

Then she turned and dished up fresh hotcakes as if nothing had happened, serving August as she climbed in a chair. His mouth watered.

"Can I help?" Zeke asked sheepishly, finally realizing he'd barged in her house with his T-shirt backward, his feet bare.

"Sure, pour the girls some milk." Paige added the condiments to the table. "And if you want coffee, mugs are in that top cabinet above the sink."

Zeke nodded, found the glasses and mugs and sipped his coffee, his gaze mesmerized by the sway of Paige's hips as she casually walked over to join them. He had a sudden image of the four of them settling down to breakfast every morning, Paige sliding her arms around his neck and nuzzling his face with her own, carrying her back to bed to make long, hot love to her after the girls climbed on the school bus. He'd take the strawberries and cream and—

"Syrup?"

The bottle clunked down in front of him, jarring him from his erotic thoughts. He hadn't realized Paige had slipped into the seat beside him. But he did notice she made a big production of tightening the belt at her waist.

The girls were already licking the last of their syrup and hotcakes. "We're taking Henrietta outside and gonna check on the kitties." August grabbed Summer's hand and they tugged the lazy dog out the door.

An awkward silence filled the room. Zeke fidgeted in his chair, vowing silently to speak to his daughters about getting him into these sticky situations. "Sorry the girls bothered you this morning. And…me, too."

Paige sipped her coffee. "So, you thought I'd let a strange guy spend the night and invite your girls in while he was here? You must not think much of me, Zeke."

Zeke immediately regretted his impulsive behavior. "Look, Paige, I'm sorry." When he saw her lick the sweet syrup from her lips, his hand stilled. "I saw the car and assumed…"

She pointed her fork at him. "I may not be mommy material, Zeke Blalock, but I'm not the kind of girl to hop in bed with just any guy, especially a drunk one. And I certainly wouldn't flaunt a lover in front of a couple of young impressionable children."

A lover? "I didn't say you would. And who ever said you weren't mommy material?"

Paige lowered her eyes, refusing to look at him. "That's what you implied."

"I never implied that." Zeke hesitated, disturbed on more than one level, but his mind took a fast track back to the man he'd thought had spent the night with Paige. "So, he's your lover?"

"That's none of your business."

Tension escalated between them as he tried to curb his questions. He didn't know very much about Paige, except judging from her kitchen, she was neat and orderly. Everything tidy and clean and in its place. It was a wonder she hadn't screamed like a banshee when she'd seen his home.

But he wanted to know more, not just the surface Paige with the neat, perfectly decorated house. He wanted to touch her, wanted to see her laugh, wanted to make her pant with passion, wanted to share a lot more than breakfast with her. Wanted her to lose that calm, cool control she wore around her like a cloak of armor. Wanted to assure her she would be a great mother...and an even better lover.

Paige plucked a strawberry from the bowl and popped the end into her mouth, her anger obviously subsiding. The sweet red juice colored her soft lips and he could practically taste the delicious juice as she sucked the ripe fruit. God, she was killing him.

"So, are you involved with this guy? What about that security consultant, Derrick?" How many boyfriends did she have?

"No, last night was our first date. And our last. Derrick and Dash were roommates at Stanford. He wanted me to get to know Dash."

Zeke's head was spinning from trying to figure out her relationships. Women! Maybe she was trying to make Derrick jealous. Or was Derrick into threesomes? He certainly wouldn't share Paige if she was his woman. "You should be careful, Paige—"

"I can take care of myself," Paige cut in.

His eyebrow shot up in surprise. "Well, if you ever need anything, I'm right next door."

She smiled as if she'd understood his double meaning

and might take him up on it, and his heartbeat picked up to an unsteady beat. ''Thanks. I'll remember that.''

Early morning light shimmered on the russet strands of her tousled hair casting a softness to her face that added to her vulnerability. Her soft voice almost shattered his control, made him forget about Derrick and Dash. She caught his gaze, and a flicker of desire darkened the centers of her beautiful green eyes. He couldn't resist the impulse to touch her.

His fingers trembled slightly as he gently rubbed her chin with his thumb. He heard her breathe, a soft whisper of desire that coiled his insides with fiery heat, then pulled her mouth to his, teasing her lips with his as he inhaled the sultry scent of her shampoo and feminine sweetness. Then he hesitated, half expecting her to pull away, but he saw the pulse hammering at the base of her neck and realized she wanted to kiss him as much as he wanted her.

She tasted of strawberries and cream and a hint of strong, delicious coffee, sweet and luscious. When her lips melded against his, he felt her need in the involuntary way she parted her lips to taste him. With a quiet sigh of feminine yearning, she accepted the invasion of his tongue into the warm cavern of her mouth and he seared her lips with his, totally claiming her. Leaning forward, he felt her body press against his, and he thrust his hand deep into the tresses of her already sleep-tousled hair, wishing for the life of him he could bury his whole body inside hers.

Her hand sank into his thick hair and he heard a low moan and realized he'd made the sound. Anxious to be closer, he scooted back his chair and slid his other arm behind her back, stroking the column of her spine, his body hardening with desire when he felt her breasts press against his chest.

"Daddy!" the girls yelled from outside.

The two of them jumped apart guiltily. He stood so abruptly his chair fell backward and hit the floor with a loud thud. Paige's creamy skin looked flushed and her lips were bruised and swollen from his kisses. Her troubled gaze locked with his, but she quickly averted her eyes and stood, then turned to the stove when August and Summer screamed for him again. He quickly stuffed his hands in his pockets.

The girls banged on the screened door, jerking him back to reality. And reminding him of the very reason he shouldn't be kissing Paige. "Daddy, come check the kitties. Fluffy's climbing out of the box!" August yelled.

"Uh, I guess I'd better go." He righted the chair, hating the way his husky voice betrayed his calm. Paige nodded, still not facing him.

"Paige?"

"Hmm?"

"Look at me."

She paused, finally meeting his gaze. Confusion clouded her expression, but he also saw the desire still nestled in its wake and his gut clenched. In spite of all the warning bells clamoring in his head, he wanted to kiss her again.

"Daddy! Hurry!"

"I...I'd better go. Thanks for breakfast."

Instantly she glanced at her hands and shoved the bowl in the sink. "Sure, no problem."

He opened his mouth to tell her the kiss was a mistake, but snapped it closed, deciding he couldn't say the words, not when he wanted to repeat the experience all over again. He remembered her hands in his hair, her voluptuous body pressed against his own rock hard one. "I'll see you later," he finally said.

She still wasn't looking at him; she only nodded in response.

"Listen, I have to go to the clinic for a while. But you've done me two favors now. The tea and breakfast. Why don't you come over tonight and the girls and I'll cook dinner for you?"

"I don't know, Zeke. I have to work and—"

"It's only dinner, Paige. A backyard barbecue. You helped us out. Now we're simply returning the favor. Besides, I found a couple of puppies that should be suitable for watchdogs, and we can pick a time to deliver them."

"Okay. But, Zeke, we'll make sure the girls know we're *only* friends." She finally faced him, her expression troubled. "I'm going to finish my degree. I don't want to get involved with a man with children, and I don't want to mislead the girls either."

He gave her a tight smile, his chest constricting at her declaration. "Right. We'll make sure they know that. See you at seven."

Then he strode to his house, more confused than ever. He'd thought Paige wanted him, and she seemed to like the twins. But like Renee, her career was more important. She didn't want the responsibility of a family.

And his family had to come first.

PAIGE FOLDED AN assortment of delicate lacy undergarments that had been shipped to the boutique and arranged them on a display table. She hadn't been able to shake Zeke from her mind. She fingered the trim on a pair of sheer black thong panties, suddenly wondering if Zeke would like them. After arranging several bottles of body liqueurs and oils on the shelf beside the lingerie, she lifted the top and sniffed one of the sample bottles. Piña colada. Hmm, yum. Would Zeke like the fruity taste?

She snapped the lid back on the bottle. Heaven help her. She'd never lusted for a man in her life. And now, she was thinking of seducing her neighbor with see-through lacy undergarments and edible body liqueurs.

Her lips still burned from Zeke's flaming kiss. She'd never reacted so strongly to a male friend as she had to Zeke. Her reaction was crazy—it wasn't as if she'd never been with a man. She and Eric had been intimate; after all, she'd spent two years with him. But looking back on their relationship, she realized he hadn't made her body yearn and burn the way Zeke's simple kiss had. Actually, she and Eric hadn't spent a lot of time alone, they'd always included Joey. Could she have made herself believe she was in love with Eric simply because she had loved his little boy?

She had to admit, she hadn't really missed Eric as much as she'd expected, and she certainly hadn't thought about his kisses for hours afterward, had never day-dreamed about taking his clothes off and making love to him the way she'd been daydreaming of Zeke all morning. Sex with Eric had been rare, and...boring. The thought of falling into bed with Zeke and devouring his tantalizing muscular body sent a shiver of wicked delight up her spine. And his reaction seemed equally volatile, making her wonder... Hmm.

"Paige! Hey!" Amelia sauntered through the door, her arms laden with expensive-looking packages.

"Hey, Amelia. Looks as if you bought out the stores."

"I'm getting ready for my honeymoon." She grinned and headed straight to the lingerie table, immediately grabbing a pair of white bikini thongs. "I'll take these."

Amelia gathered up several more undergarments, oblivious to the cost.

"How did you and Dash get along?" Amelia propped her elbow on the counter while Paige totaled up the items.

Paige wrinkled her nose. "I don't think he's my type."

"He likes to party. I thought you wanted that," Amelia said.

"I thought so, too." Paige carefully wrapped each of Amelia's purchases in flowered tissue paper. "But he and I...well, the chemistry just wasn't there."

"No animal attraction, huh?"

Paige laughed. "Yeah." *Unlike Zeke.*

"Well, we'll keep looking. Derrick has lots of friends." Amelia pulled out her credit card. "Let's see—describe your perfect man."

Paige drummed her fingers on the counter in thought. "Warm, friendly, sexy, good with kids. Tall, dark, broad shouldered, olive skin."

Amelia laughed. Paige caught herself and inwardly winced when she realized she'd described Zeke. She ran Amelia's card through the computer, then handed it back to her.

"Unattached, no kids, lots of money, free and adventuresome, right?" Amelia added.

"Right." *Free and adventuresome. Not already tied down with a family.* Paige shifted the conversation to her friend, "Listen, you want to shop tomorrow for your dress? I thought we could check the bridal shops. You can point out styles you like and we'll work up a design."

"Great!" Amelia gave her a hug. "I'm so glad you're making my wedding gown."

"I'll draw a few sketches tonight," Paige said.

"Perfect." Amelia collected her packages and hurried out the door. Paige watched her go, wishing her own life was as interesting as Amelia's.

Beverly glided in. "If you don't have plans tonight, drop by for Chinese. There's a Brad Pitt movie on cable."

Paige thumped her thumb on her chin. "Now, that's tempting, but I've been invited to dinner."

Beverly clicked her silver-polished nails on the counter. "Who's the lucky man?"

Paige gathered her purse as Beverly locked up the store. "It's not a date," Paige said, emphasizing the last word. "My neighbor's barbecuing."

"Girlfriend?"

"No, a guy."

Beverly's smile turned wicked. "A single man?"

"Yeah, he moved into Eric's old house."

"Is he good-looking?"

Paige shrugged. "If you like tall men with dark hair." *And eyes that look like chocolate kisses.*

"Sounds pretty good to me," Beverly said in a teasing voice.

Paige sighed. "No, that house is totally jinxed. He has kids and animals and dirty dishes and—"

"Responsibilities." Beverly winced and shook her head sympathetically. "Well, maybe you can eat fast and make up some excuse to leave."

Paige nodded. "Yeah, I have a project due." She touched her finger to her lips, the memory of the kiss once again surfacing. But unfortunately, she'd be going to bed alone. Because Zeke was anything but free and adventuresome. He had domesticity and homebound stamped right on his sexy forehead. And she must have stupid stamped on hers, because even with all her reservations, she couldn't shake him from her mind.

No, she *had* to. She couldn't take a chance with someone else's children. What if he left her with the girls, and something happened to them?

ON THE WAY TO the clinic that morning, Zeke had explained to his daughters about dinner and his friends-only relationship with Paige. All day though, the idea gnawed a hole in his stomach. After kissing her, *really* kissing her, could he be satisfied with a platonic relationship?

While he examined patients, the girls played with some of the pets he'd boarded for the weekend and drew pictures for the bulletin board in the waiting room. The adults seemed to get a kick out of their artwork, especially when the twins featured the clients' pets in their drawings.

"Um, Dr. Blalock." His receptionist, Clara strolled in with her clipboard. "I finished the billing, entered all the patient info for the day and checked the appointment calendar for Monday."

"I guess you're ready to leave then."

Clara smiled. "Yep. But I thought you might want to see this." His eyes bulged when he saw her holding the same crayoned flier advertising for a wife and mother his girls had posted in his neighborhood—his name and phone number in bold letters. No wonder two of his clients had invited him out for dinner. And a third woman had flirted outrageously, embarrassing him in front of Clara!

"Where did you find this?"

Clara smothered a giggle. "On the bulletin board in the cat room."

"Oh, my God. Did you check the dog room?"

She handed him a second flier. Zeke hissed through his teeth. His daughters had advertised his sexless, single life on his own bulletin board for all his clients to see!

"August! Summer! Come here!"

Both girls ran to him, their eyes widening when he waved the paper in the air.

"Why did you put this up in my office?"

"'Cause you said you and Paige was only friends," August said.

"And we wanted you to get us a mommy."

He squeezed the flier between his fingers, taking pleasure in the sound of the scrunching paper. "Get in the car."

"Uh-oh," August said.

"He looks really mad," Summer whispered.

Zeke locked up the clinic. It was going to be a long ride home.

AFTER WORK, PAIGE soaked in the bathtub with some of the strawberry-scented bath oil from the boutique, then toweled off and dressed in a clean pair of jeans and a dark green scooped neck T-shirt the same shade as her eyes. She brushed her hair and left it loose, flowing in waves around her shoulders, then slipped her feet into sandals, dreading going back to the house where she'd spent so much time with Eric and Joey. But dreading even more seeing Zeke after that spectacular kiss. Had he forgotten it—even given it a second thought?

Butterflies danced in her stomach. Ridiculous for her to be nervous. Tonight's dinner did not constitute a date. This impromptu dinner would prove to the girls they were simply friends. Then she'd ask Amelia to fix her up with another man, someone more suited to her tastes than Dash Huntington. On the way out the door, the evening light caught the gold color of the afghan Joey used to cuddle with, reminding her of her painful loss and strengthening her resolve not to get involved with Zeke.

At exactly seven, she stood on the doorstep to the Blalock house, listening to a mixture of barking and frantic voices coming from inside. August whipped the door open, her face a mass of chocolate. "Come in. We're making dinner!"

"Paige, oh, no. Is it seven already?" Zeke's harried expression was almost laughable. He was standing in the middle of the den with toys strewn around, kittens crawling all over the place, and a sleeping dachshund with bandages taped around its middle cradled in his arms. The whole room spelled crisis. And one glance told her he'd dressed in a hurry—once again, his socks didn't even match.

She should have been fashionably late. Judging from the chaos, she should also run like hell.

"Daddy's taking care of Peanut." Summer pointed to the dog. "We didn't want to leave him alone."

"He's a baby, he gets scared at night," August explained.

Paige nodded mutely, grimacing at the piles of laundry and toys littering the room.

Zeke settled the dog into a pet bed. "I'm sorry. I meant to have everything ready but Peanut had a reaction to the anesthesia and threw up all over the place and the phone's been ringing. And August wanted to make pudding."

Paige wrestled with her hands, wondering if he had a heavy-duty vacuum cleaner that could suck all the mess up in one minute. "Uh, what can I do to help?"

"Nothing."

"Take Fluffy." Summer thrust the kitten into her arms.

"And don't trip over my salamander," August said as Paige tiptoed across the array of toys. The dachshund whined and two golden retriever puppies tumbled from a box and waddled across the floor. Someone had to take charge. Obviously Zeke had lost control.

"Summer, why don't you pick up the toys while August washes up, then we'll see about dinner," Paige said.

"What about the kitties?" August asked.

"I'll put them in the box," Paige offered.

Paige faintly remembered a song she'd learned at day care when she was five. She began singing and the girls quickly joined it, "This is the way we clean up, clean up, clean up..." Within minutes, the room looked noticeably better, barring the animal chew toys and the laundry now piled in one basket instead of scattered over the furniture.

"How did you do that?" Zeke asked, staring at Paige in surprise when he saw the miraculous change.

Paige grinned. "We divided the tasks and sang—that way, it seems like fun, not work."

"I'll have to try that." Zeke led her toward the kitchen. He had steaks marinating for the grill and a bag of prepackaged salad ready to open. He tried to hide the plastic packaging and Paige hid a smile.

Summer and August ran in. "Let us butter the rolls."

"Girls, I don't know—"

"Daddy, please." Zeke gave in to their puppy dog expressions and the girls piled so much butter on the rolls Paige decided she'd be jogging forever to burn off the fat.

"How about a cold drink?" Zeke offered. "You can sit outside and talk to me while I cook the steaks."

"Sure." Paige opened a soda and followed Henrietta, the girls and the mother cat through the French doors. The girls raced around the yard playing with hula hoops. Paige tried to relax in the wrought iron chair, but Zeke's muscular physique mesmerized her, lighting a fire in her belly. The muscles in his arms rippled while he stoked the grill, his firm thighs and butt filled out his jeans to perfection. Heaven help her. Every time she looked at the man, she started lusting after his body. It was sinful for a man to look so sexy in worn-out jeans and a T-shirt. Especially a father.

"So how were things at the clinic today?" Paige asked.

Zeke flipped the steak and shot her a strange look. "The girls posted their fliers on the wall at my clinic and three women propositioned me."

Paige laughed outright.

"It wasn't funny," Zeke said. "I've had three calls since I arrived home. Those women probably think I'm some sexless, pathetic—"

"I doubt that's what they think at all." Paige immediately wished she hadn't spoken. Zeke's gaze trapped hers. Hunger burned in his eyes, the same hunger she felt for him, only it had nothing to do with the steaks that were burning.

Burning. "Zeke, the steaks!"

He whirled around and slapped at the fire with a mitt.

The sound of a car rolling into the driveway jerked their attention from the charred food. Paige wrinkled her face in confusion at Zeke's frown. "Oh, no. Not my mother."

"Grammy!" The girls raced to the Cadillac luxury car and pelted the slightly gray-haired woman with kisses as she climbed from the car. Then a much younger woman with dark hair cut in a stylish bob joined them. Was she a relative as well?

Zeke switched off the grill and shoved his hand through his hair, rumpling the long dark strands as his mother approached. "Mom, what are you doing here?"

"I was feeling better so I stopped by to see my favorite grandchildren."

Summer and August squealed with delight.

"Anyway, I thought I'd take the girls home with me for the night."

"Can we go, Daddy?" August asked.

"Pretty please," Summer begged.

"Well, sure." Zeke shifted and glanced at Paige. His mother coaxed the younger woman to join them.

"Zeke, honey, this is Edwina's daughter, Morgan."

The woman smiled coyly at Zeke and shook his hand. Zeke's mother stared at Paige with narrowed eyes, making Paige feel as if she'd been displayed on a rack for inspection like a piece of clothing. If she was a cotton dress, the other woman was a silk designer gown. She wondered if she'd measure up to his mother's perusal.

"Hi, Morgan." Zeke swept his hand toward Paige. "This is my next-door neighbor, Paige Watkins."

"She wents to the tea when you were sick, Grammy," August interjected.

"Oh, I see. That was nice of you to fill in for me."

Paige winced at her word choice. "Nice to meet you, Mrs. Blalock, Morgan."

"Do you stay at home, dear?" Mrs. Blalock asked.

"No, I'm in school and I work at a local boutique."

"Paige is gonna be a famous 'signer one day."

"Yeah, she's going to that city where Mommy wents."

"Paige is studying fashion design," Zeke explained.

Zeke's mother frowned and turned the conversation back to Morgan, bragging about her work with children. Paige felt inadequate, especially knowing Morgan was an expert on kids.

"Your mom's told me a lot about you and your twins," Morgan said.

A red flush crept up Zeke's neck. "Yeah. The girls are a handful."

"Morgan here loves kids. She's a preschool teacher." His mother tittered, then rushed on. "She was voted teacher of the year at the church school. She even has a degree in early childhood education."

"How nice," Zeke said.

Mrs. Blalock motioned to the twins. "Girls, go get your pj's and we'll head home."

"Yippee!" Summer and August squealed.

Mrs. Blalock brushed her hands down her paisley silk jogging suit. "Son, you might want to put on a pair of matching socks."

Zeke grimaced. "The girls must have messed with my clothes again."

"Daddy needs a wive to dress him," August said with a mischievous grin.

Morgan and Zeke's mother both laughed, but Zeke shifted uncomfortably. Paige backed off the patio, ready to bolt next door to her own house. With no children around, she would be alone with Zeke. Not a good idea, not after that explosive kiss. Obviously Morgan would make a better substitute mother—she was an experienced preschool teacher. And she really was attractive.

"Maybe you and Morgan can meet for dinner sometime," Zeke's mother suggested.

Zeke shrugged. "Maybe, some other time. I was making dinner for Paige tonight as a thank-you because she took your place at the tea,'' Zeke explained. ''And we have to deliver some dogs to a couple of our neighbors.''

Mrs. Blalock stared pointedly at the charred steaks. ''Well, you certainly aren't going to eat that meat, are you?''

Zeke's brown eyes darkened to black as he grabbed Paige's hand. ''No. As a matter of fact, I'm taking Paige out to dinner instead. Just as soon as you leave.''

Chapter Seven

Paige opened her mouth to protest but quickly clamped it shut when Zeke squeezed her hand firmly in his own. The warmth from his body collided with hers and in spite of the cool evening temperature, heat engulfed her.

"There's no need to be rude, son," Mrs. Blalock said, sliding her fingers through her short curls.

"I'm sorry, Mom. I didn't mean it like that." He inclined his head toward Morgan. "But you caught me off guard. I had plans this evening."

"Of course."

"We didn't mean to intrude." Morgan flashed him a brilliant smile. "I am glad to finally meet you, Zeke. I've heard so much about you. All good, of course."

So much for subtlety.

"Thanks," Zeke said in a noncommittal voice.

Paige felt like disappearing into the ground. "Zeke, we can—"

"Clean up and be ready in a few minutes. I think Mrs. Burgess and the Wileys are waiting on those puppies."

"But—" Paige started to argue that they could deliver the dogs the next day, but Zeke cut her off, squeezing her hand so hard her fingers went numb.

"We're ready, Grammy!" The girls raced down the

steps toward the car, their arms overloaded with suit-cases, stuffed animals and blanket.

"Girls, do you really need to bring all those toys?" Zeke asked.

"I can't sleep without brown bear," August said.

"And I can't sleep without blue bear," Summer added.

"And brown bear likes Pugsly the rabbit."

"And blue bear likes Sigfried Frog."

Zeke held up his hand. "Okay, I get the idea."

"Let's go, girls," Mrs. Blalock said. Zeke and Paige and Morgan followed her to the car.

"Oh, my goodness," Morgan yelped. She twisted her ankle sideways to examine her high heel. "I must have stepped in something."

"Dog poop," August confirmed.

"It's Henrietta's," Summer supplied in a matter-of-fact voice. "She gots diarrhea after she ate Daddy's hot dogs and chili."

"'Cause they was burned."

Morgan's face turned a sickly shade of green. Paige bit back a laugh. Zeke looked mortified. His mother glared at him. Then Morgan teetered sideways, grabbed Zeke's arm, balancing on one foot as she removed the offensive shoe.

"Sorry about that. Here, let me take your shoe." Zeke carried the black high heel to the grass, brushed the bottom of it on the lawn, then hosed it off, and returned it to Morgan. Water dripped from the heel. Morgan grasped it with two fingers, holding it away from her as she hobbled to the car, checking the ground as she walked.

Summer and August giggled and Zeke hugged them both goodbye. Paige's heart squeezed in her chest. Zeke Blalock was not only a handsome man, but a wonderful father. There was nothing quite as sexy or touching as a big powerful man with children.

"If Mommy calls, tell her we wants to talk to her about our birthday party," Summer said.

"Yeah, ask her if she's coming," August added.

Zeke nodded, but his shuttered expression made Paige wonder if Zeke and his ex-wife had talked about a reconciliation.

His mother drove away and he took her hand and led her inside to gather the puppies. She reminded herself they were simply friends. But Zeke gazed at her with his dark fathomless eyes full of want and she was afraid she was lying to herself, afraid she was already falling for the man.

They climbed into his minivan and she tried to reroute her wayward thoughts and forget about the fact that she was going to spend the entire evening alone with Zeke. The entire night, if she wanted.

A squeaking sound startled her. She reached under the seat and retrieved a rubber dog toy, three crushed M&M's candies and a dirty sock. A simple reminder that she'd better keep up her resolve—she and Zeke Blalock could not have a relationship or a fling. He had too much baggage, and as his mother and her friend had inadvertently reminded her, she was not mommy material.

Besides, if Zeke's ex-wife was coming for a visit, *anything* could happen.

"SORRY ABOUT THAT little scene back there." Zeke deftly maneuvered the vehicle toward Mrs. Burgess's house. "My mother makes tact sound like a four-letter word," he said, aiming for a subtle apology.

Paige chuckled. "I'm sure she means well. She's probably worried about you. And the girls, of course."

"Yeah, but I certainly don't need her throwing women at me. It's damn embarrassing." Paige laughed and he relaxed as they pulled into the neighbor's driveway.

Wanda Burgess, a widow in her late fifties, ambled out onto her front porch to greet them.

"You brought me a puppy!" The woman laughed merrily as Paige handed her the soft yellow ball of fur.

The puppy whimpered and curled into the woman's chubby arms. "He's adorable, isn't he?" Paige asked.

"It's been a long time since I've had a baby in my house." The woman dabbed at her eyes. "My children have all been gone, then I lost Harold. It's been mighty lonely around here lately."

Paige put her arm around the woman. "My house is pretty quiet, too. Sounds as if you and this little fellow will be perfect for each other."

"His shots are up-to-date," Zeke said. "Just let me know if you need anything."

The woman's eyes crinkled at the corners as she stroked the puppy's long ears. "I will, Doc. And thank you so much for finding me a dog this quickly. I've been pretty nervous these last few weeks with all this vandalism going on."

Paige and Zeke headed to the next house, not surprised when three kids barreled down the steps and met them at the car. Twelve-year-old Hannah, six-year-old Georgie and eight-year-old Samantha both grabbed for the dog at the same time.

Paige sat down on the porch, cradling the puppy in her lap. "Careful, everyone will have a chance to hold her."

"But I want him to be mine," Georgie said.

"And I want him to be mine," Samantha piped in.

Zeke laughed and Paige met his gaze, her expression amused, as she gently coaxed the children to take turns with the dog. Finally, the children's mother slipped outside, wiping her hands on a dish towel.

"I appreciate this, Dr. Blalock," Mrs. Wiley said, eyeing the kids with a grin. "The kids couldn't wait."

The children formed a circle on the ground and giggled as the pudgy puppy waddled around the grass between them.

"Had another break-in, same as before," Mrs. Wiley said. "TV, stereo, CDs. Made a mess in the house."

"It does sound like teens," Zeke said.

Mrs. Wiley scratched her head. "Poor Myrtle came in and saw her den cleaned out. She fainted on the floor, her daughter had to call the paramedics."

Paige gasped. "How awful. I'll talk to Derrick about installing a security system for her."

Zeke tensed at the mention of Derrick's name. Obviously the security consultant was still very much a part of Paige's life. But *he* had tonight with Paige. All night, since the twins weren't home. Maybe he could make her forget about the other man.

And he'd like nothing better than to coax her into spending every minute with him. He had to admit, he not only lusted after the sexy redhead, but he was really beginning to like her. Thinking back, he realized he'd never really liked Renee. Their relationship had simply been a physical attraction that had died a quick death when they'd married. And they'd only gotten hitched because she'd been pregnant. Of course, he'd never tell the girls that secret.

But he and Paige had a definite chemistry sizzling between them. Maybe he needed to help Paige see how wonderful they would be together. He suddenly couldn't wait for dinner, for the rest of the night—alone with Paige.

Several minutes later, Zeke turned down the exit, then into a small parking lot, hoping Paige would be pleased by his selection of restaurants. A log cabin structure with rocking chairs on the front porch boasted of days gone by. "This place may look old-fashioned but it's brand-new, and I've heard it has the best steaks in town."

"I've heard good things about it, too."

He slipped from the car and opened Paige's door before she could unfasten her seat belt. Like a gallant knight, he held out his hand. Paige smiled in return and dramatized the motion as if she were his princess. A vision of her wearing a full-length ball gown with glass slippers popped into his mind. Geez. He must have been reading too many fairy tales to his kids.

The hostess seated them in the corner of the quaint little room in upholstered comfy chairs situated beside a cozy fireplace. Hardwood floors and knotty pine walls enhanced the warm atmosphere, creating a feeling of country charm, with pastel linen tablecloths and pewter candlesticks adding a touch of elegance.

When Paige accepted a glass of wine and smiled at him over the dim candlelight, the red and brown streaks flickering in her hair drew his gaze, and his fantasy continued. They were dancing to some sappy tune and he was holding her in his arms, then he lifted her and carried her to his bed. Heavy drapes lined the canopy and he pushed them aside and laid her gently on satin sheets, then began undressing her ever so slowly—

"What's good to eat?" Paige asked.

You.

He coughed, then sipped his wine, wondering if he really was losing it. "Uh, the other vet I work with says the filet's great. So is the New York strip."

"I love the atmosphere, it's so charming," Paige said. "And the food smells great."

"So do you."

"What?" She almost dropped the menu.

He grinned. "What kind of perfume are you wearing?"

"I'm not." Paige fidgeted, not quite meeting his eyes. "It's the bath soap, strawberry."

"Oh." The strawberry kiss in her kitchen blazed through his mind. She obviously remembered it, too, because her gaze raced to the menu where she spent several minutes studying the items listed. Or memorizing them. Whatever, she appeared to be avoiding eye contact.

Finally the waiter arrived, breaking the strained silence. Paige ordered the filet, he the New York strip.

"So, tell me about the shop where you work, Paige."

Paige shrugged and sipped the wine. "It's called Beverly's Boutique. It's right in downtown Crabapple. We sell tailor-made women's clothing, lingerie and specialty items."

"Sounds like a nice shop," Zeke said.

"It's pretty classy. We have a few customers who make appointments for fittings during the week, but walk-ins are more common on the weekend, so Saturdays are really busy."

"And you're studying design in school? How much longer do you have?"

"Actually I'll finish this summer," Paige said. "I'm working on my final project now."

"What made you decide to study clothing design?"

"I liked to play dress up when I was a kid," Paige said with a laugh.

"So do my girls. They used to play in Renee's things.

But she didn't like the mess…'' His voice trailed off and he ran his finger around the rim of his glass.

''I used to drive my mom crazy snooping in her closet, too,'' Paige said, breezing over the awkward moment. ''But my grandma was cool. She gave me some of her old dresses and a box of costume jewelry. And she taught me to sew. We spent hours making doll clothes for all my baby dolls.''

''Where're your folks now?'' Zeke asked.

''My dad got sick when I was little. Mom had a tough time making ends meet after he died, so I took a job in high school and saved for college. Mom always wanted me to earn a degree, not have to work some menial job the way she did. She always regretted not finishing college herself.''

''Why didn't she finish?''

Paige bit down on her lip, suddenly solemn. ''Because she had me.''

He paused, his fork in midair, remembering Renee's declaration about sacrificing her career for the kids, then surprised himself by asking, ''She couldn't have done both?''

Paige shrugged. ''My dad was old-fashioned. He wanted her to stay home and she did at first. Then he got sick, and she had to work to pay bills. There was never time for her to go back.'' She twirled her fork in her salad. ''Eventually she resented the sacrifices she'd made.''

He frowned, then dug into his food, uncomfortable with the direction of the conversation. Thankfully, Paige changed the subject.

''Anyway, I always daydreamed when I was little about making Cinderella dresses, so here I am.''

His lips curved into a smile. He was mesmerized by

Paige's green eyes as they darkened in the hazy light of
the flickering flame. When she brought her lips to her
glass, he stifled a groan, slipping into his own daydream.
Paige was nearly naked, wearing skimpy lacy undergarments, panties cut high to reveal her slender thighs, a
wisp of a bra dipping low to expose her tantalizing cleav-
age. He sipped his wine and imagined dipping a finger
into the glass, stroking the rise of her breasts, circling the
rosy tips through the lace until her nipples peaked beneath his fingertip.

"How about you? Did you have any interesting cases
at the clinic today?" Paige asked.

"Huh?"

"Zeke?"

"Oh, yeah. Cases." He fidgeted in his seat, shocked
at how quickly his body had become aroused. "I stitched
up Peanut, the dachshund you saw at the house. I had a
couple of spays, a declaw and a sick bulldog." Real romantic conversation, he thought, wincing. His lack of
savvy dating skills must be obvious.

She sipped her wine again, and he concentrated on
talking instead of thinking. His fantasies were going to
get him in trouble if he wasn't careful.

"What made you decide to go into veterinary medi-
cine?" she asked.

"I always liked animals. But my dad was allergic, so
I couldn't have a pet growing up. Then Dad and Mom
divorced when I was twelve, and Mom bought me a
dog."

He saw sympathy rise in her eyes. "It was okay
though, the divorce I mean. I saw Dad on the weekends
and stuff, and he and Mom stayed on fairly good terms."

"Where he is now?"

"In Germany on business. Some kind of computer company he's considering investing in. He travels a lot."

"So, you chose your career when you were twelve?"

"No." Zeke laughed. "But I had a buddy whose dad owned an animal clinic. I worked there during the summer, you know, cleaning cages and stuff. After that... well, after watching his dad treat animals, I knew I wanted to be a vet."

"He must have made quite an impression."

"Yeah. I graduated from high school, then went to UGA. I was lucky. Got into vet school my junior year."

"I'm sure your parents are proud. So, you still like what you do?"

"Sure." Zeke polished off a roll. "Sometimes, telling little old ladies with poodles about fleas is tiresome, but every job has its downside. Mostly I enjoy the animals. And I like surgery, especially trauma cases."

He noticed her gaze stray to his hands and wondered what she was thinking. Then the waiter brought their food and they both attacked the steaks like starving animals. Either that, or they were both avoiding looking at the other one.

"Do you work on Sundays?"

Zeke shook his head. "Sometimes. I'm thinking of joining the emergency service so I won't have to go in at night. I need more time with the girls."

"Sounds like a good idea," Paige said. "So, tell me about your ex-wife."

Zeke tore off a chunk of bread, gritting his teeth. "Why do you want to know?"

Paige shrugged, cutting her steak. "The girls mentioned she's coming home."

His stomach churned. "She's supposed to return to the States next week for good."

Paige scooped up a bite of her baked potato. "I know the girls are looking forward to seeing her."

But I'm not.

"I'm sure they miss her terribly, Zeke. You must have been devastated when she left."

"The divorce was hard for everyone at first," Zeke admitted, annoyed at the subject. This was his night with Paige—he didn't intend to ruin it by discussing his failed marriage.

"Tell me about you and Derrick," he said, switching the subject.

Paige blinked. "There's not much to tell. We've known each other forever. High school sweethearts and all that."

He didn't like her answer.

He was just about to ask her if they were serious sweethearts now, but the waiter interrupted with dessert menus and the violinist serenading the couple across the room stopped in front of their table, easing into a popular romantic tune. Then Paige gazed at him with a hint of seduction and the sweet agony in her eyes obliterated any questions he'd meant to ask. He didn't want to talk about his failed marriage or Derrick tonight. He wanted to seduce Paige and end this hot torture burning between them.

"Bring us a hot fudge cake with two spoons," Zeke told the waiter, determined to end the evening on a lighter note.

Paige's eyes widened when the waiter set the huge concoction in front of them.

Zeke gave her a teasing grin. "Hey, I love strawberries and chocolate."

Their gazes locked again, and sensuous didn't begin to describe the storm of passion in her eyes. Then a sweet vulnerability shadowed her need, and he wanted to reach out and drag her into his arms and kiss her senseless until all the questions lingering between them disappeared. She nibbled at her lower lip, looking uncertain and beyond tempting, and he could almost taste the raw femininity in her heated response. The waiter set the gooey dessert in front of them and he took the spoon, scooped up a bite and practically inhaled it. Paige did the same.

When her tongue flicked the chocolate sauce off the spoon and she licked her lips, he slipped back into his fantasy. Only this time he wasn't having hot fudge cake for dessert. He was devouring Paige.

PAIGE DECIDED HOT fudge cake was her favorite dessert, that is, except for strawberries. Watching Zeke enjoy the delicious food only fueled her desire for him. She'd felt uncomfortable talking about her mother. Then Zeke had asked about Derrick and she'd been grateful for the interruption. She didn't want to mention Amelia and Derrick's engagement, for fear he'd think she was hinting at marriage.

During the ride home, Zeke turned the radio to a soft rock station, and while a blues song wafted through the car, her mind strayed to the impossible—a deliciously sinful night in bed with Zeke doing things she'd never imagined doing with a man before.

Perhaps her hormones simply needed to be readjusted.

She stole a glance at Zeke. Time to face reality. Not only was she in deep lust with the man, wanting his broad hands to roam across her body and drag her beneath him, but she actually liked him. A dangerous combination.

Her mother's past haunted her. If she allowed herself to become wrapped up in his kids, she might not finish her education, might never fulfill her dreams, might never become anything more than a salesclerk. She might end up resenting them all just as her mother had. Plus, if she accepted responsibility for the girls and something happened to them, she'd never forgive herself.

She might get her heart broken to boot.

Hadn't Zeke confirmed that his ex-wife was coming back? She'd seen the pain in his face when she'd broached the subject. Was he still in love with her? If she wanted to reconcile, he'd probably feel he owed it to the girls to try and make things work. And Paige would be left home alone with a huge hole in her heart and a house so quiet that it creaked with emptiness. She was just now getting used to being alone again, just now exorcising the sound of Joey's young chatter from her rooms.

The silence in the car seemed fraught with anticipation. Paige wrapped her arms around her middle in a protective embrace, forcing herself to curb her desires. Zeke thumped his fingers on the steering column in time with the music, his deep baritone humming the rhythm along with the song. When they pulled onto their street, she tensed, once again thinking about how delicious the hot fudge had been and wishing she could taste it again. This time on Zeke's lips.

"I guess we should be checking the neighborhood for anything suspicious." Zeke's gaze scanned the street.

Paige glanced up and down the passenger side of the road. "I don't see anything amiss. Most of the break-ins have been during the day, anyway."

"That is odd," Zeke said. "Maybe they'll catch the vandals soon. I hate to think about some of these older people being frightened."

Zeke parked in her driveway and Paige didn't wait for him to open the door but hopped out of the passenger side. He moved around the van and was standing beside her in a flash, the palm of his hand brushing her back as he escorted her up the sidewalk. "Thanks for dinner."

"You're welcome." He motioned to the porch swing and Paige hesitated, searching his face.

"I just want to talk," he said as if he'd read the concern in her eyes. His slow smile softened her reservations. She let him pull her to the swing. Lifting his feet, he gently pushed the swing so they glided slowly back and forth.

"Look, there's the North Star," she said, twisting her hands in her lap.

He caught her hands and stilled them. "When I was a kid, my dad used to take me camping. He always told me if I got lost to find that star, and it would lead me home."

Paige met his gaze. "Things were simple when we were little, weren't they?"

Zeke nodded, then lifted his thumb to her cheek and traced a path down her jawline. "Nothing's simple anymore, is it?"

"No," Paige said softly. She rubbed her hands up and down her arms, chilled from the evening air, her senses tingling from Zeke's masculine scent.

"You're beautiful, Paige," Zeke murmured. Paige felt trapped by the husky resonance of his voice, then she looked into the dark fathomless irises of his eyes and tried to remember her earlier arguments about not getting involved with him.

"Zeke, dinner was nice, but—"

Zeke gently pressed his finger to her lips. "No buts. Can't we forget about everything else for a few minutes? Simply pretend it's you and me, that nothing else matters."

His rough whisper melted her defenses like snow evaporating on a hot day. Zeke slid his arm around her and pulled her to him, his heady masculine scent sending a surge of longing through her. He tilted his head, she met his mouth. Ever so gently he placed his lips over hers, tasting, nibbling, seeking permission. Paige inhaled the sweet whisper of his breath and tasted chocolate.

His lips covered hers, pressing, seeking, urging her to taste his need, and she turned, her body pressing into his as his lips consumed her with fire. His hands encircled her waist, hers dug into his thick hair. Swallowing a moan, he plunged his tongue into her mouth, driving it deeper and increasing the pressure until she knew he felt her breasts pushing against the hard wall of his chest, until she could no longer stand simply kissing him. She arched against him and he stroked her back, then gently his hand swept around her waist and covered her breast, kneading and molding her while she melded against him. She moaned and clutched his broad shoulders, excitement coursing through her as she felt his muscles ripple and his body shudder with need.

"God, Paige," Zeke whispered softly when she finally drug her lips away from his. "You feel so good."

Paige couldn't answer, she was scorching inside and out by the flames he had ignited within her. He teased her earlobe with his tongue, then planted gentle, but hungry kisses down her neck, and she arched against him again, shamefully aching for him, moaning when he exhaled and dipped his head to nip the bud of her nipple through her blouse. His other hand slipped beneath her shirt and unclasped her bra, his fingers teasing her until she cried out his name in a husky plea. Her bare breasts felt the chill of the cool night air as he nudged up her sweater and exposed her to his dark probing eyes. Paige tensed, then clutched his head with her hands, digging her fingernails in his scalp as he lowered his mouth.

A shrill noise—a voice?—exploded between them and Paige stilled. Zeke paused, his breathing coming out in erratic pants, his tongue a fraction away from her aching, welcoming body. Moonlight spilled over her shoulder and highlighted his hungry features as he eased her shirt back down to cover her and made an attempt to calm himself.

They both glanced up to see Erma Spivy running toward them from across the street. "Paige, Dr. Blalock!"

Paige's body protested painfully, reminding her how close they'd been to seeking fulfillment in each other's arms. She'd told him she wasn't the kind of girl to hop into bed with a guy, they were supposedly only friends, and here she was practically begging him to make love to her on her front porch.

Disgusted with herself, she righted her clothing, grateful the awning obliterated Erma's view. Zeke dropped his hands to his lap, his expression solemn. "We need to talk, Paige," he said quietly.

She pushed away from him and stood. "Not now."

He grabbed her arm and swung around to face him. She shivered at the intensity in his probing eyes. "Later then. This isn't over."

She shook her head, her voice shaky. "Yes it is. What happened between us was a mistake, Zeke. We can't start a relationship—"

"Why not?"

She forced herself to tell him the truth, at least part of it. "Because you have a family and I don't want the responsibility." *I can't have it. I might let something happen to the girls. And your ex is returning to town.*

Zeke's eyes narrowed, hurt darkening his expression.

But before Paige could elaborate, Erma had crossed the street. She nearly ran over the monkey grass as she hurried toward them. "Paige, somebody broke into my house! Dwayne was so rattled he slipped and fell and knocked himself unconscious."

Paige's heart stopped. "Is he all right? Did you call the police?"

Zeke headed toward the steps, his forehead furrowed. "Is the intruder still there?"

"No, they ran off, and the police have already come and gone." She swiped a hand across her forehead, panting. "But Dwayne's lying down with a concussion, and I'm afraid to stay here by myself with him. When I saw you two drive up, I told Dwayne I'd come and get you."

Paige patted Erma's hand. "I'll be right there, Erma. Try and relax."

Zeke pressed his hand to her back, his look warning her that things weren't settled between them. But they had to be, she reminded herself, as she followed Erma.

They simply had to be.

Play **LUCKY HEARTS** for this..

exciting FREE gift!
This surprise mystery gift could be yours free

when you play **LUCKY HEARTS!**
...then continue your lucky streak with a sweetheart of a deal!

1. Play Lucky Hearts as instructed on the opposite page.

2. Send back this card and you'll receive brand-new Harlequin American Romance® novels. These books have a cover price of $4.25 each in the U.S. and $4.99 each in Canada, but they are yours to keep absolutely free.

3. There's no catch! You're under no obligation to buy anything. We charge nothing—ZERO—for your first shipment. And you don't have to make any minimum number of purchases—not even one!

4. The fact is thousands of readers enjoy receiving books by mail from the Harlequin Reader Service®. They enjoy the convenience of home delivery...they like getting the best new novels at discount prices, BEFORE they're available in stores...and they love their *Heart to Heart* subscriber newsletter featuring author news, horoscopes, recipes, book reviews and much more!

5. We hope that after receiving your free books you'll want to remain a subscriber. But the choice is yours—to continue or cancel, any time at all! So why not take us up on our invitation, with no risk of any kind. You'll be glad you did!

◆ Exciting Harlequin romance novels—FREE!

◆ Plus an exciting mystery gift—FREE!

▼ DETACH AND MAIL CARD TODAY! ▼

YES!

I have scratched off the silver card. Please send me the 2 FREE books and gift for which I qualify.
I understand I am under no obligation to purchase any books, as explained on the back and on the opposite page.

With a coin, scratch off the silver card and check below to see what we have for you.

HARLEQUIN'S

LUCKY HEARTS GAME

354 HDL CY3T

154 HDL CY3J
(H-AR-04/00)

NAME (PLEASE PRINT CLEARLY)

ADDRESS

APT.# CITY

STATE/PROV. ZIP/POSTAL CODE

Twenty-one gets you 2 free books, and a free mystery gift!

Twenty gets you 2 free books!

Nineteen gets you 1 free book!

Try Again!

Offer limited to one per household and not valid to current Harlequin American Romance® subscribers. All orders subject to approval.

The Harlequin Reader Service®—Here's how it works:

Accepting your 2 free books and gift places you under no obligation to buy anything. You may keep the books and gift and return the shipping statement marked "cancel." If you do not cancel, about a month later we'll send you 4 additional novels a bill you just $3.57 each in the U.S., or $3.96 each in Canada, plus 25¢ delivery per book and applicable taxes if any.* That's complete price and — compared to cover prices of $4.25 each in the U.S. and $4.99 each in Canada — it's quite a bargain! may cancel at any time, but if you choose to continue, every month we'll send you 4 more books, which you may either purchase at the discount price or return to us and cancel your subscription.

*Terms and prices subject to change without notice. Sales tax applicable in N.Y. Canadian residents will be charged applicab provincial taxes and GST.

Chapter Eight

Zeke watched Paige comforting the elderly woman. Derrick had shown up at the Spivys like a modern-day version of a Superman hero, installing new dead bolts and talking about the upscale security system he would install the next day. While Derrick had wowed the women with his knowledge of the latest in technology, Zeke had calmed Mr. Spivy, but now he was simply twiddling his thumbs while Lois Lane and Clark Kent saved the day.

"Thanks for coming over, Derrick," Paige said. "I know the Spivys will feel more secure with new locks."

"No problem." Derrick winked at Paige. "I'd do anything for you."

The steak Zeke had eaten earlier clumped in his stomach like leather.

"I don't know if I can fall asleep or not," Mrs. Spivy muttered. "I keep thinking about some stranger coming in my house and I start shaking."

"I know you're nervous, Mrs. Spivy. Why don't I stay here with you for a while?" Paige put her arm around the trembling woman and patted her back. "I'll rest on your couch while you lie down with Mr. Spivy and try to sleep."

Zeke admired Paige's caring attitude, but took her declaration as a dismissal of him and headed toward the door in frustration. Paige caught his arm, the imprint of her slender fingers burning through his shirt and reminding him of their evening together.

"Thanks for talking to Mr. Spivy, Zeke."

He shrugged. "It was no big deal. I care about them, too."

Paige stared at his arm where her fingers still lay, then met his gaze, the yearning in her eyes mirroring his own. "You may not realize it, but your simply sitting with him made him feel better." The corners of her mouth lifted into a smile and he wanted to reach out and touch her lips, to kiss them. "And I appreciate your coming with me."

He nodded, hoping she'd changed her mind about the two of them, but Derrick called her name and she broke the spell by pulling away and leaving him at the door alone. He walked home, puzzled over the hunger he'd seen in Paige's eyes and the distance she'd placed between them. He thought about what she'd said about her mother resenting not finishing her education. Renee had pretty much said the same thing to him about her modeling career. And now Paige...if he got involved with her and she didn't finish her degree or pursue her dreams, would she end up resenting him?

Her question about Renee bothered him. Did she think he wanted a reconciliation with his ex?

He drank in the peaceful evening night, inhaling the sweet scents of dogwood blossoms and honeysuckle in the breeze. Stars glittered and twinkled above him. Like a child, he paused and closed his eyes to make a wish—a silly wish that wouldn't come true, at least not tonight. Because he wished things weren't so damn complicated. Wished he didn't have to spend the night alone, that

Paige would come to him, that the two of them could share a night of passion that would end in promises.

No, he didn't want an affair. Having children had matured him, ending his wild roaming days. He wanted a woman who would last forever.

THE NEXT DAY Zeke still felt unsettled. After leaving his neighbors the night before, he'd tried to sleep, but the memory of Paige's body next to his fired him up, and the reality of her parting words made acid burn in his stomach. He knew it was better they hadn't slept together. Making love would have complicated a relationship apparently going nowhere. Still, he wanted her with an intensity that hurt.

Did she want a no-strings man who'd support her career and wouldn't want to tie her down with kids? Like Derrick. He raked a hand across his clean-shaven jaw in frustration; he had no choice about the family, but now he'd probably ruined chances of a friendship with Paige. Hell, who was he kidding? He couldn't simply be friends with Paige. The attraction was too strong.

Deciding he needed to distract himself from his sexy neighbor, he dressed for church. Surely he could curb his unholy feelings toward her in the place of worship.

But even in church, he found himself imagining Paige sitting next to him on the pew, her small hand folded in his, her stomach round with his baby. Maybe a boy this time, a brother for Summer and August.

A single woman named Betty Eaton slid up beside him. "I saw that flier your daughters put up in the nursery and thought we should talk."

He jerked around. She had shoulder-length blond hair, a model-thin figure, and a certain amount of sex appeal, but unfortunately, she didn't spark his interest at all. Reminded him of a silky terrier, all shiny and showy—not a real dog—not a real woman. Then her words sank in. "What? The flier?"

The church organ music began to play and an elderly man stepped up to sing a solo. "This flier your daughters tacked on the bulletin board," the woman whispered.

Zeke groaned. "They put it up here at church, too?"

Betty laughed good-naturedly and patted his arm. "Don't worry. I removed the flier." She handed him the paper and he stuffed it in his pocket, vowing to give his daughters another lecture as soon as he drove them home.

"I had no idea they'd posted this crazy advertisement in church," Zeke hissed between announcements.

"Don't worry. I work in the nursery area, you wouldn't believe some of the stuff the children tell us."

Organ music signaled the beginning of the service and Zeke opened a hymnal just as the soloist burst into a deep chorus of "Go Tell It on the Mountain."

A nervous laugh escaped him. His girls would probably be doing that next—climbing some mountain and screaming to all the people below that their father needed a wife.

As if the lady beside him had read his mind, she whispered, "So, how about lunch?"

Zeke forced himself to say yes.

An hour and a half later, when Betty had poured out the details of her nasty divorce and distrust of men, he regretted his decision. She loved children, but she also had nine cats, and when she admitted she prepared gourmet meals for them every night, a red flag waved in his head.

"They all sleep with me," she said with a light laugh that reminded him of a sick cat. "Queen Elizabeth and Elvira are due to have kittens next week."

He liked animals, but nine cats and kittens on the way seemed a little obsessive.

"And I think Winnie may need therapy."

"Excuse me?"

"A psychologist," Betty said. "She's terrified of the dark. Totally freaks out and pulls out her fur if I turn the light off at night."

"So you sleep with a light on?"

"Well, I can't very well upset her," Betty said a little defensively.

"No, I guess not." Zeke polished off his tea and decided to bring the meal to an end. "Well, lunch was nice, Ms. Eaton—"

"Call me Betty, Zeke."

"Betty, but I have to pick up the girls."

She smiled and dabbed at her freshly painted lips, blotting hot pink lipstick all over the white linen napkin. "Sure. Maybe I can cook you dinner one evening."

Maybe not. Zeke nodded and headed toward his car, feeling a hundred years old. He finally remembered what had prompted him to try marriage with Renee in the first place. Other than the fact Renee had been pregnant, he'd hated dating—all the small talk, pretense, and put-ons. He'd genuinely wanted to find someone who liked home and hearth.

Only he'd made the wrong choice in Renee. And now he'd found a woman he genuinely liked. Who liked his daughters. Was good with kids. But she didn't want a family or him. And he'd better remember it and not dwell on pursuing her, or she'd break his heart, much worse than Renee had.

He climbed in his minivan, his decision made. He would avoid his next-door neighbor. Even if it drove him crazy.

PAIGE WAS GOING crazy. She couldn't get Zeke out of her mind. Every time Amelia tried on a wedding dress, she imagined herself wearing the bridal gown. Only last night she'd dreamt about little Joey—she'd seen his small body dart in the street in front of that car. But in her dream, the car hadn't been able to stop. It was so horrible. And it had all been her fault. Then instantly the little boy had become two little girls, Summer and August. She'd woken up in a cold sweat and started shaking every time she thought about it.

"I like the neck on this dress, the bodice on that satin gown, and the train on that antique ivory dress," Amelia said, pointing to the three final gowns they'd selected. Paige quickly drew sketches of the pieces, etching in the details of the neckline, trim, beads, headpieces and trains. "Okay, I'll draw a final sketch tonight. Why don't you drop by work tomorrow and look at it. If you approve, I'll buy the material and get busy."

"It's coming up so fast!" Amelia squealed. "I can't believe it. I'm really going to have my dream wedding!"

Paige hugged her. "I'm so happy for you."

Amelia grabbed her arm. "Come on, my feet are killing me. We're meeting Derrick for drinks." She led Paige around the mall toward the Mexican restaurant.

"Amelia, I think I'll head home."

"Oh, no you don't." Amelia pushed Paige in front of her into the restaurant. Paige froze when she saw Derrick sitting with another guy at a table.

"Amelia, you set me up again."

"Yep." Amelia grinned wryly, then whispered, "He's perfect. Tall, dark, handsome, adventuresome, lots of money, and free! Exactly like the man you ordered."

Paige could have kicked herself. She'd never imagined Amelia would find someone with all those qualities. After all, she'd been thinking of Zeke when she'd made them up. Except for the last characteristic...

"Come on," Amelia said. "And flirt."

Flirt? She didn't even remember how. So Paige stood idly by, hiding her embarrassment as Derrick and Amelia kissed in a flurry of arms and heated noises.

The other man sipped his scotch and winked mischievously at Paige, ushering her into a seat beside him in a small booth. "Hi, I'm Ben."

Heat crept up her cheeks as she introduced herself. Derrick and Amelia finally loosened their lip-lock and pulled apart. Paige twisted her hands together as she surveyed the small restaurant. Southwestern paintings decorated the adobe walls and soft cushions in muted tones provided comfortable seating. A simple carnation served as the centerpiece and ferns were scattered throughout the airy room, yet the seating was tight.

"Ben learned to fly when he was in college." Amelia kicked her under the table to bring her out of her reverie. "He's been traveling all over the world since."

Paige rubbed her foot. Ben did have nice hazel eyes, a slim build, and stylishly cut black hair. He probably stood a little under six feet. Short, compared to Zeke.

Darn, she couldn't compare every man she met to Zeke.

They ordered margaritas and appetizers and Derrick and Ben reminisced about college days.

"After I finished my law degree, I spent the summer backpacking all over Europe," Ben said. "Climbed mountains, toured France and Italy. Have you traveled much, Paige?"

Paige shook her head, wondering if she and Ben had anything in common. "I worked for a while after high school, so I'm just now finishing my degree."

"You'd love Madrid. And there's nothing like hiking through the mountains in Switzerland."

They had nothing in common, Paige surmised awhile later. Nothing at all. His family owned houses in five different countries. He had visited the former Soviet Union, seen the famous Berlin Wall, and ridden an elephant in Africa. She'd been camping in the North Georgia mountains, walked through Rock City, and gone horseback riding once when she was eleven on her uncle's chicken farm.

"Wow, what an exciting life." Especially compared to her small-town girl experiences.

"Paige is studying design," Amelia interjected. "She's designing my wedding dress."

Derrick nuzzled Amelia's neck. "I can't wait to see it."

"Impressive." Ben shot her a sincere smile. "You should study in Paris. It's the fashion capital of the world."

"Yes, I've heard," Paige said. *But going to Paris takes money I don't have.* She started to explain, but Ben wouldn't understand. Apparently, money hadn't been an issue with him.

"Look at those adorable twins." Amelia pointed to the door.

Paige glanced over the row of potted plants and saw Summer and August with their grandmother. Mrs. Blalock juggled an armful of shopping bags as she ushered the girls toward a booth. Summer and August spotted her and waved frantically, then dashed around tables and wooden chairs and practically threw themselves in her lap.

"Hi, girls. Having fun?"

"Yep," August said. "Grammy's buying us lots of stuff."

"And we had ice cream," Summer added.

"I bet I can guess the flavor." Paige laughed as she wiped a chunk of chocolate from Summer's chin.

"Who's that?" August patted Ben's arm. His mouth curled in distaste when he noticed sticky brown fingerprints on his white shirt. He dabbed his napkin in his water glass and instantly brushed at the stains.

Paige introduced the children, but Mrs. Blalock hurried over. "Come on, girls. We need to eat so we can make it home before dark." She offered Paige a token hello and scurried away with the twins.

"Cute kids," Amelia said. "Derrick and I want a baby."

Derrick threaded his fingers through Amelia's fingers and grinned. "Or two."

So do I, Paige thought, surprising herself at the revelation. *But later, much later. After I've achieved my goals.*

"Not me." Ben grimaced. "I have too much to see in the world to tie myself down with a bunch of rugrats."

Paige nibbled on the chips and salsa while Ben entertained them with a story about one of his train rides through Yugoslavia. He certainly had seen the world. But he didn't want a family. And while she didn't want a ready-made one, she was warming to the idea of children. Someday she wanted a sweet baby to hold, maybe one with dark hair, dark brown eyes. A little boy like Zeke.

Shaking herself suddenly in horror, she stared at her drink and decided she should stick to water. She was losing her ever-loving mind!

"Are you busy Saturday night?" Ben asked.

Paige jerked her gaze back to Ben. "Uh, yeah, I have

plans,'' she lied. Amelia and Derrick were getting ready to leave and she wanted to scoot out with them.

Ben squeezed her hand gently. "I'm skydiving next weekend if you want to come."

"Um, I don't think so," Paige hedged. Derrick waved and he and Amelia slipped down the aisle.

Ben caught her hand. "How about bungee jumping?"

"That's not really my thing."

"Scuba diving?"'

"I'm a little claustrophobic."

"We could play tennis."

"I've always had weak arm muscles."

Ben studied his drink, swirling the liquid around. "We could see a movie." He quirked an eyebrow. "That is, unless you're afraid of dark theaters and crowds? Or are you allergic to popcorn?"

Paige laughed at his teasing tone. "A movie might be nice. Just give me a call." Then she grabbed her purse, said goodbye, and hurried out the door.

By the time she arrived home, the sun had faded to a distant sliver of orange and she'd convinced herself her dreams of marriage and a baby had only been a momentary lapse in sanity. She sat on her porch and worked on sketches of Amelia's wedding dress, then began designs for her final project. Derrick had said he'd be by at seven, and wanted her to help him check out another house.

The sound of an engine broke the peaceful quiet and Zeke pulled into his driveway. When he climbed from his van, he didn't even glance in her direction. A few minutes later, his mother drove up and the girls ran toward the house. Zeke met them in the front yard, tossing them both in the air with a hug. She heard them chattering and talking and laughing, then one of the girls called her name, and a wave of loneliness settled deep inside her. Her stomach tightened into a knot and she had the strongest urge to join them, to be a part of their little family.

But Zeke shook his head at the girls and steered them into the house. He'd obviously gotten the message that she only wanted to be friends. He was going to leave her alone and keep the girls away, too. She should have been happy. Instead, her heart cracked a notch. Even though she'd been fighting the attraction, she realized she'd already partially fallen for Zeke. Darn it.

Why couldn't she have learned from the disaster with Eric?

ZEKE TOSSED AND turned all night and woke up feeling cranky and irritable the next morning. His mood had nothing to do with seeing Derrick pull into Paige's driveway the night before, he told himself. But he knew he was lying to himself. Today he had to face her. They were having another meeting to discuss the neighborhood watch program. For the first time in his life, he actually prayed for a medical emergency so he'd have a good excuse not to attend. The telephone rang and he lunged for it. He was shocked to hear his ex-wife's voice on the other end.

"Zeke, this is Renee."

"Yeah?"

She paused. "I won't be able to make it to the States next week after all."

He muttered a curse. "Renee, look, you know the girls are looking forward to your visit. They need to see you."

"I realize that, but I simply can't come now. I have a chance to go to southern Italy for a month."

"A month? So you won't be coming at all in June?"

"That's right. It just can't be helped," Renee said as

if she expected him to understand. "I know the girls will be disappointed, but I'll send them a gift or something."

"They don't want your gifts, Renee, they want to see you."

"They'll love whatever I send them," Renee said nonchalantly.

Zeke cursed silently, but the girls picked up the phone and he bit his tongue. Renee smoothed over the news about her delayed visit, but the twins' small voices wavered with disappointment. His ex was so utterly selfish it made his blood boil. And in spite of how his girls tried to hide their disappointment from their mother, he knew he'd have to deal with the fallout after Renee hung up.

He climbed from bed, then took great pains to make homemade pancakes, hoping to ease the tension over the phone call with a special breakfast. But the girls barely ate.

"Daddy, don't you want Mommy to come back?" August asked.

Zeke paused, a flapjack in his hand. "Well, sure I do."

"You sounded mad," Summer said, her eyes wide.

They'd obviously overheard more than he thought.

"'Cause we want her to come and stay foreber," August said.

Zeke's heart clenched. He sat down and scooped them into this lap. "I know you do, and so do I."

"Then you'll be nice to Mommy when she calls so she won't leabe again?"

How could he resist those pleading sweet eyes? He raised his hand and mimicked a Boy Scouts' pledge. "I can't promise she won't leave. But I'll do whatever I can to convince her to stay."

Both girls hugged his neck and he squeezed his eyes shut, wishing he could make their dreams all come true.

They finally released him, but their chatter quickly turned to Paige. When they mentioned seeing her at the mall with two guys, his mood drastically declined. One of them definitely fit Derrick's description.

If Paige could date someone else, he should do the same. Let her have her career. He would find another woman. As the old saying went, there were lots of fish in the sea. And he'd find one who would love his daughters and him. Even if she didn't make his heart pound and the blood spin through his veins with excitement the way Paige did.

PAIGE NOTICED Zeke the moment he stepped into Mrs. Spivy's house. Their eyes locked momentarily, but he nodded briefly and glanced away, taking a chair beside Dannika. Great, the piranha of all women, Paige thought, feeling slighted that Zeke hadn't sought out her company.

Then again, why should he? She had written him off.

But Dannika definitely wasn't the motherly type; she'd have no idea how to take care of Summer and August. Not that Paige did, but heck, she would be better than the sex goddess. The mere idea of the leggy brunette all over Zeke disgusted her.

"We're growing more and more concerned about these break-ins," Mrs. Spivy said, pulling her from her troubled thoughts. "Someone in the community has to have seen or heard something."

"We don't want to point fingers," Mr. Spivy said. "But we are concerned about someone else getting hurt."

"The kids didn't make you fall, did they?" Bessie Rivers asked in horror.

Mr. Spivy shook his head. "No, but the house was so dark I tripped over the books they scattered on the floor."

"The intruders might be someone who lives outside the neighborhood," Paige suggested.

"But it's most likely someone we know," Dannika interjected. "How else would the vandals know when people are home?"

"Good point," Mr. Spivy added. "I realize a lot of the mothers in the neighborhood work. The kids are latchkey kids. They have a lot of time in the afternoon to peruse the neighborhood, to get into trouble when they're unsupervised."

Paige's temper rose. Cynthia, a divorcée, spoke across the room. "I have to work to support my kids. That doesn't mean they're juvenile delinquents."

"That's right," Paige said in her defense. "I grew up with a working mom myself. I didn't go around breaking into people's homes. Someone else could be casing the houses."

"But latchkey kids get into trouble more often than others," Dannika said. "Don't you watch the news?"

"Teens are usually rebellious no matter what kind of home they come from," Paige added, wondering if Dannika even liked children. Surely, Zeke would see through her flirtatious act and realize she wasn't kid-friendly.

A heated discussion followed. Finally Paige spoke up again. "It won't do any good for us to question one another. Let's all calm down."

Zeke stood, his powerful masculinity radiating through the room as he took charge. "I agree. The important thing here is to discover who's behind the break-ins and teach safety awareness." He and Paige worked to restore calm among the neighbors. Finally Paige excused herself and left the house, unsettled by the way Zeke kept watching her. And even more unsettled to see Dannika worming her way into Zeke's graces, and Zeke allowing her to cozy up to him.

The comments about working mothers had struck a nerve, only reinforcing her realization that she and Zeke were wrong for each other. Zeke was worried about his daughters' motherless state, a characteristic that was unbelievably charming and unsettling at the same time. Even if she could forget the horrible night with Joey and be a good mother, Zeke wanted a stay-at-home mom. And she couldn't fall into the same trap as her mother. They'd only wind up resenting one another, just the way her family had.

TWO WEEKS LATER, Zeke grimaced as he left the clinic. Friday night loomed ahead and he'd been forcing himself to date, but he quickly discovered the process grew old after a while. Compliments of his meddling mother, he had a date with Vicky Preston, a divorcée from church who'd generously offered to prepare dinner for him and the girls. She insisted on bringing her twelve-year-old son, suggesting that if the kids meshed, next time her son could baby-sit while they dined out. He'd rather go to the dentist and have teeth pulled than make small talk with a stranger tonight.

For the past weeks, he'd concentrated on the twins. He'd taken them to movies, to McDonald's restaurants, and back to the clinic at night to play with the animals—anything to avoid going home. When they asked about Paige, he explained she was busy with school and her career. They didn't like it, but they accepted it, mainly because he'd bribed them so much. Bribery—what a pathetic excuse for fathering.

To his horror, several more women had responded to his daughters' advertisements for a mother. One of his clients, Cynthia Duncan, had brought him a gourmet lunch on Monday. He'd honestly tried to find her attractive, but her high-pitched voice reminded him of a yippy terrier. In fact, all the women he met reminded him of some breed of dog. Dana Hudson made him think of a pit bull. Janet Hanley, a poodle.

He'd seen Paige go out with Derrick several times. He'd tried to ignore her, but he always ended up brooding until she arrived home. She and Derrick must be getting tighter. Dammit, he missed her. Didn't she miss him at all?

"It's your mother on line three," Clara said.

"Got it." Zeke grabbed the receiver. "Hi, Mom, what's up?"

"Well, dear, I promised the girls they could spend the night again. How about this Friday?"

He could send the girls to his mom's and he and what's-her-name could have the house to themselves. Instead, he heard himself say, "Wait till Saturday, Mom."

"Okay. I've already made their favorite cupcakes and filled the candy dish."

Zeke pinched the bridge of his nose. "Great, see you tomorrow, Mom." He hung up, annoyed with himself. Why hadn't he taken her up on the Friday night deal? He could have a night alone with his date, maybe enjoy a more adult evening. What color hair did Vicki have anyway?

He ran a hand across his stubbled jaw, trying to remember, but his mind instantly conjured images of Paige. Right now, he'd be satisfied to stay home and watch *Bambi* with the twins and his sexy neighbor. Especially if he could share a bowl of buttered popcorn with Paige.

Well, almost satisfied.

THE PAST TWO weeks, Paige had submerged herself in her design project, worked on Amelia's wedding dress and spent several evenings with Derrick house hunting. Derrick had narrowed it down to three choices. Hopefully, he'd decide on one soon. Her patience was wearing thin. She'd wanted to be choosing her own house—a new place for her and her own husband. Worse, she kept picturing Zeke's face everywhere she went—in the kitchen making coffee after a long night of lovemaking, in the shower, steaming water dribbling over his hard, angular features, in the bedroom…

She shook herself back to reality. At least Amelia's dress was almost finished. She simply needed to add the lacy trim and beads on the bodice and the veil.

Friday afternoon, she counted up the checks in the register at Bev's Boutique and sighed. She'd turned down an invitation to meet another one of Amelia's friends for happy hour, claiming work as an excuse. Instead, she'd planned a quiet night home, with a good movie and a bowl of popcorn. Now, if only she had someone to share it with, the evening would be perfect. But she remembered her nightmare about Joey and the twins, and knew Zeke couldn't be the one.

"SUMMER, AUGUST, pick up the den before Vicky and her son arrive, please." Zeke scraped the food from the leftover dishes and peeked into the den. A tornado zone. Music from *The Flintstones* drifted through the room and in spite of his request, the twins hadn't budged from the television set. How had Paige gotten them to cooperate so quickly?

"Girls, Vicky's bringing dinner any minute. Clean up now."

"I don't wanna," August complained. "Cartoons are on."

Summer curled up on the couch with her blue bear and sucked her thumb. The kittens climbed from the box where he'd put them under the stairwell and raced around the foyer. The doorbell rang, but the girls simply stared at him, then back at the TV. Henrietta grunted and continued chewing on one of her toys. Some watchdog.

"Girls, they're here!"

He hurried to the door and swung it open, hoping his girls would behave themselves. They'd been disagreeable ever since he'd told them about his date. Vicky Preston stood on his stoop wearing a short red dress and black heels. Her short dark hair spiked around her oval face. She glanced at his clothes and frowned, prompting him to check for dried blood or animal hair on the front of his shirt.

"Hi, I brought lasagna, I hope that's okay," she said in a nasally voice.

"Sounds great," Zeke said.

"And this is Timmy." She urged her frowning dark-haired son inside. He grunted when Zeke spoke to him, his face twisting with disgust when he noticed the cartoons. "Don't you have a Nintendo video system?"

"Sorry," Zeke said. "But we don't."

"Unbelievable." Joey blew out a breath, momentarily lifting his long bangs off his eyes, then curled his upper lip and gave Zeke a once-over. "Man, I've never seen anyone wear a purple shirt with green pants."

"What?" The girls had mixed up his clothes again! They were going to turn his hair completely gray before he was thirty-five. No wonder Vicky had looked at him so strangely. "Sorry, I'm color-blind. Sometimes I mismatch my clothes."

Vicky giggled, her pointed chin jutting out, as if she was grateful he had an excuse for his poor taste.

"Let's eat." Suddenly eager to hurry the evening along, Zeke called the girls. They groaned and dragged their feet. Timmy stepped on one of August's ponies and the sound of plastic cracking ripped through the room.

"He broke it on purpose," August bellowed, pointing her finger in his face.

"Did not," Timmy snarled.

"Did, too!" To his horror, August slammed her fist into Timmy's stomach.

Timmy coughed, doubling over as if he'd been mortally wounded, and Vicky threw her arms around her son.

Zeke pulled August away. "Honey, please don't hit. It's not ladylike. He's our guest."

"But he's not ladylike." Summer fisted her small hands on her hips, glaring mutinously at the boy.

"I'm not a lady!" Timmy barked.

"He's a meanie," August snapped. "He broked my toy."

"She's a stupid girl," Timmy countered.

Zeke pointed to the table, ushering them into their chairs. "Look, there's no need to start calling names. You two got off on the wrong foot, so why don't we all start over."

Vicki waved a long fingernail toward the casserole dish. "Come on and eat, girls. I think you'll like the lasagna."

The twins took their seats, their faces skeptical while Vicky dished up the main course, adding salad and bread. Zeke poured milk and tea and opened the wine, then offered Vicky a glass. He sure needed one.

"What's that green stuff?" Summer asked, picking at the food.

"It's spinach, very nutritious," Vicky said cheerfully. "We're vegetarians."

"Yuk!" August cringed.

"Double yuk!" Summer covered her mouth with her hand and ran from the table, spitting the food into the trash can with dramatically exaggerated noises. The loud commotion woke up the mama cat, who promptly leapt onto the table with a screech that jarred his eardrums.

Vicki swiped a hand at the cat. "Get down, you...you beast."

"Don't yell at Kitty!" August shouted.

Zeke reached for the cat, but she darted across the table. Vicky's face paled as the calico whipped her soft tail around, swiping the lasagna with the furry tip.

Zeke removed the animal, scolding it gently while Vicky jumped up and gathered her things. "I've never in my life seen such rude children."

Summer and August stared at Zeke, wide-eyed and innocent, then disappeared to their rooms in a streak of red T-shirts.

"I'm sorry, Vicky," Zeke said, mortified. "I don't know what's wrong with them tonight." He ordered the girls back to the table, his temper on the verge of exploding. "Come here and apologize."

The girls inched their way in, their faces contrite. Thank heavens, maybe they could salvage the evening.

"We're sorry," August said in a small voice.

"Yeah. We are." Summer held her hands up in front of her. "Since you're company, we want you to hold Juney."

"Who's Juney? One of your dollies?" Vicky slid long nails through the ends of her wispy hair, her voice suspicious.

Zeke frowned, wondering what mischief the girls were planning now. He'd never seen this mysterious Juney.

"He's our new frog we found in the backyard." Summer dropped the croaking animal in Vicky's lap with a proud grin.

Vicky screamed and jumped backward, bumping the table so hard her wineglass toppled over. It rolled across the tablecloth and bounced onto the floor with a splintering crash. Henrietta howled at the sound of the noise and the cat darted under the table, mewling like an injured panther.

"Girls!" Zeke's temper threatened to boil over when Summer and August raced out of the room again, giggling and whispering.

Vicky stood, her face grim. "Timmy, come on. Let's go. This man obviously has no control over his children."

Her hostile tone set Zeke's teeth on edge, but still, she hadn't deserved such bad treatment from his daughters. "Listen, Vicky, I'm sorry. The girls don't normally behave so badly." But he uttered the apology to the wall. Vicky and her son had disappeared, lasagna and all.

Minutes later, after he'd cleaned up the kitchen and broken glass, he strode to the twins' room, determined to discover the reason for their disruptive behavior. They must still be upset about Renee's delayed visit.

He found them sitting on the bed, their small legs dangling over the sides, their faces drawn. He sat down and folded his arms. "Girls, I need you two to explain why you misbehaved tonight."

Summer shrugged, staring at the tips of her sneakers. August simply chewed her fingernail, ignoring him, her gaze fixed on the ceiling.

He made a clicking sound with his teeth. "Come on,

out with it. Why did you intentionally ruin tonight? I thought you wanted me to find you a new mother.''

''We do but we didn't like her,'' August said.

''You didn't give her a chance,'' Zeke said, totally baffled.

Summer poked out her lips. '''Cause we don't want her. Or that stupid boy of hers.''

''We want Paige,'' August said. ''Not some dumb brother.''

''Yeah. Since our real mommy's not coming, we want Paige for a mommy.'' Summer glared at him. ''Not Icky Vicky.''

Zeke's fingers dug into the pink comforter. ''We've already talked about this. Paige is a friend, but she wants a career, not a family.''

''She can have her job and us, too,'' August said, her lower lip trembling.

''Yeah, you gots a job and us. And Toby's mommy cuts hair and Beth Ann's mommy sells drugs.''

Zeke's heart stopped. ''She does what?''

''To hospitals,'' August clarified.

His heart started beating again, but tears slipped from Summer's eyes and his chest clenched, the way it did every time he saw the girls suffering. He knelt beside the twins and wrapped his arms around them. ''It's okay, girls.''

''No, it's not!'' August yelled.

''Paige said if you wants somefin bad enuf you can figure out how to get it.''

Zeke sighed. *How he wished that was true.* But you couldn't force someone to be a mother if she didn't want to. ''I know you're upset about your mom not coming home this month, girls. And I realize you like Paige, but we'll find someone else we like, too, someone who has time to spend with all of us, who won't leave—''

"Like Mommy did?" Summer mumbled.

Zeke swallowed, forcing a calm into his voice. "Yes, sweetheart." He removed his handkerchief and gently dried tears from Summer's eyes, his heart aching as he hugged both girls. "I promise I won't ever choose any one you don't like, okay?"

The girls nodded against his shoulder. He closed his eyes and rocked them both back and forth, just as he had when they were babies. The first time he'd held them in his arms, an overwhelming sense of protectiveness had hit him. He'd believed he and Renee could make it work, that he could spare his daughters from ever being hurt, but he hadn't been able to protect them from the one person who was supposed to love them the most, their own mother. His head throbbed. He wanted to make his kids happy. And he was more determined than ever not to lead them on about Paige, to find someone else who would love the girls and him.

Still, as the girls fell asleep in his arms, despair settled over him, because Paige's face was the only one that filled his dreams. And he knew he had to forget her.

Chapter Nine

Paige finished stitching the lacy bodice of Amelia's wedding gown, rubbed her hand over her tired eyes and hung the dress over the back of the dining room door. She stepped back, admiring it, envisioning herself in the gown, with a handsome groom waiting at the end of the aisle for her. Zeke's dark eyes automatically popped into her head, and she shook herself, mentally forcing the image from her mind. Time for marriage and family later.

Disgusted with herself, she readied for bed, dragging on a new pale blue nightshirt she'd bought at the boutique. She'd just curled up in her bed with a book when she heard a noise from downstairs. Probably Henrietta again, sleeping in her kitchen. Or maybe it was the vandals.

Slipping on matching bedroom shoes and a robe, she grabbed the portable phone and a can of hair spray for protection, tiptoed down the steps warily, her heart pounding. Stifling a gasp when she spotted a shadow, she squinted to make out the form, her breath catching in her throat. Then the shadow moved and footsteps padded across the carpet, the sound of whispering voices echoing through the tense silence. She quickly heaved a sigh of relief when she recognized two small bodies scampering through her den heading toward the stairs.

"Summer, August?"

The twins froze, their small faces silhouetted in the moonlight shimmering through the front window. Their eyes widened in fright, then they recognized her and ran into her arms, promptly bursting into tears. Paige cuddled them close while they sobbed against her.

"What's wrong, girls?" Paige gently stroked their hair, her chest tightening as their small bodies heaved for air.

"We missed you," August whimpered. "But Daddy said you was too busy for us...just like Mama is."

"We won't be trouble." Tears streaked Summer's red cheeks. "Promise. Don't forget about us. We likes you."

"Oh, girls, I like you, too," Paige's voice broke as her own eyes filled with tears. She blinked back the moisture, a dull ache pressing against her chest as she ushered the girls to the sofa. She hugged them close, wishing desperately she could make all their problems disappear. Maybe when their mother returned she'd decide she couldn't leave them again and the twins would have their mom back. "Shh, shh, don't cry now. It's going to be okay," she crooned softly. "I haven't forgotten you, and I'm sure your mom hasn't either."

"She's not coming like she promised," Summer said in a tiny voice.

Paige stroked Summer's arms, the desolate expression in the little girl's eyes tearing at her. "Is that what your mother said?"

August nodded. "She told Daddy she won't be here till our birthday."

"But Daddy says he's gonna do eberthing he can to make her stay when she does come."

Paige's heart squeezed. She couldn't blame Zeke but still the realization hurt.

Summer rubbed her knuckles over her eyes. "Don't you wants to see us anymore either, Paige?"

"Of course I do, you're two of my favorite neighbors," Paige answered softly.

"Daddy says you don't wants to marry us."

Paige swallowed, wondering what exactly Zeke had told the girls. Either the twins had a very fertile imagination or they had misconstrued something Zeke had said. "Your dad's right, we aren't getting married, but we're friends. I love your visits."

"Then how come Daddy says not to come over here?" August asked, starting to hiccup from her sobs.

Paige swallowed. "Well, it's kind of complicated, sweetie. I am busy, but it doesn't mean I don't like you, 'cause I do, very much." She sighed and hugged them. "You could always call me and see if it's a good time to visit."

"We're busy, too," August said, sniffling.

"Yeah, we goes to day care."

"And to Grammy's."

"I know, honey. But you girls wanted a mommy and I guess your dad's looking around for the best one, someone who doesn't work and can stay home and take care of you all the time." *Besides, your real mom is coming back and your dad's going to try to convince her to stay. Then you can all be together again, just like you want.*

She hugged them again, wishing things were different for all of them, reassuring them that she truly cared.

"We didn't like Icky Vicky," August added.

"Timmy's a big fat meanie."

"I gots mad," August said.

"And I wanted to cry," Summer admitted.

"Icky Vicky screamed when I gave her my frog."

"Then Daddy gots rreeeeel mad."

Paige smiled as bits and pieces of their conversation gelled. "Who's Icky Vicky?"

"The girl that come over and brought yucky green 'sagna," August said.

"She gots boy's hair," Summer added.

"Oh." Vicky's car must have been the strange vehicle she'd seen in the driveway yesterday. "You know, I have something that might make you feel better. You two stay right here." She hurried to the kitchen and brought back two dolls, then squeezed between the girls on the sofa again, propping the folk dolls in her lap. "These were two of my favorite dolls when I was little."

"You gots lots of pretty dolls, don't you?" Summer asked.

"Yes," Paige said with a small laugh. "My dad used to give them to me every Christmas and birthday. We started collecting them when I was about your age." She swallowed against the lump in her throat. "Angel, the pretty one on the settee over there is my favorite. My dad brought her to me from Germany. He gave her to me right before he died."

"Do you miss your daddy?" Summer asked.

Paige ran her fingers lovingly over the little girl's cheek. "Of course I do. That's why I keep my dolls. They remind me of all the good times we had." She pressed her hand over her heart. "And I always keep him right here in my heart."

"I can keep Mommy right here," Summer said, pressing her own little fist on her chest.

August nodded. "I member the fun times with our Mommy."

Paige nodded. "I know you do. And when you feel

sad or miss her, you have to think about those good memories.''

"She's beautiful." August rubbed her fingers over one of the doll's brown ponytails.

"I named her Mad Molly," Paige explained. "When I was little and felt angry, I'd tell her my mad feelings. Then she'd hug me and make it all better." She handed the doll to August, smiling when August hugged it to her chest.

"And who's this one?" Summer reached for the doll with the yellow string hair.

"Sad Sue." Paige gently stroked the yellow braids. "Whenever I felt sad, I told her and she'd hug me and make me feel better." Summer pressed the soft cloth face to her cheek and kissed the yarn hair.

August and Summer cuddled closer to Paige and she snuggled one on each side of her, tugging a worn afghan over them. She needed to call Zeke and tell him where the girls were, but first she wanted to reassure them she cared about them. "I'll have a talk with your dad and work out some way we can all be friends." *Even if it kills me.*

"'Kay," both girls whispered.

August traced her finger over Molly's denim jumper. "Will you sing us a night-night song?"

"Sure." Paige thought for a long minute, remembering Joey's favorite song, then began singing the soft lullaby. Before she'd finished the first chorus, both girls drifted asleep, the dolls pressed tightly to their chests. She studied their precious innocent faces and her heart melted. She loved the little stinkers, but their mother would be coming soon, and they'd naturally want her with them.

And according to the girls, so did Zeke.

WHERE WERE THE twins? Zeke searched the house, his heart racing out of control. It was dark outside and the house was empty. Dammit, he was going to have a heart attack if they kept disappearing on him.

He ran out the back door to see if they'd sneaked out with Henrietta and noticed the gate swinging back and forth. Remembering their earlier argument, he knew exactly where they would be. At Paige's.

He should have known they'd pull something like this. Taking long strides, he crossed the backyard, pausing at Paige's back door, wondering what he would do if they weren't there. Call the police?

Panic seized him. He raised his hand and knocked, the long seconds that followed stealing the air from his aching lungs. Once again he'd screwed up this parenting thing. All kinds of scenarios bombarded him. The girls had wandered into the street, had gotten lost, had been picked up by some stranger… He shuddered and banged on the door again, not caring it was after midnight or that he might disturb the entire neighborhood. Finally Paige swung open the door, her robe rumpled, her green eyes heavy as if she'd been asleep.

He opened his mouth to speak but he was so frightened, his voice squeaked, ''The twins, are they here?''

Paige nodded and placed her finger to his lips, leading him to the couch where the girls lay huddled underneath a bright afghan. Zeke expelled a shaky sigh of relief. She took his hand and coaxed him out front to the porch swing, gently shutting the door behind them. ''Come on, Zeke, we need to talk.''

THE FRUSTRATION AND fear in Zeke's eyes tore at Paige but she had to caution herself against comforting him.

Zeke dropped his face into his hands and groaned. "God, I'm messing up," Zeke said in a hoarse voice.

"No, you're doing fine, Zeke. The girls are okay. Really." Paige gently tugged his hands away from his face and cupped his jaw, forcing him to look at her. "You're a wonderful, loving father and the girls are lucky to have you." Her own voice sounded thick with emotion but she didn't care. She was worried about Summer and August and Zeke. She couldn't stand not touching him another second.

She wrapped her arms around him and hugged him, aware Zeke had tensed. But slowly he relaxed against her and placed his arms around her waist, then dropped his forehead against the top of her head. She held him, letting him cling to her for support for several long minutes. His breathing was labored, his heart beating erratically beneath her ear, his big body trembling slightly. He'd truly been frightened, and she wanted to kick herself for not calling him the moment the girls had shown up.

"You don't understand," Zeke said in a rough voice. "I can't do it all, they need their mother."

"I know," Paige whispered, remembering the girls' comment. She rubbed her hands up and down his broad back, trying not to think about how wonderful his powerful muscles felt beneath her touch.

He shook his head and started to protest, but she stroked his cheek with her finger. He paused, his eyes filled with turmoil. "They ran away from me. They were both so upset. I don't know what to do to make it right."

"Just keep loving them," Paige said softly, moisture filling her eyes in spite of her determination to prevent it. "They're confused, Zeke. About us. But mostly about their mom and why she's left them. You can't do anything but be there for them."

Zeke's hands shook as he reached up and caught her hands in his. "But what if I'm not doing enough? What if…"

"You do the best you can. You love them and listen to them, watch them make mistakes, comfort them when they're hurting, and pray they'll turn out all right."

His breath heaved out in a sigh. "Yeah, but Renee called and she's not coming like she promised."

"I know." His gaze flew to hers in surprise. "The girls told me, and I know they're disappointed, Zeke. But it's not your fault."

He nodded, resignation lining his features. "But I have to deal with the fallout, every time she disappoints them, I have to pick them up and try and act like it's okay." His voice cracked. "But things aren't okay. They need her."

"I know," Paige whispered sympathetically. She brushed a curly lock of his dark hair away from his forehead. "It's not fair, Zeke. Maybe when she comes for their birthday, you can convince her to stay and you all can be a family."

"I hope so," Zeke said in a voice filled with emotions.

Paige smiled gently, ignoring the sharp pain his words brought, more certain than ever that if Zeke's ex-wife returned, he'd do anything to get her to stay there with him and the girls.

He angled his head, looking up at her warily. "What else did they tell you?"

"They told me a little about what happened tonight with…um, Vicky," she said, hesitating awkwardly.

"Icky Vicky." Zeke grimaced, his hands loosening at her waist. "What a disaster."

"I'm sorry the evening didn't work out the way you wanted."

Zeke shrugged, his hands lingering on her hips, and she suddenly realized the intimate position they were in. His hard body pressed against hers, his feet parted slightly so she fit into the crook between his legs, his arousal nudging her stomach.

"What else did they tell you?"

She swallowed, his warm breath brushing her cheek in an erotic whisper. She had to distract herself. "That Icky Vicky doesn't like frogs."

Zeke chuckled, a low rumbling sound that resonated through the night air and made heat coil in her belly. "That's putting it mildly."

Paige laughed softly at his mischievous grin, but her worries over Summer and August quickly returned. "They also wanted to know why they couldn't come over and see me, Zeke."

The tension in his shoulders returned, the brown irises of his eyes turning black in the dimness of night. Paige traced her finger along his knuckles. "I promised the girls you and I would work things out so we could all be friends."

The breath Zeke exhaled radiated with tension, then relief. He leaned back and looked into her eyes, winding a strand of hair around his finger. "Yeah?"

"Yeah. We have to bridge this gap for the girls' sake." She resisted the temptation to rest her head against his shoulder and add that she wanted to work things out so they could be together—for *her* sake.

"Yeah, for the girls," he said, disappointment lacing his voice. Silence hung between them for several seconds.

Finally Paige asked, "So what did you think about Icky Vicky?"

Zeke chuckled softly and twined the strand of hair

tighter around his finger, tugging gently. "She reminded me of a cairn terrier."

Paige laughed softly. "Is that a compliment?"

"If you like short, wiry-haired females with snippy voices." He brought the strand of hair to his nose and sniffed it gently, a slow smile spreading on his mouth. "But I prefer Irish setters myself."

Paige sighed, wondering how in the world they could remain friends when she wanted to take him inside and comfort him with loving kisses and tender touching all through the night. Zeke feathered the strands of her hair through his fingers and dropped a kiss into her hair.

"I guess I should take the girls home and let you get some sleep," Zeke said in a voice barely above a whisper.

"I suppose." She raised slightly, already missing the comfort of his body next to hers. Tilting her chin with his thumb, he brought his lips to hers. It was the sweetest, gentlest kiss Paige had ever known. Her lips melded to his, hot need awakening, then burning deep inside her. His lips felt soft and wonderful, his touch tentative and vulnerable, but as he deepened the kiss, she responded, melting into his arms. Heat and passion ignited between them. Her nipples beaded, ached, her own desire spiraled out of control. She reached for the buttons on his shirt—

"Daddy, why you kissin' Paige?" August asked from the doorway.

"You like her again?" Summer asked.

Paige and Zeke jumped apart guiltily. Zeke chuckled, dropped his arms and stood. "Yeah, I like her."

"Goody," both girls squealed.

"Now, we'd better leave and let her go to bed." Zeke

winked devilishly, but his voice sounded thick, full of sweet regret meant for Paige's ears only.

Paige watched the threesome truck across their backyard, her emotions tangled, her feelings for Zeke growing like the wildflowers in her backyard, beautiful and sweet and wild, with no order or certainty at all.

And she liked order and certainty. Everything tidy in its place. Not this chaotic tumble of emotions running rampant through her body.

ZEKE ROLLED OVER and groaned, his body aching from unfulfilled dreams—dreams of lovemaking with Paige. He'd never realized how utterly erotic simply kissing a woman could be. Innocent, yet enticing, sweet, yet provocative—the woman was driving him absolutely crazy. Just like his kids. Well, maybe not exactly like his kids, he amended, with a chuckle as he recalled Paige in his arms. She'd felt so right pressed against him, so perfect, as if their bodies would fit as one.

"Daddy! Grammy's here!"

"What?" He ran down the steps so fast he almost tripped over his own feet.

"Hi, honey," Mrs. Blalock said. She offered him a quick kiss on the cheek. "I thought I'd take the girls for breakfast before we go to my house for the night."

Summer and August jumped up and down squealing about pancakes. To his surprise, they'd already dressed themselves, packed their pink suitcases and were ready to go.

"Zeke, dear?"

"Yes, Mom?" He squinted through sleepy eyelids, wondering what she had up her sleeve.

"Morgan—you remember, that sweet schoolteacher—she's home today if you want to give her a call."

So that was the reason she'd planned this little outing. August and Summer frowned. "But Daddy's—"

"I'm busy today, Mom," he interjected, giving the girls a warning glare.

"Well, see if you can at least call her. She's a fine lady and her mother and I are best friends," Mrs. Blalock said as she turned and hurried the girls to the car.

Zeke took the steps two at a time and flew into the shower. He'd made arrangements for a substitute vet to work his clients every other Saturday so he could have more time with the twins, but since they had plans, maybe he'd surprise Paige. Maybe he could convince her to spend a romantic day with him, then maybe…the entire night.

PAIGE ROLLED OVER in bed, feeling languid and mellow, and confused. The night before, she'd lain awake for hours fantasizing about Zeke's body lying next to hers.

She liked him, his kids, his menagerie of animals, even the slimy salamander.

What was wrong with her? She couldn't give up her dreams to chance being a replacement wife and mom again. Especially knowing Zeke planned to do whatever he could to convince Renee to stay. Plus she'd had that awful dream about Joey getting hurt.

She checked the clock. 8:00. Her first Saturday off in weeks, but Derrick was due any minute for another house hunting venture. If he didn't choose between the three houses today, she'd decided to write the addresses on slips of paper, put them in a hat and make him draw one out. He was the most indecisive male she'd ever known.

Thirty minutes later, she'd showered and dressed and was sipping a hot cup of coffee when the doorbell rang. She grabbed her purse, breezed to the door and swung it

open, greeting Derrick with a hug. Then she looked up
in dismay to see Zeke frozen in her driveway, wearing a
scowl that would make grown men shake in their shoes.

ZEKE STARED AT Paige, disgusted to see the security consultant once again at her door. So much for his plans for
sweeping her off her feet and spending the day romanc-
ing her.

Paige and Derrick walked down the steps to Derrick's
car and Paige waved to him. "Good morning, Zeke.
What's up?"

My temper. "Nothing," Zeke said, shoving his hands
in the pockets of his jeans.

Paige arched an eyebrow, obviously puzzled, so he
continued, improvising with the only excuse he could
think of, "Mrs. Spivy called and wanted a dog and so
did the Jensens down the street. I thought you might like
to help me deliver them."

"Sure," Paige agreed. "What time?"

"This afternoon, maybe around four."

Paige opened Derrick's car door. "I'll make it a point
to be back by then."

Derrick lifted his hand in a wave, and Paige slipped
into his car. They sailed away, leaving Zeke all alone,
feeling as though he'd been ditched and sent to the doghouse.

"DERRICK, AMELIA WILL love this place," Paige said
convincingly. "Any woman would be wowed to know
you put so much thought into choosing a future home."

Derrick frowned in worry. "I want it to be perfect."

"Trust me, she'll love the house," Paige said, admiring the beveled glass above the garden tub. She pictured
Zeke and her climbing into the huge marble tub, bubbles

spiked to the edge, a bottle of champagne sitting on the side, the two of them undressing and slipping into the warm water...

"You don't think she'd like the Colonial better?"

Paige shook her head. "Nope, too traditional for Amelia. She'll love all this fancy molding, and that beveled glass in the front door is exquisite. Plus you have a private backyard for sunbathing." *Or for a dog.*

"Yeah, the yard is nice."

"And the two upstairs bedrooms share a bath. It would be perfect for kids." *Like Summer and August.* "And that small room would make a great office." *Or nursery.* "And you have that big bonus room for company." *Or a playroom.* "And that small room off the master for a sitting area." *Or a sewing room.*

"Okay, okay, you convinced me," Derrick said. "I'll call the agent tomorrow."

Paige sighed and shut the front door, suddenly wondering why she felt disappointed Derrick had chosen the house. After all, it was perfect for him and Amelia.

"THIS IS MAVERICK," Zeke said as he handed Paige the yellow lab's leash.

"He's adorable." Paige stooped to pet the waddling puppy, laughing when he licked her face.

"Now, you'll come back and help me train him, won't you, Doc?" Mrs. Spivy asked.

Zeke grinned. "Sure. Maybe I can trade off for some parenting lessons."

"Oh, pooh, your kids are precious," Mrs. Spivy said with a laugh.

Zeke shrugged. "Seriously though, you might want to sign up for dog obedience classes. They teach them at the community center."

"That's a good idea," Mrs. Spivy agreed.

Mr. Spivy rubbed Maverick's neck. "We're having a fence installed next week."

"Good, he's going to get pretty big. He'll need lots of room to run and play."

The Spivys both knelt to play with the puppy and Maverick dropped to the ground, sprawling with his belly up, begging for a tummy rub.

Paige laughed. "He's a sweetheart. You really know how to pick good pets, Zeke."

Better than I do women. He bit back the remark, wondering how long he and Paige had to stay with the Spivys to be polite, and wondering if Paige would balk if he suggested they spend some time alone. He hadn't been able to take his mind off of her all day.

"It's easy when you know the breeds," he said instead. "Golden retrievers and Labs are some of the most dependable ones. Irish setters are a little more feisty and temperamental, but I still think they're some of my favorites."

And I like women with fiery red hair and sparkling green eyes. The thought of her with Derrick all day had driven him mad. After holding her last night on her porch, he was determined to try and win her trust. The night before, she'd been so loving to his children and understanding to him, as if she really cared about all of them. And now, he kept studying her, watching the way she watched him, noticing the yearning in her eyes when she thought he wasn't paying attention. Paige was afraid of something. If he only knew what it was. Sure, she had reservations because of her mom, but did she still love Derrick?

Maybe if he had her alone tonight, he could figure out her secrets, if she had any, and why she couldn't be happy with him and his girls. Maybe he could wipe the fear from her eyes and replace it with hot passion and wild loving, and maybe he could convince her to stay in his bed forever.

"THE NORTH GEORGIA mountains are beautiful. I've never seen so many dogwoods in bloom." Paige parked and took their picnic supper out of the car to settle on a blanket. She still couldn't believe she'd let Zeke talk her into this evening picnic, but after watching him with the neighbors and animals, she hadn't been able to resist. He'd been sneaking heated looks at her during their neighborly visits that had made her blood boil and her imagination go wild. Her defenses had completely crumbled.

"I love the outdoors," Zeke said. "The fresh air, all the trees."

Paige grinned as a squirrel scampered up a nearby pine tree. The sound of the bubbling creek filled the air like music, and Zeke whipped out some candles and lit them, his husky voice low and simmering with barely suppressed passion. The evening picnic seemed incredibly romantic, especially with sexy, brawny Zeke Blalock turning her inside out with his mesmerizing eyes. Every time their fingers brushed, their hands touched, her body responded as if Zeke's body had engaged her senses in a slow seduction.

"Thanks for bringing me here." Paige nibbled on a grape as she desperately tried to curb her raging hormones.

Zeke stopped unpacking the picnic supplies, handed her a glass of wine. "Thanks for coming with me. The girls are great, but sometimes I get lonely for adult company."

Don't tell me that. His lazy grin blindsided her. She tried to steer the conversation to their surroundings, the weather, anything impersonal. "At least it's cooler here in the mountains."

"I can still feel the heat," he said in a sexy low voice. Paige winced at the double meaning, but he didn't give her time to reply. He raised his glass, his mouth twitching with a smile. "Let's have a toast."

Paige laughed softly as their glasses clinked. "What are we toasting to?"

Mischief sparkled in his dark eyes. "Friendship."

"To friendship." A shiver rippled up her spine at the raw sex appeal oozing from Zeke's gaze.

The candlelight flickered, highlighting his dimple, catching the dark irises of his eyes. Paige felt as if she'd been sucked into an undertow of emotions, her caution washing out with the tide. She sensed his loneliness, the pain he'd carried around since his wife's desertion, the almost urgent need for someone to hold him. She wanted to be that someone. Even if it was only for a short while.

She gently reached out and touched his hand, tracing a path over his knuckles, gasping lightly when he turned his hand palm up, then folded her small fingers in his. His skin felt warm and cool at the same time, soft but erotically rough and masculine, and the heated gaze he gave her was filled with a longing she could no longer deny. Slowly he moved toward her, his hands seeking, his mouth easing a trail of kisses over her fingers as he pressed her hand to his lips. Heat spiraled through her, engulfing her with want. Trembling, she fought a sliver of disappointment when he released her hand with a sly smile and offered her a plate.

They enjoyed the snacks, walked hand in hand along the creek edge talking about their different childhoods, then lay on the blanket and watched the bubbling brook, basking in the sounds of the night filtering through the foliage and the scents of honeysuckle and flowers and green grass that filled the warm night air.

"I bet Summer and August would love to wade in the creek," Paige said softly as they finished off the wine. *Maybe the three of you can come back,* she thought, feeling suddenly dismal.

"I'll bring them camping here sometime."

"They would love Rock City and Ruby Falls, too."

"Yeah, that sounds like fun."

Zeke threaded his fingers through hers and Paige snuggled against him, the evening temperature cooling so quickly that goose bumps shimmied up her arms. Zeke wrapped his arms around her, his embrace protective and warm, his masculine scent mingling with the outdoors, arousing her senses. She turned in his arms, silently asking for his touch.

His breath fanned her cheek, his eyes dark slits in the moonlight, and Paige shivered with arousal at the raw need she saw shining in the depths of his eyes. Then he lowered his mouth and brushed his lips across hers, tenderly, gently, so softly she arched forward, seeking more.

His hand cupped her face, angled her head so he could cover her mouth with his. He devoured her with his lips, thrusting his tongue into her mouth and hungrily tasting her. Paige clutched his arms, wedging one leg in between his thighs as she snuggled deeper into his embrace, and he cupped her bottom and dragged her against his heat, groaning. She stroked his thigh with her hand, felt the muscles ripple in his back, then arched her aching breasts forward, surrendering, begging for more.

Zeke suddenly pulled away and gazed into her eyes, his heated, passionate look making her feel heady and starved for closeness. "Come on." Zeke tugged her to a standing position. "The bugs will eat us alive us if we don't leave now. Let's go to my house."

They rode back down the mountain, listening to a soft jazz station as they wound around the curves, the anticipation and promise of passion lingering between them like the promise of food to a starving man. Zeke stroked her hand, pressed it to his thigh where he covered it with his own, brought her fingers to his lips and kissed them, seduced her with the hint of lust in his eyes. Paige relented to the mood, the purr of the music and the rich taste of the wine mellowing her resistance. Zeke elicited a hunger in her that became an almost desperate need, a want she'd never felt in her life.

Maybe she was simply tired of fighting her attraction to Zeke.

"Come in for coffee or another glass of wine," Zeke suggested when they arrived at his house.

Paige simply nodded, knowing she was agreeing to more than coffee or wine, knowing she was about to surrender her body, her heart, her soul. And not caring about the consequences.

When they entered his house, he took her in his arms, then he lowered his mouth and smothered her with a kiss that forced all reasonable thoughts from her mind. His hands slid beneath her shirt and he slowly inched her T-shirt over her head and the pure carnal lust in his eyes gave her a rush of sensations so heady she reached for his shirt with frantic fingers. His hands cupped her breasts, hers hastily unbuttoned his shirt and she slid her hands across the hard planes of his muscular chest. He brushed his lips over her mouth, then trailed kisses down her neck and lower until he reached the mounds of her breasts. Dipping his head lower, he teased her nipples to hard peaks through her bra. Paige groaned and clung to his arms, her head lolling back as sweet agony tightened her stomach.

Some distant sound vaguely broke into her consciousness, but she ignored it and let passion sweep her into its trance as Zeke stroked her back and unfastened her bra, letting her breasts spill into his hands. Her body arched toward him, the ache so painful she almost cried out with the intensity.

The sound came again, a shrill sound that rattled her nerves and penetrated the haze of desire. She felt Zeke still in her arms, his heart beating furiously.

"It's my phone," he said, his voice husky with passion.

"You have to get it?"

He leaned his forehead against hers and nodded. "It could be the clinic. Or the girls."

She nodded, her labored breathing echoing through the small foyer.

"Don't move, Paige." He kissed the tip of her nose, and hugged her to him in a tender gesture that sent a shudder through her.

Then he reached for the phone and Paige pressed her hand to her mouth, trying to steady her breathing and hide her disappointment when she heard him say his ex-wife's name.

Chapter Ten

Déjà vu struck Paige, the room spinning around her with a dizzying sickness. She righted her clothing, feeling naked and exposed in more ways than one. A few months ago she'd stood in this same room, this same house, and listened to Eric tell her he was going back to his ex-wife.

She couldn't go through that heartbreak again.

"You will be here for their birthday," Zeke said in a heated voice. "You have to come, Renee. You're their mother, the girls need you."

Paige nodded, backing toward the door. Zeke was right, they needed their mother, and obviously from the pain in Zeke's voice, he needed her, too. He glanced up, his dark eyes troubled, his shoulders slumped, and her heart squeezed, so many emotions bombarding her that she couldn't speak.

"Okay, I'll tell the girls you'll see them on their birthday." He hung up the phone, then ran his hand through his hair, tousling the dark strands as he stood, warring with his own emotions. She heard his breathing rattle across the distance and she hugged her arms around her middle when he stalked toward her.

"I'm sorry, Paige," he said in a thick voice, frowning as he stared at her shirt. "That was—"

"Your wife," Paige supplied.

"My ex-wife," he said pointedly, his dark gaze capturing hers.

"I...I'd better go, Zeke." She backed toward the door, but the turmoil in his expression stopped her.

"Why? I thought we were—"

"No." Paige cut him off. "We got carried away, but it would have been a mistake."

His expression hardened, his eyes glittering with anger. "Why do you say that?"

"Because we want different things, Zeke."

"We both wanted to make love," he said, his voice husky. "You can't deny that."

Paige shook her head, her chest tight. "No, I can't deny it, but having sex would only complicate things." She took a deep breath, finally voicing her true worries. "I can't be a fill-in for Renee, Zeke."

A muscle ticked in his jaw. "That's not what you are, Paige."

"Isn't it? The girls have been advertising for a mother, and you've obviously been dating, trying to find someone to fill your wife's shoes. Besides, Renee may come back to stay." She paced across the foyer, watching the guilt flash into his eyes. "You can't deny *that*, can you?"

Zeke fisted his hands by his sides, and gave her a long assessing look. "I hope she will, for the girls' sakes. But I want to be with you, Paige."

Paige shook her head again, the memory of the tormented way he'd looked when he'd talked to his ex-wife only minutes earlier needling her. "You want me because the girls like me, because you think they need a mother right now and I'm close by. I'm a convenient substitute."

"That's ridiculous," Zeke scoffed, his cheeks growing red with anger. "My wanting you has *nothing* to do with the girls. I wanted you the first time I saw you on my doorstep. And I've wanted you every minute since."

"I'm not saying there isn't some sort of chemistry between us—"

"At least you're not denying that!"

"But the first time you saw me the girls had posted that flier. Since they latched on to me, you thought I'd make a good candidate."

"Well, it's obvious I was wrong, wasn't I? You're just like Renee—your career is more important to you than me or the girls." His dark eyes raked over her, disappointment lacing his voice. "I guess you're right, our making love would have been a mistake, Paige. I'm not a very good judge of women, am I?"

Paige froze, his words carving a painful hole in her chest. Her legs trembling, she turned and opened the door and fled to her house, tears streaking her cheeks.

OVER THE PAST two weeks, Paige's accusations had haunted Zeke day and night. Exhausted, he slumped onto the sofa, hoping he'd be able to grab a nap before dinner. And wondering what he could have said to have made Paige change her mind. He wished for the life of him he hadn't lost his temper, that he'd taken her in his arms and proved to her that she'd been wrong about his motivations for wanting her. But he'd been too stunned, first from Renee's insensitivity to her own children, then to Paige's false assumptions about him. Couldn't the woman tell real passion when she saw it? Did she think he'd been faking his arousal? Damn, he'd almost been shaking with need every time he was around her.

Deep down in his soul, he knew Paige wasn't like Renee. She honestly cared for the girls; he could tell in the tender, loving way she treated and respected them. But she wanted her career, too, didn't want the responsibility—or was she afraid of it?

Heck, he was being old-fashioned. No, archaic. Perhaps, he needed to rethink his views on working mothers.

The girls were happy at day care, and if Paige worked nearby, she would still be with him and the girls in the evening. Maybe he could handle having a working wife if she loved the girls and him, too. But how did Paige feel about him?

His beeper sounded and he checked the number. The clinic. An emergency. He called in the number and told the hysterical woman on the phone he'd meet her at his clinic. Her German shepherd had been hit by a car.

"Summer, August," he yelled from the bottom of the steps. "I have to go back to the clinic." The girls barreled down the steps.

"Can we go to Paige's?"

He shook his head, knowing his sporadic on-off friendship with Paige confused them. "I'll call Grandma."

He phoned, but his mother was out for the evening and with the vandals still at large, he didn't feel comfortable using a teen baby-sitter. He'd have to ask Paige to help him, and hope she didn't shut the door in his face when he turned up, asking for a baby-sitter. And he prayed she didn't see his request as a confirmation of her accusations.

PAIGE FINISHED tacking the hem on the halter dress and smiled, pleased with the way the design had turned out. For her final project, she'd designed a series of outfits for the traveling woman, keeping in mind the economy of packing and the various social occasions and business functions a woman would need. For ease of coordinating accessories, she'd chosen a black and white color scheme which could be elegant enough for after dinner as well as suitable for work. Classy and sophisticated. The black crepe halter dress had a softly flared side slit on the skirt and would make a perfect outfit for dinner. A white fitted sheath dress with a black jacket worked for the office. Removing the jacket would make the transition into an evening outfit as well. A broomstick skirt made in georgette and black jeans lent to more casual attire, both ensembles being paired with a white poet's blouse of cotton poplin. Black pumps and simple silver bangle bracelets and earrings completed the collection.

She rubbed her eyes and stretched, her vision blurring from working with the tiny stitches. Exhausted, she left the outfits spread across the table and headed to the kitchen to clean up the dirty dishes. Beverly and Amelia had eaten spaghetti with her earlier, and they'd gotten so caught up looking at the wedding dress designs, she'd left the dishes for later.

She yawned, deciding she had to forget Zeke or she'd never sleep again. The doorbell rang and Paige hurried to answer it. When she opened the door, she was surprised to see the man who haunted her dreams standing on the porch.

"Paige!" both girls shrieked and ran into her arms. She hugged them both, eyeing Zeke over their small heads. He was watching her, a guarded expression on his face, his dark eyes blazing heat up and down her body with his scorching perusal. She shivered slightly, wondering if he could possibly have read her mind earlier and come running to her house to pronounce his love.

"I hate to bother you, but I have an emergency," he said, his voice low and throaty.

"Grammy can't come over," Summer said.

"And we wants to stay with you, Paige."

"Can we?" Summer pleaded.

Disappointment suddenly ballooned in Paige's stomach, but she met Zeke's steady gaze, determined not to reveal her emotions. And trying not to panic that she'd have full responsibility for his children. "Sure, girls. You can stay here," she heard herself say.

"I really hate to ask, Paige, but with the vandals still on the loose—"

"It's okay, Zeke. I don't mind baby-sitting," Paige said pointedly.

His jaw tightened, and he opened his mouth to argue, but his beeper sounded again.

"Better go, Daddy," Summer said.

"Don't let that doggie die," August added.

Zeke hugged both girls for reassurance. "I'll do my best," he said in a gruff voice.

"I don't know what time it will be," he said, his gaze locking with hers. "I may have to do surgery."

"Don't worry about the time." Paige searched his face for some sign he still wanted her. "I'll put them to bed in the guest room if you're not back in a while."

He nodded, his thumb absentmindedly rubbing the beeper at his belt. "Thanks, Paige. I really appreciate this."

She nodded and forced a smile, her chin up, then closed the door. Her heart broke when he drove away. She'd been right. She was just a baby-sitter. Zeke had probably realized he didn't have to date her or bed her to ask her to baby-sit. All he had to do was to walk next door.

"What 'ya doing?" Summer and Paige both asked when they saw her sewing supplies spread on the table.

"Working on my project."

The girls squealed when they noticed the bags of material and ribbons and rickrack. Summer examined several decorative buttons and August draped a long red piece of silk around her head.

"Hey, look, I'm Little Red Riding Hood."

Seeing their excitement, she realized they weren't ready for bed, so Paige dragged out a box of scraps to entertain them. "Would you girls like to learn how to sew? We could make doll blankets for Molly and Sue."

"Yeah!" both girls exclaimed.

Summer and August searched through the scraps. "I like this purple 'terial," Summer said.

"And I want the blue striped."

"Great. Now, we'll turn the edges down and sew them to make a blanket." She pinned the folds and threaded a needle, then taught them how to make a simple hem stitch.

"This is hard," Summer said. She reached for the big scissors to snip a loose thread but Paige grabbed them first and quickly warned the girls about using her sharp scissors.

"You're getting the hang of it, Summer," Paige said in an encouraging voice. "Your stitches are getting straighter every time.

"Look at mine," August said.

"Mad Molly will love it," Paige exclaimed. Both girls beamed proudly, tugging at her heart.

"Can we make clothes next time?" August asked.

"Sure. We can make anything you want."

When the girls finally finished, Paige praised them both. The stitches were crooked and big, but it didn't matter. They had put a lot of effort into the work.

"Come on, let's get ready for bed, then we'll have a story."

The three trudged into the kitchen for water first and Paige gasped. "Henrietta, stop!"

"Oh, no!" Summer and August screamed.

Henrietta had knocked the spaghetti bowl off the table and was digging in with her paws. "Catch her!" August screamed.

But Henrietta took off running, streaking the floor with her spaghetti-red paws.

"Not there!" Paige yelled.

"Henrietta!" August shouted. "Wait!"

"Come back here!" Summer screamed.

It was too late. Henrietta ran into the dining room and jumped up on the table, skittered across it, then sprawled on top of Paige's white dress, smearing her red spaghetti-stained paws all across her final project.

Paige froze in absolute horror. Henrietta had completely ruined her project.

Summer and August reached for Henrietta, but Henrietta scurried across the pieces on the table, smashing gooey spaghetti into the fine fabric, then leapt off the table and raced through the house, marring the floor with her messy footprints. They almost caught her in the hallway, but she barreled back to the kitchen and ran outside through the pet door. Paige checked to make sure Henrietta had run into the backyard instead of the street, then returned to the house to find the twins washing the black-and-white dress in the sink. Paige groaned silently. Wetting the dry-clean only fabric had simply smeared the red sauce into bigger splotches. Black bled onto the white sections, turning the material into a murky gray.

Summer and August stared at her wide-eyed as she surveyed the damage. "Oh, my gosh!" August's chin quivered.

"Can you fix it?" Summer sloshed soapy water everywhere as she attempted to catch a tear from her cheek.

Paige hugged them both, murmuring comforting words, but she felt like crying herself. All those long hours of tedious work and her final project had been destroyed within minutes. Not only was the black crepe and white poplin splattered and streaked with red spaghetti, but Henrietta's claws had picked the material beyond repair.

"Paige?"

"Sorry," Summer whimpered, bursting into tears.

Paige glanced at the girls' sorrowful expressions and her heart ached. Her mother would have had a fit if she'd seen the messy floor. Once upon a time, Paige would have also cringed, too. But the project and her house didn't matter nearly as much as the little girls. She knelt and folded them into her embrace.

"I'm sorry," August whispered.

"We didn't mean to be so much trouble," Summer cried.

"Don't leabe us like Mommy did." The girls' sobs tore at her heart and Paige stroked them and crooned comforting words. "Mommy hated anmuls, 'specially Henrietta."

"Shh, it's okay. It wasn't your fault, sweetheart, it was an accident." She brushed back their hand. "And I don't hate Henrietta. She's just being a dog."

"But Henrietta's our dog," August argued.

"And we should've watched her better." Summer gulped.

"And I shouldn't have left the spaghetti out so she could get to it. And I should have hung up the clothes instead of leaving them on the table," Paige added, accepting full blame. She hugged them against her, wiping away their tears.

"You're not mad at us?" Summer said.

"You won't go away?" August asked.

Paige shook her head. "I love you, girls. And, no, I'm not mad, and I'm not going anywhere." She glanced at the ruined dress, ignoring the despair settling in her chest.

Summer and August threw their arms around her. "We love you, Paige."

Paige smiled and hugged them again. "I love you, too." She gestured toward the stained material. "Now, let's clean up this mess before your dad gets back and thinks we're a bunch of little animals ourselves."

August giggled. "'Kay, Paige."

Summer swiped at her nose and nodded. Between the three of them, they finished cleaning the kitchen and floor, then Paige gathered the outfits and dropped them in the trash.

"But what will you do for your prospect?" August asked.

"My project," Paige clarified.

"Will they drop you out of school?"

"No, honey, don't worry." Paige stuck her hands on her hips, her mind racing for a solution. She only had a few pieces of material left, not nearly enough to redo the first project. "I don't know what I'll do for the project yet, but I'll think of something. Come on, it's nearly ten—you two are going to bed." She tucked them into the guest bed, gave them two rag dolls from the shelf to cuddle with, sang them a lullaby, then tiptoed out into the hallway, wishing she could be a part of the little girls' lives forever.

Paige lingered at the door, listening to them whisper. While she waited on them to settle down, her gaze rested on one of her dolls perched on her bedroom dresser. She suddenly had a brainstorm. She'd design a child's wardrobe. She had enough material for smaller articles of clothing, and if she kept the patterns simple, no zippers or elaborate stitching or gathers, she could finish them in one night. And she could give the clothes to the girls when she'd finished. Using the girls as her inspiration, she set to work, excited about the new designs whirling in her brain.

Zeke called about midnight to tell her he needed to watch the German shepherd through the night.

"The girls are sleeping. Just leave them here for the night," Paige told him, purposefully omitting the details of her project crisis. And the fact that she would be up all night making a new one.

"I appreciate this," Zeke said, sounding tired.

"Don't worry about the girls. You can pick them up in the morning." They said good-night and Paige grabbed the scissors, grateful she had work to do to keep her mind off Zeke.

WHEN THE DOORBELL rang at seven o'clock the next morning, Paige staggered to the door holding a cup of coffee.

"Morning." Zeke sauntered in, looking sleepy-eyed and rumpled in the same jeans and shirt he'd worn the night before. He stared at her, his forehead furrowing. "What's wrong, Paige? You look exhausted."

Paige yawned. "I am tired. I had a late night."

Zeke tensed, his panicked gaze shooting over her shoulder to scan the room. "How come? Did one of the girls get sick?"

Paige shook her head. The girls bounced in, full of early morning energy. "Daddy, we made doll blankets for Molly and Sue.'' They held up their creations, their faces glowing with pride.

"We sewed 'em ourselves last night with Paige!" August exclaimed.

"Great work." Zeke examined the small stitches, then grinned at Paige appreciatively. "It was really nice of you to teach them how to sew. And to let them spend the night."

"No problem." Paige poured herself a fresh cup of coffee and gestured in offering toward Zeke. He shrugged no.

The girls scrunched their faces, whispering amongst themselves. Finally August piped up. "Did you tell Daddy about the mess?"

Paige shook her head and whispered, "Shh. It's okay."

"Did she tell daddy about what mess?" Zeke asked.

Summer tugged on Zeke's hand and pointed to the trash. "Henrietta messed up Paige's dresses. She had to throw 'em away."

The girls talked at once, both giving elaborate versions of the harrowing night. When they were finished, Zeke shuffled on his feet, looked mortified. "Paige, I'm sorry. What can I do to fix it?"

"Nothing, Zeke. Everything worked out okay."

"Did you make a new dress?" the girls asked.

Paige yawned. "Yep, a couple of new ones. I finished early this morning."

"You couldn't have asked for more time?" Zeke asked.

"It's the end of the summer session, my last project." She showed them the children's outfits—a black broomstick skirt and small white blouse, a pair of shorts and tunic top and a full-length black jacket over a simple white jumper.

"They're so cute!" August said.

"I love the skirt," Summer cried. "Daddy, can we get one like it?"

"Tell you what." Paige knelt to hug both girls. "After my professor grades the project, you can have the outfits."

The girls squealed in delight.

"You're creative and way too generous," Zeke said. "Especially after my dog caused you so much trouble."

A million emotions swirled through Paige, but she was too exhausted to explore them. She suddenly felt vulnerable and exposed again, as if they were both replaying snippets of their last disastrous conversation. He hadn't called her generous then, but selfish. And she'd accused him of using her to baby-sit.

The antique grandfather clock in the hallway chimed and Paige startled, realizing she had to dress for class. "I have to go," she said, hoping Zeke would say more.

But he studied her for a long moment, then nodded and said goodbye. And she was left in her big, suddenly too quiet house, wishing things were different, and suddenly feeling achingly alone.

"WHAT?" PAIGE COULD hardly believe the compliments her final project had received. When Professor Davidson had asked her to stay after class to discuss her project, she was afraid he was going to give her a bad grade.

"We need more designers in the children's field," her professor said. "Someone who not only knows fashion, but understands children and their needs. I'm giving you an A on the project." Professor Davidson pulled out a business card. "And I'd like you to call and make an appointment with Blythe Johnson. She's a fashion consultant who might be able to help you if you're interested in this field. I think you have some real talent."

"*If* I'm interested," Paige said, growing more and more excited. "I'd love to talk to her."

"She might even have an apprenticeship for you. If she likes your work, a showing at the Atlanta Apparel Mart might not be too far off in the future."

"You're kidding! That would be incredible."

Professor Higdon nodded, her glasses wiggling on the tip of her nose. "I'm also putting your name in for one of the overseas grants. Good luck, Ms. Watkins."

Paige thanked the young black woman and walked outside in a state of shock. Maybe the catastrophe last night with her first project had been a blessing in disguise. She couldn't wait to tell the girls! And Beverly. But what about Zeke? Would he be happy for her?

She climbed in the VW and drove to the boutique, almost shouting the news to Beverly as she entered the shop.

"Wonderful!" Beverly said. "I knew you could do it."

"Well, I have to meet with that Ms. Johnson first, but just thinking about a showing at the Apparel Mart is so exciting. And a chance to study abroad."

Beverly tapped her thumb against her bottom lip. "You know, I've been thinking about adding on to the store. Maybe a mother-daughter section."

"You're kidding?"

"No." Beverly grinned. "As a matter of fact, I've had several requests from women for mother/daughter dresses in coordinating fabrics, for special occasions like Easter and Christmas."

"I could work up some designs," Paige offered, her mind already spinning with visions of smocked dresses with elaborate stitched borders. Lacy collars, cross-stitched bunnies, hearts for Valentines...

"Then get busy, girl. We'll make a special corner for

the display models, even have an open house. Can you make at least three different designs, then stitch them up in several sizes? We can advertise and take custom orders, too.''

''Sure. How soon do you want them?''

''Last week!''

They both laughed. The rest of the afternoon spun by with a whirlwind of excited activity. Paige called the lady her professor suggested and set up an appointment. From the tone of the woman's voice on the phone, she felt confident they would work something out. And she loved the idea of the mother-daughter dress designs!

''Why don't you leave a little early?'' Beverly suggested. ''Go celebrate.''

''Thanks,'' Paige said. She wanted to share the news. Then she paused, wondering what Zeke and the twins would say.

Strains of a melancholy jazz song filled the silence as Paige drove, her earlier excitement fading as she approached home. Her empty house, the quiet, lonely rooms, the big yard with no children of her own to play in it, her dreams of designing clothes, all the long hours of working and planning—all for what?

She was so distracted she pulled into the driveway, barely sparing a glance around the house and yard as she ambled up the sidewalk, her feet heavy, her mind contemplating why the happiness and elation she thought she would be experiencing felt diluted.

Then she stuck her key in the door to unlock it, gasping in shock when the door swung open and she saw the contents of her home scattered across the floor. The vandalism had spread to her house, and the culprits had left a path of destruction in their wake.

Chapter Eleven

Zeke had just stepped from the shower when he heard someone pounding on his back door. The twins had gone home with a friend from day care and weren't supposed be home until nine. Maybe it was Paige. No, he wouldn't hope for that. Maybe Renee had changed her mind and decided to come home early. Or was it someone else responding to that confounded ad his daughters had displayed everywhere?

The pounding grew louder so he hurriedly threw on a shirt and tugged on his jeans, barely zipping the pants and leaving the shirt hanging open. Whoever was knocking certainly was impatient. He took the steps two at a time, then swung the door open, still towel-drying his hair.

Paige stood on his stoop, looking shaken and distressed, her green eyes filled with tears. His heart slammed against his ribs. "Paige, what's wrong?"

She collapsed in his arms, her voice a whisper against his bare chest. He wrapped his arms around her and soothed her with tender strokes. "Shh, what's wrong? Are you hurt? Did something happen?"

She sniffled, then pulled back slightly, still nestled in

his embrace, but far enough so he could see into her eyes. "Someone broke into my house."

Panic sliced through him. He pushed her away from him, searching her for injuries. "Are you okay?"

"Yes." She moved into his arms again as if she needed his reassurance. She felt soft and vulnerable, the wispy tendrils of her hair brushing across his chest. "It was those kids again, I guess."

"Did you see anyone?" he asked, his voice husky.

"No," she whispered. "But they left a mess. My...my dolls, some of them are broken."

He swallowed, not grasping the full meaning of her loss, but realizing the doll collection he'd seen must have some kind of sentimental value.

"And they smashed my sewing machine and painted ugly words on my walls."

His temper flared, the senseless destruction now taking on a personal nature. The vandals had hurt Paige; they had hurt him. He cupped her face in his hands and gently kissed her forehead, easing her hair from her face and trying to soothe her with soft words. "Have you called the police?"

She shook her head. A strange burst of male pride assaulted him—she'd come to him first. Not the police, and not her security guard boyfriend.

She shivered in his arms and he rubbed his hands over her shoulders, nuzzling his face into the thick tresses of her hair. "You want me to call them?"

As if she just realized where she was, she glanced around the kitchen. "Where are the girls?"

"They're at a friend's house. They won't be home until later."

She sighed, obviously relieved. "Good. I don't want them to see the house like it is."

Again, anger churned through him. He realized with a great deal of admiration that in spite of Paige's own personal upheaval, she'd wanted to protect the girls first. Shame hit him for ever comparing her to Renee.

"I'll call the police," he said. "Then I'll go with you to your house to meet them, okay?"

A small smile of relief curved her mouth and he had the desperate urge to kiss her senseless and lay her down and make love to her until all her reservations had disappeared, until she knew that the two of them belonged together. But now wasn't the time. If they wanted to catch these hoodlum kids they needed to act quickly.

"Here, sit down and drink some water while I phone the police," he suggested, tucking her into one of his wooden chairs while he called.

A few minutes later, his anger surfaced again when he witnessed the destruction in Paige's house. Books and clothes were strewn everywhere. They had dumped food items on the floor and spread ketchup on the counters, used lipstick to write foul words on the walls, and broken three of her dolls. "My dad gave me this one right before he died," Paige said quietly as she stared at the shredded doll clothes.

"We'll dust for prints," the officer said. "But in the other break-ins we haven't had any luck."

Paige trembled as she nodded at the officer. "I appreciate whatever you can do."

When the officers had completed their work and left, Paige turned to Zeke, her eyes still misty. "Thanks for coming with me, Zeke."

He pulled her into his arms. "I'm sorry they did this to you, Paige, so sorry."

"I guess I should start cleaning up." Paige wrapped her arms around his waist, then laid her head on his chest.

He inhaled the sweet scent of her shampoo, the feminine scent of Paige that coiled his body into knots, and he silently wished he never had to let her go.

He gently brushed her hair from her face. "Why don't you let me call a cleaning service? You can come over to my house and relax while they take care of it."

Paige gazed at him, her eyes shadowed with vulnerability. "Thanks, Zeke, I'd like that."

WHEN THE CLEANING crew arrived, Zeke took Paige's hand and led her back across the yard to his house. The girls arrived at the same time and raced into the house, both jabbering about their visit with Betsy.

"Paige is going to have pizza with us," Zeke said when they'd finally exhausted their chatter.

"Goody," both girls squealed.

Paige explained about the vandals breaking into the house. Zeke used the break-in as a perfect reminder to the girls as to why they shouldn't go running off. Paige jumped in, warning them to always stay close to an adult and not to talk to strangers.

"Did they break Angel?" Summer asked, her voice wobbly.

Paige nodded. "I'm afraid so, and they destroyed two of my other dolls, too."

August threw her arms around Paige's neck. "I'm sorry, Paige. Maybe you can fix it. You can spend the night with us if you're scared to go back."

"Yeah, we can have a slumber party," Summer suggested, tears pooling in our eyes.

"Yeah, tomorrow's the Fourth of July!"

Zeke and Paige exchanged surprised looks, then Zeke stuttered, "Well, I don't know. If she wants to stay over that's fine. I can sleep on the couch."

"Oh, Daddy," Summer said with a giggle. "Don't be silly. Paige is a girl. She can sleep with us."

"Please, Daddy, it'll be part of our birthday present," August begged.

Zeke hid a smile behind his hand at Paige's agitated look. "But your birthday's not for three more weeks."

"It'll be an early present," August argued.

"Paige?"

"I guess it would be okay," she said. "I'll need to lock up my house first."

"I'll go with you."

His daughters pulled at his hands. "Then Paige can spend the night?"

"Okay, but only if Paige agrees." *And because I'm worried your mom won't show. And I don't want Paige to go home either.*

They walked next door and dismissed the cleaning crew, then locked Paige's house. The four of them spent the rest of the evening relaxing, laughing and talking like old friends as they sprawled on the floor, gobbling pizza and popcorn while they watched *The Wizard of Oz.*

Zeke glanced at Paige and gave her a sexy grin, their fingers brushing occasionally when they reached into the popcorn bowl. Each time, Zeke let his linger on hers for a brief moment, watching the pupils of her eyes dilate at the heat in his touch. He remembered the night they'd shared a romantic picnic in the mountains, the night they'd almost made love in his house, and he had to tear his gaze from Paige's lips to keep his body in control.

Near the end of the movie, Summer and August put on their red patent leather shoes. When Dorothy clicked her heels together, reciting the famous lines, "There's no place like home," the girls imitated the movements, reciting the words along with Dorothy.

Afterward, Paige told them about her children's designs and the girls were ecstatic that she would be making and selling clothes in town.

Maybe that means she'll be sticking around, Zeke thought, hope burgeoning in his chest. Then she mentioned the possible grant and his hopes deflated. Finally both girls dozed off and Paige helped him carry them to their bedrooms.

"I guess I should go," Paige whispered as they tucked them in bed.

Summer popped an eye open. "No, Paige, you promised."

August rolled over. "You said you wouldn't leabe us."

Uncertainty crossed Paige's face, but she caressed Summer lovingly. Zeke read the questions in her eyes. "I'll explain if you don't want to stay," he said softly, hoping she would stay and he could coax her downstairs and into his arms for a while.

"No, I did promise." She brushed her fingers across August's forehead. "And I don't break my promises." Then she scooted down and lay beside Summer. His throat closed at the sight of the three redheads cuddled together. Moonlight rippled through the miniblinds, casting shadows and streaks of golden light on his daughters' angelic faces and highlighting the soft, sensual curve of Paige's cheeks. Then both his daughters snuggled up beside Paige and he had to leave the room—before he joined them.

ZEKE SAT FOR a long time in his bedroom, the image of Paige and his girls lying side by side tearing at his heart. Paige was partly right—he did want a mother for his girls. But he didn't want just anyone. He wanted Paige

Watkins. He'd never met a more loving, giving, sexy and talented woman and he wanted her in his life, not just for his daughters' sake, but for himself. She was the type of woman he wanted his daughters to become—strong, independent, self-confident, ambitious, but loving and nurturing at the same time.

Why had he ever thought a woman couldn't mix a family and a career? Men did it all the time. He knew beyond a shadow of a doubt Paige could handle both roles. She fit perfectly in their family. Didn't she see it?

And she would fit perfectly with him. He took off his clothes and slid under the covers, wearing nothing but his boxers, imagining Paige lying beside him, cuddled next to his naked body. He wanted her whispering sweet nothings to him all night long instead of sleeping with his children, and he wanted to tear off her clothes and make love to her until she couldn't speak, could only breathe his name on a contented sigh.

But how could he convince her he was sincere? He had four weeks until Renee came to visit; he'd have to use them to persuade Paige they were right for each other. A knot of dread tightened his stomach as he thought about his ex-wife flying in. The girls would be devastated if she didn't come for their birthday, but they couldn't count on her. Not like Paige. When Paige gave a promise, he knew she'd do anything within her power to keep it.

But what would his ex-wife's appearance do to him, other than reopen old wounds and scrape them raw again? And how would her appearance affect his already shaky relationship with Paige?

PAIGE WOKE TO Summer sitting on her stomach and August blowing bubbles above her head. Henrietta lay snoring at their feet. She groaned, then laughed. "Today's the parade, today's the parade," Summer chanted.

Paige rose and finger-combed her hair from her face, motioning for the twins to follow her to the kitchen. They tiptoed down the stairs and she made French toast for the girls, touched when they gave her a handmade invitation to their birthday party. She had just seated herself with a cup of coffee when Zeke stumbled into the kitchen, his hair still damp from the shower, the scent of his after-shave and soapy skin almost bowling her over with its masculinity. At least he had the good sense to put on a shirt, even if it wasn't completely buttoned.

"You're still here?" he said as if he'd expected differently.

"I'm getting ready to go home," Paige said, apologizing quickly.

"Don't leave on my account," he said in a sexy drawl. Paige shivered at the heated gaze he shot her. She sipped her coffee, feeling a heated blush creep up her cheeks.

"Are you coming to the parade, Paige?" Summer asked.

"Come with us," August begged. "Can she, Daddy?"

"That's a great idea," Zeke said with an easy grin.

"Then I'd better go shower." Paige jumped up and hurried from the kitchen, Zeke's teasing, flirtatious smile almost scorching her back as she disappeared to the safety of her own house. But Zeke caught up with her, ordering her and the twins to stay outside while he checked her house to make sure the vandals hadn't returned.

Such a hero, Paige thought, with ridiculous pleasure, when he strode out and told her the coast was clear. Her feelings for him grew even more when he leaned sideways and dropped a sexy whisper in her ear. Then he winked and the heated promises in his eyes made her think of fireworks—not the kind they were going to see at the town parade.

THREE WEEKS LATER, Paige could no longer deny she was totally in love with Zeke Blalock. She wasn't sure when it had happened, the night she'd spent the night for the impromptu slumber party, the moment she'd fallen into Zeke's arms when her house had been vandalized, or snippets of treasured moments they'd shared over the past few weeks. They hadn't been alone, but the tension burning between them every time they saw one another was more exciting than any night she'd ever spent with another man. She was dying to sleep with him, aching to know if his passion was as strong as the heady promises she saw in his eyes.

But today would be the test. Zeke's ex was coming home.

Her stomach pitched, totally protesting any breakfast, and she quickly wrapped the small sewing baskets she'd bought for the girls in decorative paper, then carefully placed dress-up clothes in a small trunk for the twins.

She'd wanted desperately to be alone with Zeke over the past few weeks, had craved the final intimacy that would bond them as a couple, but she'd kept the distance between them in spite of the fact Zeke had subtly hinted for more, forcing herself to wait until today, to see for herself how he reacted to his ex. Because once she gave herself to Zeke, her body and heart, she would never be able to withstand the pain of his loss. Already the strength of her feelings for him went way beyond the feelings she'd had for Eric.

Taking a deep breath for courage, she picked up her presents and peeked out the window, grateful not to find a strange car in his driveway, knowing when she did, his ex would be back in his life. And wondering if it would mean that she was no longer a part of it.

ZEKE'S HEAD spun from blowing up balloons, preparing for twenty four-year-olds to arrive for Summer and August's party, and wondering if indeed, it was going to take him half a lifetime to win Paige. They had helped the neighbors, taken the girls on a picnic, and even discussed the girls' party, but he'd yet to have a moment alone with Paige. The tension was killing him.

His ex would return any time and he'd wanted Paige to know how he felt before Renee blew back into the picture. He'd wanted to make love to her, too, but she kept pushing him away.

He could scream like a wild man. Watching her house before had been an exercise in torture, but being with her and not touching her was even worse. He wanted to tease and explore all her sensitive areas, find the hidden places on her body that drove her crazy and make her writhe beneath him. Then he wanted to slap a ring on her finger, tie her to his bed and make love to her until she promised to never leave him. He was scared out of his ever-loving mind.

What if she didn't love him? He'd failed once, what if he failed again? And what if Renee didn't show for the girls' birthday party?

"Daddy, the kids are here!" August screamed.

"It's time for the party," Summer cried.

The girls jumped up and down and Zeke's stomach did somersaults. He hoped he could pull this party off without a hitch. If only Renee had taken an earlier flight. The girls had asked several hundred times already when she would arrive and he'd used every stalling technique he could think of. Maybe he was going overboard with the party, hoping to compensate for Renee. A swift surge of panic hit him when cars started to arrive.

The doorbell began ringing and kids filled the room, their excited whispers and chattering creating a crescendo of noise as they piled presents everywhere. Soon the kids were running circles around the den, screaming and laughing and chasing each other and his house had erupted into total bedlam. He had no idea what to do.

"Looks like you can use a little help." For a moment Paige looked stricken at the sight of the unruly youngsters, but she quickly masked her emotions, slipping into the house with presents.

"I'm open to suggestions," he yelled over the noise.

Three girls ran in circles around them. The kittens chased and swiped at the bows on the presents, and Henrietta dived into the corner and hid beneath a chair. Another girl threw her headband across the room like a Frisbee toy. Somebody popped three balloons, having a domino effect as it sent a series of squeals renting the air. The headband pinged across the room again, barely missing Zeke's nose.

Paige gestured to one of her gifts. "Why don't you let them open this big box? The kids can play with the things inside while you set up the refreshments."

Zeke swiped sweat from his brow. "Thanks, Paige."

Within seconds, Paige had organized the children in a circle. Summer and August opened the big trunk, their faces animated when they discovered Paige had made them a dress-up box filled with assorted dress-up items, including colorful scarves, hats, costume jewelry, old dance costumes, capes, western vests and cowboy chaps and shoes.

"Everyone find an outfit and we'll have a fashion show," Paige suggested.

The kids squealed and Zeke marveled at Paige's calm take-charge approach. He watched as she made an impromptu runway, served as master of ceremonies. Soon, he was videotaping the fashion show, laughing, and actually enjoying himself.

"Time for cake," he finally announced. The children gathered at the table, taking seats and watching in awe as he lit the candles. "Now, make a birthday wish."

Summer and August both closed their eyes, "Please give us a mommy for our birthday," they whispered. Zeke's chest tightened with a surge of sorrow. When he saw the concerned look on Paige's face, he realized she'd heard the wish, too.

He checked the door every thirty seconds in anticipation of Renee's arrival, moving on autopilot as he and Paige served ice cream and cake.

"Can we open gifts now?" August begged.

"We should wait for Mommy," Summer said, her face suddenly crestfallen.

"I think we should go ahead and open the gifts before the parents arrive," Zeke said, his gut tightening with every passing minute.

Paige gave him a sympathetic look. An undercurrent of tension and sexual awareness rippled between them. Zeke's mother arrived, camera in hand, and shrieks and laughter filled the air as everyone crowded around to look at the gifts.

"This is for my two precious angels," Mrs. Blalock said. The girls opened the bright pink bags and jumped up and down.

"Gift 'tificates from the toy store!" August yelled.

"And this is a flier telling all about the horseback riding lessons I bought for you," Mrs. Blalock said.

"Yippee!" the girls squealed.

"Can we go riding now?" August asked.

"We should wait for Mommy," Summer said again.

Mrs. Blalock patted her brown curls into place. "I'll take you by the stables tonight if you want." She gestured toward Zeke, then spoke softly. "Renee called and said she wouldn't be arriving until tomorrow. Her flight was delayed in Germany."

"I wonder why she didn't call here," Zeke muttered.

"She said your phone must be off the hook." Zeke glanced at the desk and noticed the phone was indeed lying out of the cradle.

He cursed under his breath, then realized his mother had purposely showed up with the riding lessons to smooth over Renee's disappointing no-show. When the party died down and the parents arrived to pick up the guests, Mrs. Blalock helped the girls pack an overnight bag.

"Daddy, what if Mommy comes and we're not back?" Summer asked worriedly.

"Yeah, what if she comes and leaves and we misses her?" August asked.

Zeke's hands tightened around a paper cup, crushing it in his fist. "I won't let her leave without seeing you," he said. "I promise."

Summer swiped at a tear. "She said she'd be here for our party."

"Yeah, she broked her promise," August added, her chin drooping.

"I know and I'm sorry." Zeke knelt and hugged both girls to his chest, his own heart ripping in two. "But she is on her way and I promise I'll keep her here for the two of you.'' He tipped their small chins up with his thumbs. ''You believe me, don't you?''

The girls nodded solemnly and he caught Paige's eye, confused by the clouded expression on her face.

''Now, have fun with Grammy,'' Zeke said as they went out the door.

''Don't worry, girls,'' Mrs. Blalock said cheerfully as she followed them outside. ''I'll have you back before your mother arrives.''

Zeke waved to his daughters and his mother, then turned and saw Paige watching him. He was finally alone with her and after all these days and nights of craving her, he didn't know if he could keep himself from touching her. Renee would be here tomorrow, wreaking havoc with his life, but tonight belonged to him and Paige. He intended to show her how much he loved her, with every part of his body, his heart, and his mind.

PAIGE POURED herself a cup of coffee, hoping to occupy her hands to keep from touching Zeke. The last few weeks had been torturous and the yearning she'd seen in his eyes all day had nearly driven her insane with desire. Tomorrow his ex would arrive. He'd promised the girls he'd do anything to convince Renee to stay. Did that also mean he'd try to reconcile with her? If he did, Paige had to face the reality that she would be a fleeting memory in his life. But tonight he wanted her, and not just for his daughters' sake. There was no mistaking the feral sexual interest in his chocolate-colored eyes.

And she wanted him. If only for tonight.

The long silence between them stretched, every nerve cell in Paige's body screaming for him to touch her. He cleared the table, then turned to her, his mouth set, his jaw determined.

"Do…you have plans tonight?" he asked.

She shook her head slowly.

His lips curved into a sexy smile that made her heart flutter ridiculously. "I'd like to be with you," he said candidly.

She swallowed, perspiration dotting her forehead.

"We'll do anything you want tonight, Paige."

"I want to be with you, too, Zeke."

His loud sigh filled her ears, then he was crushing her to him, cupping her face in his big hands and savagely kissing her. As if he was starved for her, he plundered her mouth, teasing and tasting and nibbling at her lips, his hands stroking her back, her waist, the curve of her hips, his body frantically pulling her into his heat. "I've wanted you for weeks," he whispered in a ragged voice.

"And I want you, Zeke," Paige whispered against his neck.

He threaded his fingers through her hair, his breath hot on her cheek, then gently pulled her face back and forced her to look into his eyes. "You really want this?"

The uncertainty in his voice surprised her, shocked her to the core, and she realized that Zeke was vulnerable himself. He'd been hurt as much as she had in the past. Tonight she wanted to take that hurt away, erase both their past and all the baggage creating roadblocks in their relationship.

"I really, really want you, Zeke," she whispered, nibbling at his lower lip.

A loud sigh of relief escaped him and he threw his head back and chuckled. "Do you know I've dreamt about this so many times I don't know where to start? I can't decide whether to throw you down and attack you or go so slow you'll be beg me to finish before I even undress you."

His provocative words sent heat sizzling through her, pooling in her belly. However he wanted to take her, she would surrender. "We have all night. We could try it both ways," she whispered in his ear.

His dark eyes grew smoky, his lids lowering to reveal long dark lashes that no man should ever possess, and the honest, raw need in his face startled her. "I want you every way possible," he said in a husky voice.

Then he scooped her into his arms and carried her to his bedroom, pausing only long enough to kick the door closed behind him. Paige traced her fingertip around his mouth, memorizing the small cleft in his chin, the curve of his lips, the strong, firm line of his jaw, every detail of his handsome face.

With a low growl he lowered his mouth, his hunger subsiding into something gentle and tender and so loving she almost wept with the intensity of it.

The late evening sun was setting and slivers of red and gold light streamed through the blinds, streaking his hair with golden highlights and setting his skin in bronze tones that resembled the burning embers of a fire. The long lonely nights without him flashed through her mind and she knew that once he possessed her, she would never want to be apart from him again. But she couldn't think about tomorrow…

"I thought about you all night," he whispered roughly. "Every night."

His eyes were dark and unfathomable, his sexy words sending her reservations to the far recesses of her mind. She lifted her fingers, the anticipation making her fumble with his buttons. Taking a deep breath, she eased the buttons from their encasements and parted his shirt so she could run her hands across the soft dark mat of hair covering his bare chest. His sharp intake of breath made her quiver inside and the heat radiating through her felt deliciously sinful and right. He stood stock-still, his eyes closing briefly as if he was savoring having her hands washing across his flat stomach. When her hands roamed to the waistband of his jeans, he trapped them in his own.

"Not yet. I want to look at you."

Paige's breath caught as he stroked the tangled threads of her hair away from her face and gently unbuttoned her pink blouse. He took his time, his gaze trapping hers so he could see every nuance of her expression, so his breath mingled with hers. She savored the harsh whisper of his voice when he finally drew away the fabric. His dark gaze seemed to penetrate her skin as he raked his eyes over her body, his breathing slowing as he gently traced the soft swell of her breasts above the lacy-thin fabric of her bra. He seemed to be drinking in the sight of her and she suddenly felt self-conscious. She started to cover herself, but he caught her hands again and shook his head. He slowly reached up and unfastened the front clasp, his breath faltering when the thin fabric fell away.

"You're so beautiful you make me hurt," he said roughly.

"I want to look at you, too," she whispered.

He smiled and stripped off his shirt, tossing it to the floor, as if he was honored to have her stare at his naked chest. His gaze moved over her heavy breasts and then lower, where she had already started to ache for him. Gently he reached out and cupped her weight in his hands. Throwing his head back, he groaned and kneaded her flesh, his mouth nibbling and trailing kisses down her neck, beside her ears, then lower still.

"Zeke?"

"God, Paige. Don't you know how much I've wanted to do this?"

She caught her bottom lip between her teeth and suddenly he grabbed her and encircled her with his arms. "I need you, Paige," he whispered against her ear.

He stopped talking with words and used his hands and his mouth to tell her exactly how he felt. They shifted against the bed, and he shoved her shorts off her hips so they fell in a heap at her bare feet. Shaking with need, he shucked his jeans and underwear in one quick movement and stood before her.

"Oh, Zeke."

He fingered her hair away from her cheeks, brushing her shoulders lightly with his fingertips. "You want me, darling?"

The endearment made her shiver with want. "Yes, I want you." She leaned into his arms, reveling at the feel of her tight nipples pressed against his bare chest. "I can't help it, Zeke, all I've thought about lately is you."

"I can't stop thinking about you. I want you beneath me. On top of me. I want to be inside you. Over and over and over." He swooped her up in his arms, his patience evaporating. Raw need swirled inside her as he caressed her body with his hands, stroking every inch of her until she groaned and begged him to touch her more. His lips found her breasts, his tongue sought her nipples and he laved and suckled her until her body throbbed with a need for release. Then he slipped his fingers into the heart of her, his gaze capturing hers so he could watch the passion flare across her face.

Paige groaned and pleaded and bucked against his hand, her own hands squeezing and kneading his muscles, cupping his buttocks and pulling him close so his arousal brushed against her thighs. He seared her with hot, hungry kisses, swallowing her moans as his tongue plunged into her mouth, his body mimicking the movement of his hand and tongue. Paige cried out and clutched his back, her fingernails digging into his skin as convulsions swept through her in a rage of sweet release and emotions that brought tears to her eyes.

Then Zeke pulled back and gazed into her eyes. "Look at me, Paige. I want to see you when I'm inside you." Paige could hardly breathe. Zeke quickly donned protection, then slowly thrust inside her. She cried out, arching forward to receive the whole of him. Zeke's breath became erratic and he pushed himself deeper within her, filling her and stretching her until her muscles convulsed again. She whispered his name, and they began to move, until she came apart in his arms.

He drove his mouth over hers, tasting and consuming the fire she emitted, taking solace in her arms and the warm acceptance of her body, his breath mingling with hers. She whispered his name again, murmuring words of how much she wanted him. A surge of emotions almost blinded her as he finally moved with a guttural sound that sent shivers up and down her spine.

They lay still, panting and reveling in the aftermath of their lovemaking, for a long time. Paige knew that she'd been truly possessed, body, soul and heart, but had it been that way for Zeke? She'd never thought lovemaking could be such an emotional experience. She'd bared her whole heart to Zeke. But could she dare tell him how she felt? Especially knowing his wife would arrive the next day, knowing how much the girls wanted Renee to stay?

He curled his hand around her neck and drew her into his embrace, stroking her back and hair, whispering sweet nothings to her, telling her how much pleasure she'd given him and how he hoped he'd pleased her as well. Finally they drifted off to sleep, sated and content in each other's arms.

When Zeke woke an hour later with Paige nestled in his arms, he drew in the sweet scent of her skin and stared at her gloriously beautiful body. He had never had such an emotional sexual experience. It scared the hell out of him. His relationship with his ex-wife had been totally young lust. He had never loved her. Not the way he...

Did he love Paige? He was certain he did, more than he'd ever loved another woman in his entire life. Which meant she had the power to hurt him, even more than Renee had. He'd already made one terrible mistake in his life—and now his two precious children were suffering for it. Could he afford another?

He studied Paige's soft smile and the way she snuggled into his arms, and knew one thing for sure—what had happened between them was so good, he had to take a chance on it. Telling himself their relationship had nothing to do with the girls was ridiculous. Everything in his life had to do with the girls, because they were a part of him. Whomever he found to share his life had to fit with them.

But it wasn't only the girls. He'd been attracted to Paige from the start. Her soft laugh, her sweet voice, her understanding nature, her fondness for kids and animals, her creativity. He only hoped she'd felt his love when he'd been inside her, that she would remember those feelings tomorrow when his ex returned. He was afraid to speak of marriage, afraid he'd scare her off.

But just to make sure she couldn't doubt that he wanted her, he dropped tender kisses all over her breasts and stomach until she stirred and smiled at him languidly. Then he started loving her all over again, determined not to waste a second of their precious time together and hoping when the night was over, Paige would feel bonded to him forever.

Chapter Twelve

Paige woke, feeling totally sated and light-headed from their wonderful night of lovemaking. She had never been more fully loved and satisfied in her life. Zeke was a sensual lover, attentive, tender, but aggressive enough to make her feel as if his passion for her had been feverish. During the night, they'd made love again and again, taking the time to explore, to arouse, to give each other pleasure. But morning sunshine peeked through the windows, dotting the room with slivers of light, reminding her their fantasy night had come to an end.

She stretched and lay on her side, pausing to watch Zeke sleeping for a minute before she forced herself to leave his side. Dark stubble grazed his strong jaw and the dark hair on his chest was so inviting she had to tangle her fingers in its softness just one more time.

"Good morning." Zeke smiled lazily as he snatched her hand and moved it lower.

Paige's eyes widened when he suddenly rolled over and pulled her beneath him, covering her with a kiss that woke up the rest of her body in a delicious way. His lips brushed hers, then lowered to kiss the sensitive column of her neck, then he brushed them over her nipples until the rosy peaks hardened and ached. She writhed beneath him, eager to touch his skin, reveling in the way his body responded to her touch. Within minutes, he'd awakened her senses to a crescendo with his heady explorations. She was so aroused she pleaded with him to end the torture.

He rose above her, his hands braced beside her head and stared into her eyes, smiling smugly as his throbbing fullness nudged her heat.

"Zeke, please," she whispered.

He grinned, his eyes smoky as he drove himself inside her in one slow thrust, then slowly pulled away, teasing her. Rising on his arms, he thrust inside her again with a loud groan. His breath hissed out as he filled her again and again, his expression tight with restraint. Hypnotized by his touch, she was helpless to do anything but savor the sensations his body evoked. She dug her nails in his back, her mind screaming with pleasure as he taught her the depth of her own need. When she soared to the stars, he moaned his pleasure in erotic words she would never forget. And as the turbulence of his passion erupted, she clung to him, aware the intimacy they had shared would bond her to him forever.

Minutes later, he lay spent on top of her, his breathing erratic, his body still magically tucked inside hers, when the sharp peal of the phone invaded their moment of sanctity.

"Damn," he muttered against her neck. "I wish I could throw that thing out the window."

Paige chuckled. "Me, too." She nibbled at his neck and he caught her hand, kissing her fingers one by one. "You are wicked, you know that." Then he dipped his head and tasted her nipple before finally grabbing the phone.

"Hello."

Paige propped herself on her side, studying the stark beauty of his nakedness as he stood beside the bed.

"Yeah, Mom, I hear you." His tone of voice became clipped and Paige sat up. Suddenly uncomfortable, she searched for something to put on, knowing their romantic interlude had been broken and that the girls were on the way home. And that their mother probably would be, too.

"I DON'T WANT you to go," Zeke said a few minutes later when they were dressed and standing in the kitchen drinking coffee.

"Look, Zeke, we've been over this. You and the girls both need some time alone with Renee."

Zeke grimaced, his stomach rolling, his chest tight with emotions. "I don't even want to see her, not after the way she's hurt the girls."

Paige rubbed her fingers over his hands, noticing how tense he'd become since the phone call. An awkwardness had developed between them that she wasn't sure how to read. "I know you're angry with her right now, but for the girls' sakes, you two have to talk. She's the twins' mother and they need her."

Zeke frowned, knowing there was something about Paige's tone of voice that was bothering him. And remembering the promise he'd made to the girls. But he was too upset over the anticipation of seeing Renee again and dealing with whatever fallout she created this time to fully dissect Paige's reactions.

A car sounded in the driveway and Paige pulled away, her stomach churning when she noticed a small, red convertible pulling into the driveway with a tall, beautiful blonde at the wheel. Zeke's mother and the girls parked behind them and they all exited their cars at once, Summer and August shrieking and running into their mother's arms excitedly. Zeke's jaw tightened, emotions clouding his eyes.

Tears clogged Paige's throat at the touching sight of the homecoming scene. She clenched her hands into fists, her nails biting into her palms. She called herself all kinds of names for not rushing home sooner so she could have avoided the scene entirely.

The door swung open and suddenly Summer and August bounced inside, yelling happily. "Mommy's here, Mommy's here!"

The blonde breezed into the house wearing a short, tight skirt and a tank top that accentuated her generous bosom. She threw her arms around Zeke and kissed him with a mind-boggling passion that sent Paige's hopes sinking to the hardwood floor. With her heart in her throat and Zeke in his ex-wife's arms, Paige slipped out the back door without even being noticed.

"I TOLD YOU the house was jinxed," Paige told Amelia two days later as they sipped margaritas on her patio.

"I can't believe he'd take her back," Amelia said, licking the salt around her glass. "Not after the way she hurt those poor little girls. She doesn't deserve it."

"I don't know what he's going to do," Paige admitted, feeling hopeless. Especially since Renee had been staying at the Blalocks night and day since she arrived. "Zeke's a great father, a wonderful man. He'd do anything for his children."

"Yeah, but he doesn't have to reconcile with his ex. They could stay divorced and divide up the time."

"That's what we said about Eric," Paige said, her fears growing sharper.

"I'm sorry." Amelia poured Paige another drink. "But

just because Eric was a dog doesn't mean Zeke is. Have you even talked to him?''

"No. Renee has been sleeping over ever since she arrived." That had hurt the worst. Knowing another woman was in his house, maybe in his bed.

"Maybe they're not sleeping together," Amelia suggested in a weak voice.

"Maybe. But you didn't see his face when his ex kissed him. And she's so beautiful." Paige sighed, tears stinging her eyes. "Summer and August were so excited, too. *I* even wanted their mother to stay, just so they'd be happy."

Amelia patted her hand sympathetically. "You are such a mush, Paige."

"I know." She threw up her hands and stood, brushing the moisture from her damp cheeks. "Enough about my troubles. You want to try on your wedding dress?"

Amelia jumped up, her bracelets jangling. "Of course. I can't believe the wedding's almost here."

Only three days, Paige thought, glancing at the collection of bracelets dangling around Amelia's arm. "And this time you're getting a ring, not another bracelet."

"Yep," Amelia agreed. "This wedding's going to come off without a hitch."

ZEKE'S HANDS tightened on the windowsill as he stared at Paige's house, wondering why she'd disappeared the minute Renee had arrived. She hadn't even said goodbye. He watched her house, hoping for some sign of life, but the shutters were drawn, the house dark, almost as if Paige had dismissed him from her life.

Then, Derrick's car pulled into the driveway and his blood began to boil. Surely Paige would tell him to get lost. She'd made love to Zeke—she couldn't possibly consider seeing that man again. Could she?

Scrubbing a hand over his face in confusion, he sighed. When Renee had first arrived, the girls had been ecstatic to finally see her. Then Renee had bulldozed her way into staying in the guest room and he hadn't known what to say, not with Summer and August pleading for him to agree.

He'd never forget how upset they'd been when Renee left the first time, and he'd never forgive her for hurting them. He'd hoped Paige would hang around for moral support, especially after they'd made love all night, but it was as if she'd slept with him, then trotted back home to her own life. He'd thought they'd bonded that night, had hoped she loved him.

Her front door opened and Derrick stepped inside. Dammit.

His heart thudded in a dull rhythm as he listened to Summer and August's excited chatter and Renee's shrill voice. She'd showered the girls with expensive gifts and wowed them with her international tales, but not once had she said she loved them or mentioned moving back for good. How had he ever thought he loved such a shallow, selfish woman?

"Mommy, can we go back to Parrish with you?" Summer asked.

"It's Paris," Renee enunciated the word carefully. "And no, Paris isn't really a good place for kids."

Yeah, it might cramp your style.

"Then you're gonna stay here with us, right?" August asked.

Zeke's heart stopped, his chest aching with the pressure as he waited on Renee's reply.

"Actually, honey, I'm flying back in a couple of days.

I'm modeling for a photo shoot in Italy—one of their glamour magazines is going to feature me on the cover.''

Oh, good, the girls can pick up a copy and see a picture of their mom instead of really being with her.

He saw the telltale signs of disappointment already in the twins' big, sad eyes. *Damn, Renee. How can you hurt them like this?*

"Look, I brought you both a silk scarf from France," Renee tittered.

Zeke opened the door and walked outside, anxious for some fresh air and a reprieve from his ex-wife. He automatically started toward Paige's house, wanting desperately to have her fold him in her arms and tell him everything was going to be all right. He wanted to hold her, to kiss her, to love her and feel the passion in her response. He wanted to tell her he loved her, to know she would be his forever. He wanted to know she hadn't accepted that internship abroad.

An uneasy feeling skated up his spine, but he shook it away and lingered on the porch. No, he couldn't go to Paige just yet. He'd have to hang in there until Renee left, then he'd see about making Paige his wife.

THE NEXT DAY as Paige helped Amelia finalize the wedding arrangements, she fantasized about her own wedding. Then reality returned with a horrendous crash and her dreams died. She couldn't help but wonder if Renee had wormed her way back into Zeke's life…bed and all. She'd seen the girls in the backyard a couple of times and they'd both said their mother was staying.

Foreber, Summer and August had said.

Paige could still see the joy in their precious little eyes when they'd told her.

She was so upset when she got to work, she tagged all

the sale items the wrong price and had to redo them twice.

"Maybe you'd better call it a day," Beverly said sympathetically. "You don't look so well, Paige. You might be coming down with something."

Yeah, heartbreak fever. "Thanks, Bev. I am pretty tired. I think I will go home."

Weary and confused, Paige drove straight to her house, determined to put Zeke out of her mind. But as soon as she pulled into her driveway, her gaze strayed to his house. She breathed a sigh of relief when she noticed the driveway, void of Renee's little sports car, but then tensed when she saw Zeke walking toward her.

She slowly climbed from the car, averting her gaze when he followed her onto the porch. His tentative smile only proved how much ground they'd lost since she'd last seen him.

"Paige, we have to talk."

Paige nodded and sank into the porch glider. He jammed his hands in the pockets of his khaki pants. "I want us to talk, but first I have to do something. I hate to ask you this, Paige, but I wondered if the girls could stay here with you for a little while."

Paige's gaze swung to his in shock. He wanted her to baby-sit?

"I know this is awkward, but I need to settle things with Renee." He gestured toward the house. "And there's no way we can talk with the girls underfoot."

A knot of dread ballooned in Paige's chest, but she forced herself to take a calming breath. She had to be a big girl. Although inside, her mind was screaming—did you sleep with her? Are you taking her back?

"Paige?" His voice sounded rusty, and dark shadows lined his eyes. Darn it, she couldn't feel sorry for him.

"Sure, you can bring the girls over."

His breath whistled out as he leaned against the wooden porch rail. His broad shoulders looked even broader tonight, the muscles in his arms and legs tight as he held himself rigid. "When I finish with Renee, I want to see you."

She studied his eyes, but the dark brown centers appeared tired and dull, not giving away any of his emotions.

"Paige, I wish you'd say something."

He wanted her to make it easy on him. Eric had wanted the same thing. But he was the one who'd been sharing his house with his former wife the past few days while she hadn't heard a word from him.

If she had nothing left, she had her pride. "All right." She stood and brushed past him, wincing when her arm accidentally touched his elbow as she passed. "Just let me know when you want to talk."

He nodded, then started down the stairs. "I'll bring the girls over in a minute."

Paige forced a smile. "Good, I'd like to see them." Chin up, she stepped inside, her heart breaking. Zeke had looked so solemn, so troubled, so restrained, nothing like the flirty, fun-loving father she'd seen. And nothing like the tender, tough lover who'd brought her to ecstasy only a few short days ago.

"YOU'RE WHAT?" Zeke sat his water glass down with a thunk, appalled by his ex's latest news. The waiter instantly rushed over and swiped up the mess, then refilled it. Zeke's stromboli sat untouched, his appetite gone.

"I'm moving to Europe permanently." Renee calmly sipped her wine. "If I want to make it in the modeling profession, I have to be there. This magazine shoot is just the beginning.''

A sour taste filled Zeke's mouth. ''Have you told the girls yet?''

Renee shook her head, her long blond hair swaying across her bare shoulders. ''I thought I'd let you tell them, Zeke.'' She fluttered her overly made-up eyelashes. ''After all, you're so good with them. So domestic.''

Bile rose in his throat and he swallowed in a concentrated effort to control his temper. He didn't want to create a scene and people were already staring at his voluptuous ex-wife.

Renee grinned and pushed away her small salad, as if the mere idea of food would destroy her perfect figure.

His gaze fastened on her outfit and his stomach churned. The blouse, if you could actually call the skimpy piece of silk a blouse, looked sinful, revealing the mounds of her artificial bosoms for anyone and everyone to see. And soon, she would be baring them for the entire world, that is, if her dreams of posing for full-cover nude shots panned out.

The idea made him sick. As did his ex.

And he would have to break the news to the twins. They would think he'd let them down.

ONCE SUMMER AND August arrived, Paige realized they obviously knew something important was brewing between their parents. They vacillated between chattering one minute and lapsing into long, silences that tore at Paige's heartstrings. She'd brought out blueberries and ingredients for homemade blueberry muffins. They danced around the kitchen to the Dixie Chicks while the muffins baked. Henrietta lay on the floor, wolfing down a muffin of her own.

August and Summer were filling their stomachs with their third round of batter when Paige heard a loud commotion in the backyard. It sounded like metal garbage cans rattling. She eased the back door open and scanned both her yard and Zeke's. The noise once again pierced the quiet. Then Henrietta howled, a gut-wrenching long yelp that made Paige's heart skip a beat. The girls barely noticed as another song rocked the room. "Girls, stay here and watch Henrietta. I'll be right back."

The girls grinned, dipping their fingers into the batter and picking at the berries. Paige grabbed the cell phone and the broom from the back stoop and slowly inched toward the backyard. Her yard was empty, but the sounds grew louder, as if they were coming from Zeke's. Maybe a stray cat?

She walked slowly, planning to simply peek over the fence. If she saw something suspicious, she'd run home and dial 911. The girls were her first priority.

But as she reached for the gate, it suddenly creaked forward. Paige paused, clenching the bat at her side as she saw Zeke's back door standing open. Voices drifted over the row of bushes flanking the line between their property. Boys' voices. Shouting.

Someone was in Zeke's house.

She clutched the phone and pivoted to head back home when suddenly August and Summer raced up, then flew past her, chasing Henrietta. Henrietta darted toward Zeke's back door, Paige's wooden cooking spoon wedged in her mouth.

"Henrietta, stop!" the girls yelled. "Come back here!"

"No, Summer, August, don't go in there!" Paige took off running after them.

But August ignored her and ran for the house. She

barreled over a ball in the yard, then tripped and fell into the doorway. Summer tagged behind her sister so closely she tumbled over August and sprawled on top of her. To Paige's horror, she saw a teenage boy wearing scruffy jeans and a long, black jacket step into the doorway from the kitchen. He grabbed August by the shirt and clutched Summer's arm.

Paige froze, her heart thumping wildly at the frightened look in the girls' eyes. The teenage boy didn't look much better. His face seemed abnormally pale in contrast to his spiked black hair and the black eyes that radiated anger. And fear. He was also about six feet tall and way stronger in physique than she or the girls.

She had to calm him. To do something so he wouldn't panic and hurt the girls.

"Get out of here!" the young boy yelled to Paige.

"Let us go!" Summer and August both squirmed and wiggled, kicking at him, but the boy jerked them both in front of him and shook them.

"Shut up, you little brats."

"Wait, don't panic." Paige forced a calm to her voice. "Look, I'm not going to hurt you, just let the girls go and you can get out of here. No questions asked."

A second boy appeared behind him, a pip-squeak of a kid with baggy jeans, pimples and an earring in his left ear. Then Paige heard the sound of a car and realized Zeke and Renee were home. The engine died and the boy's eyes grew even wider. If only she could warn them.

"Daddy!" the girls screamed. "Help!"

"Shut up!" The boy shook them harder, sending both girls into tears.

The second boy jerked at his friend's arm. "Come on, man, let's get out of here!"

"Go on," Paige coaxed. "Let the girls go and leave. You can escape before they come in."

But the boy wasn't fast enough. The door swung open and Zeke walked in, pausing in the kitchen when he noticed the intruders. He moved up behind the boys, a fraction to the right so Paige caught his shocked look when he realized the bully had hold of his daughters. Then he saw her on the other side in the doorway and his jaw clenched, a dozen emotions riding across his features. Renee rushed in, momentarily oblivious to the situation. Zeke held out his arm to warn her to stop but she saw the boys and let out a bloodcurdling scream.

The boys jumped, both stricken. The big one released Summer and August and ran toward Paige, almost tripping over the girls in his haste. He shoved Paige aside, knocking her down as he pushed past her to escape out the back door. His buddy darted after him, but Zeke quickly nabbed him by the back of his shirt. With Zeke's strength and size advantage, he dangled the smaller boy like a sack of potatoes.

"I'm not running, don't hurt me," the boy squeaked.

"Then you'd better cooperate," Zeke barked.

"Girls!" Renee screamed. "Oh, my God, are you all right?"

The girls ran into their mother's arms, then burst into tears. Renee began to sob and the three of them huddled together on the floor, almost hysterical. Paige picked herself up and tried to catch her breath.

"I'll call 911." She punched in the number, her stomach plummeting at the dark look Zeke shot her. As if by rote, she gave the operator the information, her hands trembling when she saw Zeke glance worriedly at the girls, then back at her. As if to blame her.

He was right. She'd been responsible for the girls.

She'd let them place themselves in danger. Oh, God, it was happening again.

She felt the trembling start deep within her stomach and rise to her throat. Her skin felt clammy, nausea rose to her throat, hysteria slithered through her and rose to the brink. What if that boy had hurt Summer and August? She swayed, staggered against the wall and caught herself.

She absolutely could not fall apart with the twins and Renee all sobbing hysterically.

Zeke shoved the boy into one of the kitchen chairs. "You, buddy, are going to tell me who the hell your friend is."

The boy visibly quaked in his clothes and nodded. "Don't hurt me, I'll tell you everything."

Zeke folded his arms across his broad chest and glared at the kid. "You'll tell it to the cops, just as soon as they get here. Now don't move."

The boy nodded shakily and Zeke knelt to pat the girls. She saw him keeping an eye on the boy as he put his arms around the twins and hugged them. "Shh, girls, calm down now. Everything's all right."

"We was scared," Summer sobbed.

"We're glad you got here," August said.

Zeke helped Renee to stand and move into a chair, handing her a stack of napkins to wipe her face. "Try to calm down now, okay? We're all right. It's over."

"Yes, thank goodness we came in. Thank goodness you were here, Zeke." Renee squeezed his hand and Zeke returned the gesture. Paige swayed again, déjà vu once again striking her.

Within minutes, the police arrived, the boy spilled his guts and a search warrant was issued for the second boy. A few minutes later, the police informed Zeke they would contact the minors' parents to meet them at the police station. The boy had confessed that he and his friend were members of a club; the various members were responsible for all the vandalism. While the police questioned the boy, Zeke paced back and forth between Renee and the girls and the interrogation. Not once had he spoken to Paige.

Paige went over and poured water for the twins and offered Renee a glass, then knelt and consoled both girls.

"You're okay, girls?" she asked Summer, then August.

"Yeah, but we was scared," Summer admitted.

"I was gonna punch his lights out," August said.

Renee frowned up at her. "How could you let this happen? You were supposed to be watching them."

Paige felt as if she'd been hit herself. She opened her mouth to explain, but realized she couldn't. Renee was right to blame her.

"It wasn't Paige's fault," August argued.

"Yeah, we was chasing Henrietta," Summer said.

"She had Paige's spoon."

"We was making muffins. And Paige told us to watch Henrietta."

"That damn dog," Renee muttered.

Summer and August traded horrified looks. "Mommy, Don't get mad at Henrietta. She liked Paige's muffins."

"Shh, it's okay now." Paige patted them both. When she glanced up, Zeke had left the officer and was standing beside her, watching the scene intently. Summer and August both bolted in to his arms and he hugged them fiercely.

"You scared the daylights out of me, girls," he muttered, his voice rough with unshed tears.

Paige's throat closed as Renee stood and encircled the

three of them as if they were all a family. Once again
déjà vu struck her. The episode with Joey had brought
Eric and his wife back together, made them realize how
petty they'd been during their separation. How they
needed one more time to try and be a family. Would this
scary incident do the same thing for Zeke and his ex-
wife?

Finally Zeke turned to Paige. Emotions, dark and troubled, swirled in the depths of his eyes, and she caught
her bottom lip between her teeth to keep herself from
crying out. He hated her; he had to. She'd put his kids
in danger. ''Are you all right?''

Paige wrapped her arms around herself and nodded,
surprised at the question. ''I'm fine.''

''What happened?''

Paige swallowed, aware her voice was shaky when she
finally spoke. But she told him about hearing the noise
and coming over to check on his house.

''My God, Paige, what were you thinking? You were
going to protect yourself with a broom?'' Anger radiated
through his voice and Paige clenched her hands into fists
at her side. She started to defend herself, but knew she
couldn't. Because he was right.

She'd been stupid to leave the girls. Because of her,
they might have been hurt. She'd been telling him she
wasn't mother material. And now, she'd proven it.

ZEKE GROWLED, tugged on his shoes and glanced at the
clock. Dammit, it was midnight and he still hadn't had
time to talk to Paige. She'd disappeared as soon as the
police had finished questioning her. Between Renee's
hysteria and his daughter's fears, he'd had his hands full
for the last two hours calming them all. Finally, after he'd
promised Henrietta wouldn't be punished, the girls had

drifted to sleep. He'd fixed Renee a good stiff whiskey and ordered her to lie down in the guest room. For someone who'd told him she was moving thousands of miles away from her daughters, she certainly had acted hysterical. Of course, Renee always basked in the limelight. He hadn't missed the way she'd blamed Paige for the incident when he knew Paige would do anything within her power to protect his daughters.

But what about Paige? Was she all right?

She'd seemed calm and cool, had looked as if she had the situation with the young boys halfway under control when Renee had screamed and scared the boys into a panic. He'd been torn between chasing down the kid who'd put his filthy paws on his innocent little girls, making sure Paige was all right after the jerk had pushed her down and comforting his girls when the situation had finally ended. But Paige had been strong.

He'd had to go to Summer and August. Then Renee had made things all the more complicated by being her overdramatic self. But all the while, he'd ached to hold Paige and make sure she hadn't been harmed. He'd admired her composure, the way she'd taken charge and consoled the girls, even his hysterical ex-wife.

He splashed cold water on his face in the bathroom, buttoned his oxford shirt as he strode toward the door, then headed toward Paige's, hoping she was still up. He wanted to hold her for a few minutes, hear her voice, kiss her good-night, then he might be able to fall asleep himself.

He slipped out the back door as quietly as possible, hurried across their backyards and paused at her back door, surprised when he saw her kitchen lights still on. The door was cracked so the evening breeze fluttered through the back door, but the screen was locked. He heard her soft lilty voice on the phone. She was talking in a hushed voice, fumbling with the phone cord. He heard her say Derrick's name. Hell.

"Yes, Derrick. I decided to take the internship in Paris."

He froze, his heart pounding. What?

"The wedding dress is almost ready, and beautiful if I do say so myself. Lots of ivory lace and pearl buttons."

He wiped a bead of sweat from his forehead.

She laughed softly. "I know you'll enjoy taking your time with those little buttons."

Nausea churned in his stomach.

"Sure, what woman wouldn't love diamonds?"

The color completely drained from his face.

"I'll pick up the rings from the jewelry store." She laughed. "Yeah, Paris sounds like the perfect honeymoon spot. And the wedding should come off without a hitch."

"Yeah, right. I love you, too," Paige said with a light laugh.

She loved Derrick? Her words cut him to the quick. How could she say that to another man after making love with *him?* Unless she hadn't felt anything, unless their act of intimacy had simply been sex to her?

He felt like a complete fool. She'd told him she didn't want the responsibility of kids. After tonight, the frightening deal with the intruders and his ex, he guessed he couldn't blame her. But did she have to run off to Paris and marry Derrick?

PAIGE FORCED herself to sound upbeat for Derrick. First she'd called to tell him about the vandalism and get advice on a home security system, relaying the story in a detached voice, as if the incident hadn't affected her so deeply. Hopefully, the police would catch the group of kids responsible and the neighborhood would return to its safe small-town atmosphere. Then Derrick had shifted the conversation to his wedding and she'd had to sound cheery for her best friend's sake.

But as soon as she hung up, memories of the episode at Zeke's flashed through her mind and her shakes returned. She made herself a cup of herbal tea, took a long hot shower, then climbed into bed and curled into a fetal position.

And finally let the tears fall.

Tears for the terror she'd felt when she'd seen that guy grab Summer and August. Tears for the fear and anger she'd seen in Zeke's eyes. Tears of guilt for putting Summer and August in danger.

Tears for the future she couldn't have with Zeke.

Chapter Thirteen

"Yes, everything's set for the wedding," Paige told Derrick, who'd called her again for reasssurance. "I finished the dress this morning." She paced back and forth with the phone cradled beneath her ear, aware the twins were watching her, wide-eyed and curious. Summer pointed to Amelia's wedding dress. Paige had tried it on to make certain the hem was straight and hadn't had time to change.

"It's beautiful," August said. "It's a Cinderella's dress."

Except Cinderella won her man, Paige thought morosely, tuning Derrick out as her mind strayed to Zeke. Summer simply stared at the dress, then back at Paige, a big frown marring her little face.

"Yes, I have the rings in a safe place. I'll see you at the rehearsal." Paige hung up, then offered the girls some freshly baked chocolate chip cookies. The girls grabbed a handful and munched on them as if they hadn't eaten for days.

"Who's Derrick?" August asked.

"One of the guys you saw me with at the mall."

"The one with the fuzzy face?"

Paige laughed. "Yes, that's the one."

The girls nodded, then shared a secret look Paige didn't understand. Maybe they'd come to tell her they couldn't visit her anymore, that their mom was moving back in. History repeating itself. When Eric had reconciled with his ex, Joey had come running next door to break the news before Eric had gotten up the nerve. "How was preschool today?" she said, hoping to divert their attention.

"We didn't go," Summer mumbled.

"Oh?"

"We went shopping with Mommy," August said.

Summer ran back into the kitchen. "See what she brought us from Europe."

Paige's throat felt thick when she stared at the beautiful, very expensive porcelain dolls Renee had given them. "They're gorgeous, girls. Really fancy."

"But Mommy says we can't play with them," August said.

"They're break dolls," Summer whispered. "But we wanted to show 'em to you."

"Since you collect dolls," August added.

"They're lovely," Paige said sincerely, taking time to notice the details of the elaborate clothing. "That was really special of your mother."

Summer frowned. "Not really, she says the airport's full of souvenir dolls."

"Mommy's over there talking to Daddy."

"She gots something portant to tell him."

"She wanted some pri…vacy."

"We think she's movin' back for good."

"She kissed Daddy."

"But we gots to go," August said.

Paige nodded, each word confirming her earlier fears. "Okay, girls. Tell your dad hello for me."

The girls scampered across the yard, carrying their new porcelain dolls beneath their arms. Paige closed her eyes, refusing to give into the lonely ache settling in her chest. She didn't have time to feel sorry for herself. She needed to find someone to rent her house, pack, get a passport. She should be excited—her dreams of traveling were finally coming true.

Her dreams—or were they her mother's dreams?

Her mother had always talked about traveling and seeing the world. But Paige loved Crabapple. Would *she* resent staying in this small town with the girls and Zeke, designing children's clothes right here with Beverly at the boutique?

The end of *The Wizard of Oz* flashed into Paige's mind and she suddenly wondered if she would be like Dorothy, if she'd travel all the way around the world looking for happiness when she already had everything she wanted right here at home. Next door, to be exact.

Confused and troubled by her thoughts, she forced them away. It didn't matter; she'd accepted the internship. Besides, she wasn't fit to even be Summer and August's part-time mom. What if those boys had been dangerous men—what if they'd had a gun or knife?

Shivering at the thought, she pushed aside the incident. She had to get ready for Amelia's rehearsal dinner. At least *someone* was marrying the man she loved. Maybe Amelia would give her her bracelet collection as a bridesmaid's gift.

"WHAT'S A HEARSAL?" August asked as she dipped a french fry in a glob of ketchup.

Zeke arched an eyebrow, trying to eat the soggy hamburger in front of him, his mind raw with concern. The girls had been alarmingly quiet when Renee had left and had accepted the news of her move to Europe with only a few tears. They'd been excited about the new dolls Renee had produced, but their lack of emotion over her departure worried him even more than a tantrum would have. He'd brought hamburgers home for dinner, and he was waiting for the storm to explode. "You mean a rehearsal?"

"Yeah, that's it." Summer bit into her plain hamburger.

"It's a practice, like when you practice a play at school. Why, are you girls having a rehearsal at school?"

August shook her head, her red ponytail brushing the shoulder of her overalls. "No, Paige gots one tonight."

"For the wedding," Summer said, through a mouthful of burger.

Zeke dropped his food on the paper wrapper, his appetite completely gone. "She talked to you about the wedding?"

Both girls shook their heads. "She gots a beautiful dress," August said.

"It looks like a princess dress," Summer said, her lower lip quivering slightly.

"And she gots the rings on her counter," August added.

Summer sniffled. "Daddy, we wanted Paige to marry us."

Zeke's own eyes felt moist. Then the dam he'd been expecting suddenly opened, the gates flooding as his little girls burst into tears and sobbed their hearts out. Zeke scooped them both into his arms and carried them to the sofa, letting them curl against him and vent their emotions. He stroked and petted them, whispering soothing words, feeling helpless as hell and trying to forget his own shattered heart. How could Paige possibly marry another man after making love to him? How could she leave them, too?

Sure she wanted a career, but she wasn't like Renee. She loved the girls, he knew she did. So why couldn't they compromise? Didn't she love him?

Finally the girls' tears subsided and he coaxed them into watching a movie, not *The Wizard of Oz* as they both remembered watching it with Paige. Instead they watched *The Little Mermaid,* a glorified romantic fairy tale he decided, forty-five minutes into the film. But in this case, the man would win the woman. It definitely didn't happen in real life.

The girls curled on the couch, snuggling with the rag dolls Paige had given them, and he finally dozed off, dreaming about Paige and wedding gowns and rings. When the movie credits rolled, he woke up, and realized in dismay he'd been dreaming. He'd been telling Paige he loved her, and he'd been begging her not to marry the other man, struggling to get the words out. Had he spoken aloud?

He squinted through the darkness, shuddering at the dream, then studied the girls snuggled beside him. The dream had been an omen, a reminder of how he'd lost his pride when he'd begged Renee not to leave them the first time she'd walked out. He'd sworn never to love another woman, and certainly never to lose his pride like that again.

But could he stand by and watch Paige marry another man?

WHEN ZEKE SAW Paige leave the house the next morning, all dressed up in some fancy silky white blouse, he felt like putting his fist through the wall. Instead, he gritted his teeth, and helped August and Summer fix a box for the turtle they'd found in the yard. The girls had been moping around all morning so he'd tried to interest them in a ball game in the yard, but they'd discovered the little animal and had been playing with it, confiding their troubles to the reptile. It was another exciting family morning at home.

"He gots a little bitty tail," August said. "Let's name him Bitty."

"Why does he stick his head under the shell?" Summer asked.

"To protect himself," Zeke explained. *Like I should have done with Paige.* Instead, he'd not only shared her bed, he'd let her worm her way inside his heart. The attraction had been too powerful to avoid. He'd fallen head over heels in love with her.

He should have seen the danger coming; he should have stayed in his house and avoided her the way the turtle stayed inside his shell when he sensed danger. Damn animal had a brain the size of a pea, yet it was smarter than him.

Summer complained about the sweltering heat so they went inside. "Let's watch a movie," August said, suddenly shifting into her mopey stage again.

Summer crawled on the sofa with the Sad Sue doll, her lower lip pouting.

"What do you want to watch?" he asked.

"*Cinderella,*" both girls chimed.

He rolled his eyes and settled back to watch the fairy tale with them, recalling the movie last night and the dream he'd had. "Why don't we watch something else?" he suggested.

"Why, Daddy?"

"We like Cinderella," August said.

"Yeah, she's pretty like Paige."

He silently groaned, but Summer's eyes filled with tears.

"Honey, I'm sorry. We'll watch whatever you want. I know you miss Paige and your mommy."

August sniffled. "We didn't want Mommy to leabe again."

"And we're sorry we ruined Paige's stuff so she don't wants us anymore either."

"And we ran after Henrietta and Mommy yelled at Paige."

Zeke curled his hands around the remote. "What?"

"That's why Paige's is marrying that man with the fuzzy face," August said brokenly.

Zeke shook his head, trying to follow their logic. "No, sweetheart," he said, pulling them into his arms. "If Paige is marrying someone else, it has nothing to do with you."

"But we messed up her stuff."

"That was an accident and Paige knows it, honey. Besides, remember she fixed her project and she was excited about making those children's clothes."

Summer scrubbed her hand beneath her nose. "Then why don't she like us anymore?"

"She does like you," Zeke said softly.

"But she's not marrying us," August complained.

Zeke shrugged, mentally trying to form his words. "Honey, Paige likes you both. But when a man and a woman get married, it should be because they love each other."

"Do you and Mommy love each other?"

Zeke sighed, wondering if he'd just made things worse. He stroked both girls' hair away from their foreheads gently. "Your mom and I both love you, and we care about each other. But no, I'm afraid we don't have the kind of love to make a marriage work. We want different things in life. Remember we talked about this when your mom left the first time.''

''So you and Paige don't loves each other?'' August asked.

Zeke's hand stilled. He couldn't very well lie to his children. ''Honey, it's not that I don't love Paige—''

Summer's eyes widened. ''Then you do loves her?''

''Well, yes—''

''And you told her you loves her?''

''Well, no—''

''Then how does she know?''

''Yeah, maybe she thinks you don't loves her either.''

''That's why she's marrying that fuzzy faced man.''

''But, girls—''

''Go get her to marry us, Daddy.''

If only it were that simple. ''But I don't know if *she* loves me,'' he said gently.

August's green eyes glittered with tears. ''Of course she loves you, Daddy.''

''Yeah, you're the bestest daddy in the whole world. She gots to love you.''

Zeke closed his eyes as the girls threw themselves into his arms. Could his daughters possibly be right? He remembered the way Paige had felt in his arms, the soft words of passion she'd whispered in the dark, the way she'd given herself to him so completely.

It was when Renee returned that she'd started acting strangely. He'd always sensed she was afraid of something, but what?

He had heard her tell Derrick she loved him. They'd been high school sweethearts.

''Go get her, Daddy,'' August whispered.

''Yeah, Daddy, go get her,'' Summer chimed.

"You gots to at least tell her you loves her."

"Yeah, you gots to at least tell her that."

August thumped her finger on her chin. "You tolded me not to give up so easy when I wanted to learn to ride my bike."

"You shouldn't oughta give up so easy either," Summer added.

"Yeah, Paige said if you want something bad enuf, you can figure out a way to get it."

Did he want Paige bad enough?

Zeke's pulse raced. Maybe he should fight for Paige. "Okay, girls, let's go see if we can find her."

"AMELIA, YOU LOOK beautiful." Paige patted at the tears pooling in her eyes.

"Thanks to you," Amelia said. "I'm so glad we decided not to elope. I'll always remember this day." She hugged Paige, both of them laughing through their tears. "The dress is perfect."

Paige smiled proudly. "It looks great on you." With Amelia's tiny waist, small bust and slim hips, the lace bodice and V-shaped hipline accentuated her slight curves. And the delicate heart-shaped neckline looked stunning with the diamond pendant dangling over the low-cut lacy neckline.

"Your husband-to-be is waiting," Paige said. She'd designed herself a soft peach taffeta skirt with a pearl-trimmed ivory lace blouse, but she desperately wanted to be the bride.

Amelia's mother and father walked in and hugged her, then soft piano music began to play, signaling the arrival of the guests. Amelia's mom kissed her one last time and hurried into the chapel. Her father extended his arm and

Amelia took it. "Okay, Paige, here goes," Amelia said. "The most exciting day of my life."

Paige smiled, trying not to dwell on the fact that her own romance hadn't worked out so well. She grabbed her flowers and hurried to take her place. As the wedding march played, she walked slowly down the aisle, smiling at Derrick, and scanning the small crowd of visitors, silently wishing Zeke was standing at the altar waiting for her.

When she reached the end of the aisle, she took her place across from Derrick and Dash, the best man. Piano music signaled the wedding march and Amelia started her procession down the aisle. Derrick beamed with pride as he watched his bride approach. A feeling of envy stirred deep within Paige.

Finally the couple joined hands and the preacher began reading from the Bible. From the back of the church, someone cleared their throat loudly, breaking into the reverent ceremony. Heavy footsteps clattered on the polished wood floor. A deep voice cut through the room, shocking everyone.

"Wait. You can't marry him."

Paige glanced up in horror to see Zeke hurrying up the aisle, with Summer and August close behind him.

"ZEKE?" PAIGE'S shocked whisper reverberated through the flower-scented room. A round of gasps echoed off the ten-foot chapel walls.

Zeke stood at the far end, clutching his daughters' hands, shaking in his Sunday shoes. The bride turned with a gasp. He held his breath, prepared to witness Paige pledging herself to another man. But a strange woman's face peeked from behind the veil.

The room suddenly spun around him. Paige wasn't the

bride! He glanced through the sea of people swimming in front of him and found Paige standing beside the bride, wearing some kind of orange skirt and a white blouse, her mouth hanging open in horror. Even color-blind, he could tell her cheeks were scarlet.

"Who are you?" Amelia asked.

"What the hell is going on?" Derrick bellowed.

"Zeke, what are you doing?" Paige squeaked.

"Young man, I think you should leave," Amelia's mother snapped, fanning her face with her hand.

Amelia's father stepped into the aisle and glared at Zeke. "I'll take care of him."

Dozens of pairs of eyes burned through Zeke as if he was a raging lunatic. Which he supposed he was.

Paige picked up the hem of her long skirt, and hurried toward him. The swishing of taffeta seemed ominous in the tense silence of the chapel. "Zeke, what are you doing?"

"Uh…" Zeke wanted to crawl under one of the pews and slither out of sight. He'd not only interrupted Derrick's wedding to a woman he didn't know, but he'd made a complete idiot of himself in front of Paige and a churchful of strangers. How was he going to explain his way out of this?

Paige quickly turned to her friends and forced a smile. "Zeke is a friend of mine. I'm sure this is some silly mistake." She turned to Zeke with a beseeching look. "Isn't it, Zeke?"

Zeke nodded, too dumbfounded at his own blunder to speak.

"Are the girls okay?"

Zeke nodded again. The girls peeked out from behind his jacket.

Paige held up a hand to Amelia. "Give me a minute,

please." Paige quickly dragged Zeke to the back of the church.

When they were all huddled behind the doorway, August pointed to Derrick. "We comes to stop you from marrying that man."

"Yeah, we asked for you to be our mommy for our birthday wish," Summer whispered.

Paige's expression softened. "Honey, I'm not marrying Derrick. My best friend, Amelia, is."

"You made that princess dress for her?"

"Yes, sweetie, I did."

"And those pretty rings—"

"Are for them, too. I'm the bridesmaid so I was keeping the rings for them for today."

Summer grinned and August squealed in delight. "Goodie, then you can marry us."

Paige's smile faded as she raised her gaze to Zeke.

Zeke cleared his throat, finally finding his voice. "I'm sorry, Paige. I thought…"

"You thought I was going to marry Derrick?"

"You never told me he was engaged to your best friend."

"I didn't mention their wedding because I didn't want you to think I was hinting."

Zeke's mouth fell open. "Believe me, that thought never occurred to me."

"Where's Renee?"

"She's gone," Zeke said.

"Back over the ocean," August said.

"I'm sorry, girls, so sorry. I know you wanted your mommy to stay."

Summer's lip trembled but August jutted her chin up, trying to look stubborn and strong, but failing miserably.

Paige's chest clenched. "The girls were upset because Renee left, right?"

"Well, yeah, but—"

"The twins talked you into coming down here, didn't they?"

Zeke heard heated whispers from the front, and the crowd fidgeted nervously. He was completely mortified. "Well, yes, but...but I wanted to come."

Paige shook her head, tears filling her eyes. "Zeke, don't you see?" she whispered. "You can't marry someone just for your daughters' sake."

"I know that," he said, his voice filled with frustration. "Better than anyone I know that, Paige."

"Besides, I wouldn't make a good mother. Look what happened the other night when you left the girls with me."

Zeke's eyes narrowed suspiciously. "Is that what this is all about?"

Paige shrugged. "It happened before, with Eric's little boy. I was supposed to be watching him, but I looked away for a minute and he ran into the road. He fell in the street and almost got hit by a car." Her voice broke with unshed tears and she looked away, unable to meet his eyes. "I can't handle that kind of responsibility."

Zeke reached out and tipped her face toward him. "You're afraid, God knows I understand that, Paige. Parenting is scary, but remember what you told me about doing the best you could?" He gently stroked her cheek with his fingertip. "And the accident with that little boy wasn't your fault, Paige. Kids do that, they don't always listen—"

She shook her head in denial. "But I was in charge, just like the other night with the girls. Don't you see, Summer and August were almost hurt because of *me*, I could never forgive myself if anything happened to them.'' She swiped at tears she didn't even realize had fallen, then rested her hand on Zeke's. ''I'm not their real mother and I'd make a poor substitute.''

''Paige, look at me, darling.'' Zeke brushed a strand of hair from her face, his voice husky. ''You've been more of a real mother to them the past few weeks than Renee has in the past year. You taught them to sew, went to that tea with them, *for* them. You've sung to them, read to them, tucked them in bed—''

''Zeke, don't. You were mad that night, you can't deny it. You wouldn't even speak to me when you saw those boys.''

''I was scared out of my mind, Paige.'' His voice choked. ''Not only for the girls, but I was scared for you, I didn't come to you then because I was afraid I'd break down and lose control.'' He ran a hand through his hair. ''Then everything went crazy, the girls were upset and Renee was hysterical. But you were great, you were strong and calm, exactly the kind of woman I want my girls to be when they grow up.''

''No, I wasn't, I was scared, too, Zeke,'' Paige's voice quivered as she pushed his hand away. She brushed her fingers gently over each of the girls' forlorn little faces.

Tears pooled in their eyes as they clutched their daddy's side. ''Daddy, tell her you loves her,'' Summer whispered, tugging on his sleeve.

''I do.'' Zeke said. ''I love you, Paige. I want to marry you.''

Tears streamed down Paige's cheeks, her voice filled with disbelief and regret. ''I'm sorry, Zeke. But it wouldn't work. We'd only be getting married for the girls. Marriages like that never last.''

A lesson he'd learned the painful way. And now, he'd

confessed his love, put aside his pride again for a woman, and discovered the truth—she didn't love him.

The preacher tried to quiet the increasingly annoyed crowd, and he glanced up through blurry eyes to see Amelia's father fast approaching, an angry scowl on his face.

He grabbed the girls' hands and cleared his throat, his heart breaking. "I'm sorry I interrupted, Paige. You're right, of course," he said, resigned. "We'll go now."

"But Daddy!" Summer and August both protested.

"Shh." He slowly urged them toward the door before he completely lost his self-respect and begged Paige to marry him anyway. "Everything's going to be all right." Then he walked outside and closed his eyes against the sunshine, and the pain he felt inside.

Chapter Fourteen

Paige wiped away her tears and hurried back to her place beside Amelia, her heart breaking.

"What was that all about?" Amelia whispered.

"I'm so sorry. I'll explain later," Paige said softly.

"Can we get on with this wedding?" Amelia's father snapped.

Paige nodded, her face heating. "Yes. Sorry for the interruption."

She listened to Derrick and Amelia repeat their vows of love, thinking about Zeke's declaration and wishing desperately his proposal had been sincere. If he really loved her, if could forgive her what happened to the girls, if he didn't blame her...

"Paige, um, the rings." Amelia poked her elbow and Paige jerked her mind back to the ceremony, tears blurring her vision when the preacher pronounced her friends man and wife. Amelia's diamond bracelet glittered in the light as she and Derrick strolled down the aisle.

As soon as people had stopped flocking to congratulate Amelia and Derrick at the reception, Amelia pulled her aside.

"Okay, spill it, Paige," Amelia ordered, her eyes sparkling with curiosity. "What did Zeke say?"

Paige fumbled with her fingers as she reiterated the conversation.

"That is so romantic," Amelia squealed.

"You're kidding. He thought you and I were…um, the two of us were…?" Derrick stuttered.

Paige nodded. "Can you believe it? I don't know how he got that idea."

Derrick laughed. "No wonder he kept giving me the evil eye at all those neighborhood watch meetings."

"What do you mean?" Paige asked.

"God, Paige, he couldn't take his eyes off of you."

"He really said he loved you?" Amelia asked. "And what did you tell him?"

"That it wouldn't work," Paige said in a low voice.

"Sweet heavens, why not?" Amelia asked. "You're in love with him."

Paige swallowed. "He only wants me because his daughters like me, and they're upset about their real mother leaving."

"You're crazy, Paige. That guy is nuts about you." Derrick cleared his throat, his voice suggestive. "Believe me, from a man's point of view, I don't think it has anything to do with his kids."

Paige's gaze swung to Derrick's, a fleeting memory of Zeke saying something similar when he'd admitted he wanted to make love to her. Could Derrick be right? "Why do you say that, Derrick?"

Derrick chuckled. "Look, Paige, a guy knows." He curved his arm around Amelia's waist. "I could tell by the way he looks at you. But I didn't realize you were serious about him."

"You have to go after him," Amelia said, pushing up the lacy sleeves of her wedding gown.

"But what if you're wrong?" Paige asked, for the first

time allowing herself to feel a sliver of hope. She explained about the incident with the vandals.

"Oh, sweetie, you have to stop blaming yourself for everything. You can't control the world."

"Yeah, if you love those kids, you'll make a great mom."

"No parent is perfect," Amelia reminded her. "For goodness' sakes, look at ours."

She was right. Paige's mother had made mistakes, had filled her with guilt, but Paige had loved her anyway. A fleeting memory of a time when she'd wandered away from her mom at the local shopping mall crept to the back of her mind. All parents made mistakes…

"You have to take a chance," Amelia coaxed. "Stop being afraid. After all, look how it turned out for us." Paige caught the twinkle of Amelia's diamond bracelet as she raised her hand to Derrick's face to kiss him. Strains of a love song began to play softly in the background, and Amelia and Derrick turned goo-goo eyes on one another and headed for the dance floor. Paige nodded, picked up her skirt, then waved and ran for the door.

IT TOOK PAIGE exactly five minutes to formulate a plan. And another five to implement it. She hurriedly dressed in her running clothes and started out the front door. As she stepped outside, dusk settled on the horizon and she inhaled the sweet scent of honeysuckle and fresh flowers blooming, then smiled when she saw Summer and August sitting out in the front yard on a blanket, coloring. Maybe she would make a fool out of herself, but she had let her fears overrule her heart. She might be taking a chance but Zeke and August and Summer were worth it. And if Zeke could forgive her for putting them in danger, she could forgive herself.

She approached them cautiously, taking a quick glimpse at the pictures they were drawing. Both seemed to be moping, sketching their own versions of the wedding they'd just witnessed. Her heart squeezed when they glanced up at her with big doelike eyes filled with sadness and uncertainty.

"Hi," she said in a soft voice.

"Hi," both girls chimed, their eyes slightly red-rimmed and swollen from crying.

Paige eased herself down beside them, guilt spreading a dull ache through her.

"Did you have fun at that wedding?" August asked.

Paige nodded. "Yeah, it was nice to see my friends so happy."

Summer simply stared at her, her heart in her eyes.

"I'm sorry if I upset you or your daddy," Paige said, patting Summer's back.

Summer's lip trembled. August folded her arms across her pink T-shirt. "We're sorry we messed up your stuff. We promise we won't do it again if you'll love Daddy."

Paige blinked against the moisture pooling in her eyes. "Honey, I'm not upset over that project. I told you I fixed the dress and it's forgotten."

"And we'll listen better next time. Daddy said you won't marry us 'cause you was scared."

Paige swallowed at that revelation. He'd been right on that score.

"But we told him you said if you wanted somefin bad enuf, you'd find a way to get it."

"So he said that means you don't luvs him bad enuf?"

Paige heaved a painful sigh. How could Zeke not know she loved him?

"How come you don't loves Daddy?" Summer asked, her shoulders slumped.

"Our daddy's lots of fun," August argued.

"He smells bad sometimes," Summer said. "But that's 'cause he's saving doggies' and kitties' lives. He's a hero."

"We can make him take a shower."

Paige laughed softly. "Honey, I do like your daddy—he's wonderful. But when a man and woman get married, it should be because they love each other."

"That's what Daddy said," Summer whispered.

"So you don't luvs our dad?" August asked.

Paige swallowed, knowing she couldn't lie to these innocent girls. Or to herself or Zeke any more. Not because of her fears. "Yes, I do love him."

August sighed, her expression older than her years, then threw up her hands. "Then I don't get it. What's the probwem?"

"Yeah, Daddy loves you, too," Summer said.

"He tolded you that," August said as if Paige were crazy.

"We heard him say it in his sleep," Summer said.

"You did?"

Both girls nodded.

"He sounded all goofy," Summer added.

"Like he was having a dream," August interjected. "He was begging you to marry him."

"And he was crying on the way home from the church."

"He was?"

Summer shrugged. "He said he wasn't, but he kept rubbin' his eyes. Said he had dust in 'em."

"'Cept I think he was 'barrassed, 'cause he thinks boys don't sposed to cry."

"Yeah, he sniffled, too. Like this." Summer wrinkled her nose and made an exaggerated sniffling sound.

Paige studied the twins' faces. Bits and pieces of conversations with Zeke splintered through her mind, the way he'd looked at her when they'd made love, the husky way he'd murmured her name, the tender way he'd loved her over and over in the heat of the night. But she'd sent him away, foolishly dismissing their love because she'd been afraid. He'd said he wanted the girls to be like her when they grew up, but so far, she'd been a coward.

Well, she'd swallow her pride and teach the girls that her words weren't hollow—she loved Zeke bad enough to do anything to get him back.

"Can I borrow a piece of paper?" Paige asked.

August wrinkled her nose in confusion, but Summer nodded and tore off a blank page. Paige grabbed a red crayon and began to write. When she finished she read the flier to the girls, laughing when they jumped up and down, squealing with delight. "Come on, let's show this to your daddy," she whispered.

The girls beat her to the door and ran inside. "Daddy, Daddy, come here, Paige wants to talk to you."

"Hurry," Summer called. Both girls giggled, clasping hands and swinging them back and forth.

Zeke stumbled to the door, looking tired and rumpled in jeans and a Braves T-shirt. His eyes were wary as he gazed at her, his expression guarded, a sadness about him she'd never seen before. Paige almost lost her nerve, but Summer tugged at her hand. "Go ahead, Paige show him."

Paige smiled hesitantly. "Hi."

"Hi," Zeke said in that incredibly deep and sexy voice of his.

"I wondered if the girls might help me," Paige said. "I wanted to hang this flier and I couldn't find my hammer."

Zeke frowned, running a hand through the dark strands of his hair. "Having a garage sale so you can get ready to move?" Zeke reached for the flier and Paige placed it in his hand, her heart pausing painfully.

She saw the minute comprehension dawned on Zeke's face. His mouth dropped open and his eyes transformed into two dark circles of fire.

Zeke silently read the flier and his jaw dropped, hope yanking at him.

Husband and family wanted for single female
Makes great chocolate chip cookies
Likes to sew little girls' clothes
Loves kids & pets, even frogs
Call 555-7780

What the hell was she doing, advertising for a family? The woman had lost her mind! Then he reread the message and an inkling of wonder crept into his head.

"Paige, are you serious?" His throat tightened when he saw the smile curving her mouth.

"Yes," she said in a low voice. "I love you, Zeke."

Zeke lost his breath as he looked into her sea green eyes. "You do?"

"Yeah, I do."

Zeke's chest filled with emotions. He glanced down at his mischievous girls, afraid to breathe, to hope, but wanting so badly to take Paige in his arms his hands twitched by his sides. "You're not just saying this for them?"

Paige shook her head. "I told you it wouldn't work if the twins were the only reason, and I do love them," she said, putting her arms around the twins' shoulders, "but

I love you, too.'' Her voice broke and she tried to steady it. "I have for a long time.''

His voice came out gritty, "But at the church you said…I thought—''

"I was scared," Paige admitted in a low voice. "After what happened with Eric and Joey, I didn't think I could bear to lose another family.''

"You loved him that much?''

Paige shook her head, biting down on her lip. "I love you that much.''

"You don't have to be afraid," Zeke said, his voice husky. He reached for her, brushing her cheek with his finger. "I love you, Paige, with all my heart. I'll never hurt you, sweetheart, I promise.''

Tears filled Paige's eyes. "I love you, too, Zeke, and I will *never, ever* leave you.'' She covered his hand with her own. "Not as long as you want me.''

"We want to keep you foreber," the girls chimed.

Paige laughed through her tears. Zeke took her hand in his trembling one and kissed her fingers, then swept her into his arms with a shout of joy. "Yeah, we want to keep you forever.'' He dropped excited kisses on her face, then scalded her mouth with his lips. When they finally pulled away, he whispered breathlessly, "Will you marry us, Paige? I mean, me?''

Summer and August hissed out a tiny breath of anticipation.

"Of course, I'll marry you.'' Paige threw her arms around Zeke, then pulled the girls in between them, sandwiching them into their hug. "I'll marry all of you. And I'll try to be a good stepmom.''

The girls squealed and jumped up and down. Zeke covered her face with kisses, whispering words of love and longing. "You'll make a wonderful wife and stepmom. We have to get married right away. I can't stand being without you." He threaded his hands through her hair, pulling her close to nuzzle her neck and nibble at the sensitive skin behind her ear.

"I can't stand it either." Paige melted against him.

"I joined the emergency service at work so I'll be home more with the twins. And if you want us to hire a nanny so you can travel or a housekeeper to give us both more time or if you want to move to Paris to do that internship, we'll go with you—"

Paige closed her lips over to his to quiet him, then she whispered so low he had to strain to hear it. "I want to design children's clothes right here in Crabapple," Paige said softly. "After all, there's no place like home."

Summer and August giggled but Zeke tightened his hold around her. "Are you sure? 'Cause we'll do anything you want—"

"I want to marry you right away," Paige said.

"Yippee! We got our birthday wish," August yelled.

Zeke licked the tip of her ear, whispering against her neck, "You've given me, us, so much, Paige. I wish I could give you something in return."

Paige pulled back and toyed with the hair at the nape of his neck. "Well, there is one thing you could give me that I don't have," she said slowly.

Zeke froze, inhaling her sweet scent and knowing he would promise her the moon if he could give it to her. "What, sweetheart?"

Paige ran a sexy finger down his arm. "A little boy."

Now, that he could do. He nodded, cupping her face and angling it so he could kiss her deeply. "No problem. I think we should get started right away."

"A baby?" Summer asked.

August clapped her hands. "You're getting us a brother?"

Paige and Zeke traded secret looks, both grinning when the twins wrinkled their noses, perplexed.

"Not yet. But maybe some day," Paige said softly.

"Daddy," August asked. "Where do babies come from?"

Oh, boy. Zeke stared into Paige's twinkling eyes. "I think I'll let your new *mom* answer that question."

HARLEQUIN®

AMERICAN ◆ ROMANCE®

presents

CAUGHT WITH A COWBOY

A new duo by
Charlotte Maclay

Two sisters looking for love
in all the wrong places...
Their search ultimately leads them
to the wrong bed, where they
each unexpectedly find
the cowboy of their dreams!

THE RIGHT COWBOY'S BED (#821)
ON SALE APRIL 2000

IN A COWBOY'S EMBRACE (#825)
ON SALE MAY 2000

Available at your favorite retail outlet.

HARLEQUIN®
Makes any time special ™

Visit us at www.romance.net

HARCWC

COMING NEXT MONTH

#821 THE RIGHT COWBOY'S BED by Charlotte Maclay
Caught with a Cowboy!
Though Ella Papadakis found herself in the wrong bed, she'd found the right cowboy. Now, if she could just convince Bryant Swain that they were meant to be together. With their baby on the way, Bryant agreed to a marriage in name only, but Ella wasn't going to rest until she lassoed the cowboy into admitting he wanted happily-ever-after, too!

#822 LAST-MINUTE MARRIAGE by Karen Toller Whittenburg
Brad Keneally's overprotective ways drove Zoë Martin crazy. But when Brad suddenly asked Zoë to pretend to be his wife for two weeks, she said yes! Being close to Brad forced Zoë to admit the truth—she'd secretly loved him for years. Was it too late to turn a last-minute marriage into the love of a lifetime?

#823 A PRECIOUS INHERITANCE by Emily Dalton
An unexpected tragedy had landed three little girls in Spencer Jones's custody—and Alexandra Ethington into his life. As a small-town doctor, Spencer valued the importance of family and he was ready to make Alexandra his wife...until he learned she was the girls' aunt. Did Alexandra just want custody, or was she genuinely interested in Spencer?

#824 HAVING THE BILLIONAIRE'S BABY by Anne Haven
With Child...
He was rich, he was sexy...and he was going to be a daddy! When Serena Jones realized that her brief affair with business tycoon Graham Richards had resulted in a bundle of joy, her protective instincts told her to keep the child a secret. After all, the last thing Graham wanted was a family, right?

Visit us at www.romance.net

CNM0300